P9-ELW-385

Tea for Two

"Dixon was known for his philanthropy?" asked Theodosia.

"And for being an all-around good guy," replied Detective Tidwell. He smiled at her, then helped himself to an almond scone. "Lovely," he muttered under his breath.

He's not given me an ounce of useful information, thought Theodosia. She sighed. Conversations with Tidwell were always of the cat-and-mouse variety.

"You realize," she began, "there is a long-standing feud between the Dixons and the Cantrells." She watched him as her words sank in. He gave her nothing.

"The feud began back in the 1880s," she said. "The heads of the two families fought a duel to the death."

"Mm hmmm." Tidwell took another bite from his pastry, but Theodosia knew she had his attention. She seized the moment.

"Do you know much about antique pistols?"

A Tea Shop Mystery
Don't miss the first novel in this charming series,

Death by Darjeeling . . .

Tea Shop Mysteries by Laura Childs

DEATH BY DARJEELING
GUNPOWDER GREEN

Gunpowder Green

LAURA CHILDS

BERKLEY PRIME CRIME, NEW YORK

If you purchased this book without a cover, you should be aware that this book is stolen property. It was reported as "unsold and destroyed" to the publisher, and neither the author nor the publisher has received any payment for this "stripped book."

This is a work of fiction. Names, characters, places, and incidents either are the product of the author's imagination or are used fictitiously, and any resemblance to actual persons, living or dead, business establishments, events, or locales is entirely coincidental.

GUNPOWDER GREEN

A Berkley Prime Crime Book / published by arrangement with the author

PRINTING HISTORY
Berkley Prime Crime mass-market edition / March 2002

All rights reserved.
Copyright © 2002 by The Berkley Publishing Group.
Cover art by Stephanie Henderson.

This book, or parts thereof, may not be reproduced in any form without permission.
For information address: The Berkley Publishing Group,
a division of Penguin Putnam Inc.,
375 Hudson Street, New York, New York 10014.

Visit our website at
www.penguinputnam.com

ISBN: 0-425-18405-6

Berkley Prime Crime Books are published
by The Berkley Publishing Group,
a division of Penguin Putnam Inc.,
375 Hudson Street, New York, New York 10014.
The name BERKLEY PRIME CRIME and
the BERKLEY PRIME CRIME design
are trademarks belonging to Penguin Putnam Inc.

PRINTED IN THE UNITED STATES OF AMERICA

10 9 8 7 6 5 4 3

ACKNOWLEDGMENTS

Heartfelt thanks to my editor, Kim Waltemyer; agent extraordinaire, Grace Morgan; publicity whiz, Julia Fleischaker; and the rest of the wonderful people at Berkley. Thanks, too, to my husband, Dr. Robert Poor, for all his ideas, suggestions, and support.

CHAPTER I

❈❈❈

*T*HEODOSIA BROWNING REACHED up and removed the tortoiseshell clip that held her auburn locks tightly in place. As if on cue, the brisk wind from Charleston Harbor lifted her hair, just as it did the graceful, undulating flags that flew from the masts of the yachts bobbing in the harbor.

It won't be long now, Theodosia decided, shading her eyes against the brilliance of the midafternoon sun. Off in the distance, she could see dozens of sleek J-24s hurtling down the slot between Patriots Point and Fort Sumter. Masts straining, spinnakers billowing, the yachts and their four-man crews were fighting to capture every gust of wind, coaxing every bit of performance from their boats. Twenty minutes more, and the two hundred or so picnickers gathered here in White Point Gardens at the tip of Charleston's historic peninsula would know the outcome of this year's Isle of Palms Yacht Race.

Theodosia noted that most of the picnickers had drawn into cozy little circles of conversation, lulled by the warm April weather, sated by an abundance of food and drink.

There had been a crazed hubbub when the sailboats from the competing yacht clubs took off, of course: cheering throngs, glasses held high in toasts, and loud boasts from both sailing teams. But once the flotilla of sailboats had zigzagged their way across Charleston Harbor and rounded the outermost marker buoy on their way toward the Isle of Palms, they were out of sight.

Which also meant out of mind.

The remaining yacht club members, with their abundance of friends, families, and well-wishers, most of whom lived in the elegant Georgian, Federal, and Victorian homes in the nearby historic district, had settled down to a merry romp in the verdant gardens that made Charleston's Battery so utterly appealing.

As proprietor of the Indigo Tea Shop, located just a few short blocks away on Church Street, Theodosia had been invited to cater this "tea by the sea" for the Charleston Yacht Club, the host for this year's race. She'd been pleased that Drayton Conneley and Haley Parker, her dear friends and employees, had displayed their usual over-the-top creativity in event and menu planning, and had enthusiastically jumped into the fray to lend a hand on this spectacularly beautiful Sunday afternoon.

Gulls wheeled gracefully overhead, and fat, pink clouds scudded across the horizon as Theodosia cinched her apron tighter about her slim waist and let her eyes rove across the two long tables that were draped with white linen tablecloths and laden with refreshments. Satisfied that everything was near perfect, Theodosia's broad, intelligent face with its high cheekbones and aquiline nose finally assumed a look of repose.

Yes, it *was* perfect, Theodosia told herself. Wire baskets held golden breadsticks, while fresh cracked crab claws rested on platters of shaved ice. Smoked salmon on miniature bagels was garnished with cream cheese and candied ginger. And the chocolate-dipped strawberries with crème fraîche were . . . oh my . . . disappearing at an alarming rate.

Hoisting a silver pitcher, Theodosia poured out a stream of pungent yellow green iced tea into a glass filled with crushed ice. She took a sip and savored the brisk, thirst-quenching blend of Chinese gunpowder green tea and fresh mint.

Drayton Conneley, her assistant and master tea blender, had created the tea especially for this race-day picnic. The Chinese gunpowder green tea was aptly named since, once dried, the tiny leaves curled up into small, tight pellets re-sembling gunpowder, unfurling only when subjected to boiling water. The fresh mint had been plucked yesterday from her aunt Libby's garden out in South Carolina's low country.

Theodosia had decided to name the new tea White Point Green, a nod to the tea's debut today in White Point Gardens. And judging from the number of pitchers that had al-ready been consumed, this tea would definitely be packaged up and offered for sale in her tea shop.

"Your table reminds me of a still life by Cézanne: po-etic, elegant, almost too beautiful to eat." Delaine Dish, owner of the Cotton Duck Clothing Shop, hovered at Theodosia's elbow. Her long, raven-colored hair was wound up in a Psyche knot atop her head, accenting her heart-shaped face.

Theodosia sighed inwardly. Cotton Duck was just a few doors down from the Indigo Tea Shop, and Delaine, though a kindhearted soul and true dynamo when it came to volunteering for civic and social events, was also the ac-knowledged neighborhood gossip.

"I mean it, Theodosia, this is an amazing bounty," cooed Delaine. Ever the fashion plate, Delaine was turned out today in a robin's egg blue silk blouse and elegant ta-pered cream slacks.

Theodosia wiped her hands on her apron and peeked

down at Delaine's feet. They were shod in dyed-to-match robin's egg blue python flats. Of course Delaine would be coordinated, Theodosia decided. She was *always* coordinated.

Dipping an enormous ripe strawberry into a bowl of crème fraîche, Delaine stood with the luscious fruit poised inches from her mouth. "Did you ever think of switching to full-time catering, Theodosia?" she said as if the thought had just struck like a bolt from the blue. "Because you'd be *brilliant* at it."

"Abandon my tea shop? No, thank you," Theodosia declared fervently, for she had literally created the Indigo Tea Shop from the ground up. Starting with a somewhat dreary and abandoned little shop on Church Street, she had stripped away layers of grime and decades of ill-advised improvements such as cork tile, fluorescent lights, and linoleum. Somewhere along the way, Theodosia's vision took hold with a vengeance, and she sketched and dreamed and haunted antique shops for just the right fixtures and accoutrements until the results yielded a gem of a shop. Now her little tea shop exuded an elegant, old-world charm. Pegged wooded floors highlighted exposed beams and brick walls. Antique tables and chairs, porcelain teapots, and copper teakettles added to the rich patina and keen sense of history.

Floor-to-ceiling wooden cubbyholes held tins and glass jars filled with loose teas. Coppery munnar from the southern tip of India, floral keeman from China's Anhui province, a peaches and honey–flavored Formosan oolong. All the tea in China, as Drayton often remarked with pride. Plus teas from Japan, Tibet, Nepal, Turkey, Indonesia, and Africa. Even South Carolina was represented here with their marvelous, rich American Classic tea grown on the Charleston Tea Plantation, just twenty-five miles south on the subtropical island of Wadmalaw.

The tea shop had been Theodosia's exit strategy from

the cutthroat world of media and marketing. She'd spent fourteen years in client services, years that had taken their toll. She grew exhausted working for others and not for herself. Theodosia was determined never to climb aboard that merry-go-round again.

"I bet you'd make more money in catering," cajoled Delaine. "Think of all the social tête-à-têtes that go on here in Charleston."

"A foray into food service just isn't for me," said Theodosia. "I've got my hands full just running the tea shop. Plus our Web site is up, and Internet sales have been surprisingly brisk. Of course, Drayton is constantly blending new teas to add to our line, and he's making plans to offer specialty tea events, too."

"Pray tell, what are specialty tea events?" asked Delaine.

"Chamber music teas, bridal shower teas, mystery teas—"

"A *mystery* tea!" exclaimed Delaine. "What's that?"

"Come and find out," invited Theodosia. "Drayton's got one planned for next Saturday evening."

Theodosia knew that she and Delaine Dish were a breed apart. She had abandoned the fast track of competing for clients and was deliciously satisfied with the little oasis of calm her tea shop afforded her. Delaine, on the other hand, thrived on spotting new trends and employed sharklike techniques with customers. When a woman walked into Cotton Duck for a new blouse, Delaine had a knack for sending her home with a skirt, shoes, handbag, and jewelry, too. And if Delaine had really worked up a full head of steam that day, the woman's purchase would probably include a couple of silk scarves.

"Hello, Drayton," purred Delaine as Drayton Conneley, Theodosia's right-hand man, approached, bearing a silver tray. "Aren't you just full of surprises."

Drayton Conneley arranged his face in a polite smile for

Delaine, exchanging air kisses with her even as he raised an eyebrow at Theodosia.

"I was telling Delaine about your upcoming mystery tea," explained Theodosia.

"Of course." Drayton set his tray down and grasped Delaine's hands in a friendly gesture. "You must come," he urged her.

Theodosia smiled to herself. Drayton could schmooze with the best of them. But then again, he'd had years of experience. Drayton had worked as a tea trader in Amsterdam, where the world's major tea auctions were held. He had been hospitality director at a very prestigious Charleston inn until she'd talked him into coming to work for her. And Drayton Conneley was currently on the board of directors for the Charleston Heritage Society.

Of course, what Drayton did best was conduct tea tastings, educating their guests on the many varieties of tea and their steeping times, helping them understand little tea nuances such as bake, oxidation, and fermentation.

As much as Theodosia knew the tea shop was her creation, she often felt that Drayton was the engine that drove it. And, at sixty-one years of age, he reveled in his role as elder statesman.

Delaine reached out and brushed her French-manicured fingertips across the lapels of Drayton's sport coat. "Egyptian linen. Nice." She threw an approving glance toward Theodosia. "You can always tell a gentleman by the way he's turned out," she drawled.

"Drayton's straight from the pages of *Town and Country*," Theodosia agreed wryly, knowing that Delaine's affectations were beginning to set Drayton's teeth on edge.

"Theo, are there any more cucumber and lobster salad sandwiches?" asked Drayton as he rummaged through the wicker picnic hampers and coolers that had been stuck under the tables. "Oh, never mind, here they are." Drayton pulled out a fresh tray of the tiny, artfully prepared sandwiches. "We've been getting requests. And"—he paused, the first real look of genuine pleasure on his face—"would you believe it, Lolly Lauder just located an artisan from Savannah who assures her he can restore the molded wooden cornices on her portico and still preserve their integrity!"

Drayton adjusted his bow tie, smiled perfunctorily at the two women, then sped off, eager to exchange architectural gossip. He looked, Theodosia thought to herself, all the world like the perpetually hurried and harried White Rabbit from *Alice in Wonderland*.

Besides tea and gardening, Drayton's mission in life was historical preservation, and he enjoyed nothing better than to share tales of tuck pointing and tabby walls with his friends and neighbors who lived in the elegant old mansions that lined Charleston's Battery. Drayton himself lived in a tiny but historically accurate Civil War–era home just blocks from White Point Gardens.

"Do you see who's sitting over there?" asked Delaine in a low voice. Her violet eyes were fairly glimmering, her perfectly waxed brows arched expectantly.

Theodosia had been busy refilling tea pitchers and arranging more strawberries on the platter. "Delaine," she said, struggling to keep her sense of humor, "in case you haven't noticed, I've been working, not socializing."

"No need to get snippy, dear. Just look over my shoulder and to your left. No, a little more left. There. Do you see them? That's Doe Belvedere and Oliver Dixon."

"That's Doe Belvedere?" exclaimed Theodosia. "My goodness, the girl can't be more than twenty-five."

The Belvedere-Dixon wedding had been the talk of Charleston a couple months ago. Doe Belvedere and Oliver Dixon had staged a lavish wedding in the courtyard garden of the splendidly Victorian Kentshire Mansion. They had utterly dazzled guests with their horse-drawn carriages, champagne and caviar, and strolling musicians costumed like eighteenth-century French courtiers. Afterward, the newlyweds had dashed off to Morocco for a three-week honeymoon, leaving all of Charleston to relive the details of their sumptuous wedding in the society pages of the *Charleston Post and Courier*. Aside from those grainy black and white photos, this was the first time Theodosia had laid eyes on the happy couple.

"She's twenty-five," purred Delaine. "And Oliver Dixon is sixty-six."

"Really," said Theodosia.

"But honey," continued Delaine, "Oliver Dixon supposedly has piles of money. Did you read where he's about to launch a new high-tech company? Something to do with those handheld wireless gizmos that let you make phone calls or get on the Internet. That's probably what kept him in the running for Doe, don't you think?"

"I'm sure she loves him very much," said Theodosia generously.

Delaine gazed speculatively at the couple. "Yes, but money does give a man a certain, shall we say, *patina*."

"Who are you two whispering about?" asked Haley as she came up behind Theodosia and Delaine. Haley Parker was Theodosia's shop clerk and baker extraordinaire. At twenty-four, Haley was a self-proclaimed perpetual night school student and caustic wit. She was also the youthful sprite who ran the small kitchen at the rear of the Indigo Tea Shop with the precision and unquestioned authority of a Prussian general, turning out mouthwatering baked goods that drew customers in by the carload. Haley carefully supervised the choice of flour, sugar, cream, and eggs, and often went down to Charleston's open-air market herself to select only the finest apples, currants, sourwood honey, and fig syrup from local growers. And her unflagging high standards always paid off. Haley's peach tarts and apple butter scones were in constant demand. The poppy seed stuffing she infused in her lighter-than-air profiteroles was to die for.

"We were discussing Doe Belvedere," said Delaine conspiratorially. "You know, she just married Oliver Dixon."

Haley squinted in the direction of the pretty young woman with the flowing blond hair who sat chatting animatedly with well-wishers, even as she grasped the hand of her new husband.

"So *that's* Doe Belvedere," exclaimed Haley. She narrowed her eyes, studying the girl. "I've certainly heard enough about her. I mean, she's virtually a *legend* on the University of Charleston campus. Doe Belvedere was homecoming queen, prom queen, and magnolia princess all in one year. Talk about popular," sniffed Haley.

"That's nothing," said Delaine. "Doe was Miss South Carolina three years ago."

"Sure beats Miss Grits or Miss She-Crab," said Haley with a wicked laugh.

"You got that right," said Delaine with a straight face.

"As I recall," said Haley, "Doe Belvedere was offered a contract to model in New York."

"With the Eileen Ford Agency," said Delaine with delight. "But she passed on it. For *him.*"

"I guess Oliver Dixon is one lucky guy, huh?" said Haley in a dubious tone.

"Oliver is supposed to be filthy rich," drawled Delaine. "How else could he afford that enormous house on Archdale Street?" Delaine nodded in the direction of Oliver Dixon's yellow-brick mansion. "I bet Timothy Neville positively had a *cat* when Oliver Dixon bought a mansion bigger than his, then built on another huge wing!"

Haley squinted at Doe and Oliver. "Think they're planning a family?" she asked.

"Haley!" said Theodosia.

"Hey, I was just wondering," shrugged Haley with a mischievous look.

"Genteel women do not wonder about such things in public," teased Theodosia as Haley's blush spread across her freckled cheeks.

"Who told you I was a genteel woman?" quipped Haley, with typical youthful bravado.

"Your mother," said Theodosia.

"Oh." Tears sprang quickly to Haley's eyes, for her mother had passed away just two years ago. "You're right. Sometimes I'm a little too . . ." Haley fumbled for the correct word. ". . . forthright . . . for my own good."

"We love you just the way you are, dear." Theodosia put an arm around Haley's slim shoulders. Although Theodosia was only thirty-five herself, she often felt very protective of her young employee. Haley was prone to plunging ahead, often before formulating a clear plan. A case in point, she'd already shifted her college major four times.

"Come along," urged Delaine, "I'll introduce you. Maybe that roving photographer from the *Post and Courier* will even snap your picture." She reached out and grabbed Haley's hand.

"Okay," Haley agreed and scampered off with Delaine.

Well, I'm not going to stand here like a bump on a log, decided Theodosia. She picked up a plate of tiny, crustless sandwiches and was about to set off into the crowd, when a man's voice called to her.

"Say there, ma'am?"

Theodosia whirled about, finally glancing down toward the shore. One of the workers, a young man with dark, curly hair, the same one who'd helped set chairs up earlier, was struggling with a metal folding table. One end of the table seemed fine, but the legs on the other end were locked in place. "Do you have . . ." the man gave the table a disgusted kick. ". . . another of those cloths?"

Theodosia set her tray down, wandered a few steps closer to him. "You mean a tablecloth?"

"Yeah," he said, swiping an arm across his brow. "I'm supposed to set up the trophies and stuff here."

Theodosia walked back to her picnic hampers and snatched up the extra tablecloth she'd tucked in with her catering gear, just in case.

Wandering back down the bank, she saw that the worker had finally stabilized the table amid the sand and rocks. "This should do nicely," she said, unfurling the white linen tablecloth, letting the wind do most of the work. It settled gently atop the metal table.

"It's a warm day," said Theodosia. "Can I offer you a glass of iced tea, Mr. . . . ?"

"Billy," said the man. "Billy Manolo. I work over at the yacht club." He gestured toward a faraway cluster of bobbing masts barely visible down the shoreline. "I better not; lots to do yet." And off he strode.

Grabbing her tray of sandwiches again, Theodosia wandered among the picnickers, offering seconds. The day was a stunner, and White Point Gardens never looked as beautiful as it did this time of year. Magnolia, crape myrtle, and begonias bloomed riotously, and palmettos swayed gracefully, caressed by the Atlantic's warm breezes. In the early days, when Charleston had been known as Charles Town, pirates had been strung up here on roughly built gallows, and wars had been played out on these grounds. Now hundreds of couples came here to get married, and thousands more came to stroll the peaceful grounds that seemed to provide nourishment for the soul.

"This kingdom by the sea," Theodosia murmured to herself, recalling the famous line from Edgar Allan Poe's poem "Annabel Lee," which had so aptly and romantically described the city of Charleston.

For Charleston truly was a kingdom. No fewer than 180

church spires, steeples, and turrets pierced her sky. Across from White Point Gardens, crowding up against The Battery, shoulder to elegant shoulder, was a veritable parade of enormous, grande dame homes. Like wedding cakes, they were draped and ornamented with cornices, balustrades, frets, and finials. Most were painted in pastel colors of salmon pink, alabaster white, and pale blue; a romantic, French palette. Behind these homes lay another twenty-three-block tapestry of historic homes and shops, Charleston's architectural preserve, complete with cobbled streets, wrought-iron gates, and sequestered gardens.

"You're the tea shop lady, aren't you?" A rich, baritone voice interrupted Theodosia's reverie.

Theodosia turned with a smile and found herself staring into alert, dark brown eyes set in smooth, olive skin. A neatly clipped mustache draped over full, sensuous lips.

"You have the advantage, sir," she said, then realized immediately that she sounded far more formal than she'd intended.

But the man wasn't a bit put off and swept his Panama straw hat off his head in a gallant gesture that was pure Rhett Butler. "Giovanni Loard, at your service, ma'am."

The name sounded faintly familiar to Theodosia as she stood gazing at this interesting man who smiled broadly back at her, even as he dug hastily in the pocket of his navy blazer for a business card.

Theodosia accepted his card, squinted at tiny, old English type. "Loard Antiquarian Shop. Oh, of course," she said as comprehension suddenly dawned. "Down on King Street."

"In the antiques district," Giovanni Loard added helpfully.

"Drayton Conneley *raved* about your shop," she told him enthusiastically. "He said you had the finest collection of eighteenth- and nineteenth-century paintings in all of Charleston. Wonderful estate jewelry, too. I keep meaning

to get down there but never seem to find the time," Theodosia lamented. "I've got this one wall—"

"That's *begging* for a truly great painting!" finished
Giovanni Loard.

"Exactly," agreed Theodosia.

"Then, dear lady, you simply must *make* time," Giovanni admonished. "Or better yet, come open a second tea
shop in our neighborhood. It would be a most welcome ad-
dition."

"I'm not sure I've got the first one under control yet,"
Theodosia admitted, "but it's a fun idea to entertain."
Theodosia smiled up at Giovanni Loard, amused by this
colorful, slightly quirky fellow and suddenly found him
gazing in the direction of Doe and Oliver Dixon.

"My cousin," Giovanni Loard offered by way of explanation. "The groom."

"Oliver Dixon is your cousin?" asked Theodosia.

"Actually, second cousin," said Giovanni. "Oliver is my
mother's first cousin."

Theodosia maintained her smile even as her eyes began
to glaze over. In Charleston, especially in the historic district, it often seemed that everyone was related to everyone
else. People literally went on for hours explaining the tan-
gled web of second cousins, great-great-grandparents, and
grandaunts.

Thankfully, Giovanni Loard didn't launch into a disser-
tation on his lineage. Instead, he gently plucked the tray of
sandwiches from Theodosia's hands.

"Allow me," he said with a twinkle in his eye. "I'm sure
you have other items to attend to." And Giovanni wandered off into the crowd, an impromptu waiter.

So surprised was Theodosia that she stood rooted to the
spot, blinking after him.

"At sixes and sevens?" said Drayton's voice in her ear.
She whirled to find him clutching two empty pitchers in

one hand, a tray bearing a single, lonely sandwich balanced in the other. He gazed at her quizzically.

"That antique dealer you told me about, Giovanni Loard?" Theodosia gestured after Giovanni. "He offered to help. *Nobody* ever offers to help."

Drayton peered through the crowd. "Remarkable. Do you know that the Center for Disease Control in Atlanta has rated South Carolinians as having the most sedentary lifestyle in the country?"

"Hey," said Haley as she joined them, "I'm about ready for a sedentary lifestyle. My feet are tired, and I think I just got my first sunburn of the year. But first things first. Who *was* that cute guy, anyway?"

"Giovanni Loard," said Theodosia. "He runs an antique shop down on King Street."

They watched Giovanni pick his way through the crowd, dispensing sandwiches, talking animatedly with guests. "Personable chap, isn't he?" remarked Drayton.

Giovanni wound his way to Doe and Oliver Dixon's table, where Delaine was still seated, and offered sandwiches all around.

Suddenly, a man with flaming red hair swaggered up behind him. Although Theodosia, Drayton, and Haley were far enough away that they couldn't hear the exact words spoken, they could obviously see that the red-haired man was angry. Very angry. Oliver Dixon whirled about to confront him, and now both men were talking excitedly. A low murmur ran through the crowd.

"The guy with the red hair," said Haley. "What's his problem?"

"Don't know," said Theodosia.

"Do you know who he is?" asked Drayton as he pursed his lips and peered speculatively at the two men whose argument appeared to escalate by the second.

"That's Ford Cantrell," said Theodosia. She knew him, knew *of* him, anyway. Ford Cantrell was from the low-country, that vast area of woods, old rice plantations, and swampland just south of Charleston. He was a farmer by trade, although his ancestors would have been called plantation owners.

"He's been drinking," hissed Drayton. "Have you ever seen anyone drunk at an afternoon tea?"

Theodosia's eyes flickered back to the hotheaded, swaggering Ford Cantrell. He had one hand stuck out in front of him as he spoke angrily to Oliver Dixon. Then he gave Oliver Dixon a rough shove and stalked off.

"Yes," she finally answered. "I have."

Now another excited voice rose from a small group of onlookers gathered down by the shore. "Here they come!"

Two hundred people jumped from their chairs en masse and began pushing toward the water.

No, thought Theodosia. *Make that one hundred ninety-nine.* Ford Cantrell was hustling off in the opposite direction. She watched as he veered around a group of Civil War cannons, then set off toward the bandstand. Ford Cantrell appeared to be walking steadily, not staggering, but the back of his neck glowed red. A been-drinking-too-much red, not an out-in-the-sun red.

Why had the seemingly mild-mannered Oliver Dixon been embroiled in an argument with Ford Cantrell? An argument that looked like it could have erupted into a knock-down-drag-out fight? *What got those two men so fired up?* wondered Theodosia.

"Theodosia, come on," called Haley. "The sailboats are heading for the final markers!"

Theodosia shook off her consternation with Ford Cantrell and turned her attention to Charleston Harbor. She could see that a half-dozen boats had managed to gain a commanding lead and were bearing down on the two red buoys that pitched wildly back and forth in the billowing waves.

Somewhere out there, Jory Davis was skippering his

J-24, Theodosia told herself. Jory was an attorney with her father's old firm, Ligget, Hume, Hartwell, and she'd been dating him off and on for the past few months. She hoped his yacht, *Rubicon*, was one of the handful of boats jockeying for finishing-line position.

Theodosia strode across the newly greened grass, picking up dropped napkins and flatware as she went. When she finally caught up with the crowd, they were packed into a tight knot near what was left of the old seawall that had been pummeled by Hurricane Hugo back in 1989. The onlookers were whistling and cheering as the sailboats fought their way through the strong crosscurrents that marked the confluence of the Ashley and Cooper rivers.

Theodosia cleared the half-dozen empty platters from the long buffet table and glanced toward the sailboats again. Once this race ended, and it looked like it would end soon, folks would wander over to the Charleston Yacht Club for cold beer, fried catfish, or she-crab soup. Some would retire to private courtyard gardens in the historic district for mint juleps and, later, enjoy elegantly prepared dinners on bone china. Her task here was almost done.

"Oliver, over here!" An officious-looking man with a shock of white hair and a too-tight white commodore's blazer trimmed in gold braid waved broadly to Oliver Dixon. He took the wooden box that had been tucked carefully under one arm and laid it on the table Billy Manolo had set up down at the shore. Then the man motioned to Oliver Dixon again. "C'mon, Oliver," he urged insistently.

Theodosia paused in her cleanup to watch as the highly excited commodore opened a rather lovely rosewood box and gently removed a pistol. It was old, she decided, antique, with brass fittings that glinted in the sun and a long, curved barrel. How nice, she thought, that Oliver Dixon was being given the honor of officiating at the finish line.

All the yachts had rounded the markers now, and two yachts had pushed out in front, gaining a substantial lead.

One of the leaders flew a white mainsail that read *Topper*; the other had a blue and white striped sail printed with the numbers *N-271*. Neck and neck, they bore down toward the finishing-line buoy.

More cheers rose from the crowd. The wind had risen and was driving the two boats furiously toward the finish line.

Thirty feet to Theodosia's left, Oliver Dixon stood poised on the rocky shore, next to the table. His fine silver hair riffled in the wind, his eyes were fixed on the boat with the blue and white striped sail, *N-271*. That yacht seemed to have gained a slight advantage over *Topper* as it skimmed across the waves.

Now everyone on shore could see the crews working madly to fine-tune the trim of their sails even as they hung out over the sides, using body weight to balance their craft.

The two lead boats were closing in, *N-271*, the boat with the blue and white striped sail, still enjoying its small lead. So close were they now that Theodosia could even see the faces of the crew members pulled into grimaces, betraying their hard work and exhilaration.

Oliver Dixon stood at the ready, poised to fire the pistol as the winner hurtled across the finish line.

Theodosia picked up a silver pitcher and was about to empty it, when the finish-line gun sounded with a tremendous explosion.

A sudden hush swept through the crowd, as though someone had pulled the plug.

Then a single, anguished cry pierced the stillness. Beginning as a sob, Doe Belvedere Dixon's voice rose in a horrified scream as blood poured forth from Oliver Dixon's head, and she watched helplessly as her husband of nine weeks crumpled to the ground.

CHAPTER 2

❧❧❧

D *RAYTON STAGGERED TOWARD* Theodosia and grabbed her arm roughly. "No one's doing anything!" he said in a choked whisper.

Theodosia gazed about as the ghastly scene seemed to reveal itself in slow motion. Drayton was right. Everyone was just standing there. Picnickers who had been in such high spirits moments earlier seemed frozen in place. Most of the crowd gaped openly at Oliver Dixon's splayed-out body; a few grimaced and covered their eyes.

Out of the corner of her eye, Theodosia was aware of a woman collapsed on the ground. She considered the possibility that the young wife, Doe, had fainted and figured her hunch was correct.

Theodosia found her voice. "Someone call 911!" she yelled. Her words rang out loud and commanding.

Giovanni Loard was suddenly next to her, frantically punching buttons on his cell phone. He barked into it, a harsh, urgent request for the operator to dispatch an ambulance and medical team to White Point Gardens.

Frustrated, feeling the need to do something, anything,

Theodosia rushed over to where Oliver Dixon's body lay. Staring down, she inadvertently flinched at the sight of silver hair flecked with drops of blood. The poor man had pitched face forward onto the table, then slithered down. And, while his head now rested on the sandy shore, the lower half of his body was partially submerged. Water lapped insistently, gently rocking him back and forth in the surf.

Seconds later, Theodosia pulled herself together. Bending down, she gently touched her index and middle fingers to the side of Oliver Dixon's throat. There was nothing. No throb of a pulse, no breath sounds.

"The ambulance is on its way. What else can we do?" Giovanni Loard had joined her again. His breath was coming in short gasps; he was pale and seemed on the verge of hyperventilating.

"Nothing," replied Theodosia as she stared at the bright crimson stain on Oliver Dixon's mortally wounded head. "I'm afraid there's nothing we *can* do."

What seemed like an eternity was really only three minutes, according to Drayton's ancient Piaget watch, before screams from the ambulance erupted just blocks away.

"Theodosia, come over here."

"What?" Theodosia looked up into Drayton's lined countenance. He bore the sad look of a betrayed bloodhound.

"Come over here while they tend to him," Drayton urged.

She was suddenly aware that her feet were cold, and her long, silk skirt had somehow gotten wet and now trailed sadly. Drayton pulled her away from Oliver Dixon's body as a team of paramedics pushed past them, kicking the table out of their way. White blankets fluttered, and Theodosia heard the clatter of the metal gurney against rock. It made an ugly, scraping sound.

Drayton led her to one of the chairs and forced her to sit

down. *Minutes earlier, carefree revelers had sat here,* she thought to herself. People had been enjoying iced tea and hors d'oeuvres—*her* iced tea and hors d'oeuvres. The crowd began to disperse and mill around. People spoke in hushed tones, but still no one seemed to know quite what to do.

Delaine wandered over and collapsed in a chair across from Theodosia. Her teeth were chattering, and her hair swung down in untidy tendrils. Eyes the size of saucers, she stared at Theodosia. "My God," she moaned, "did you see that poor man's *face?*"

"Hush," snapped Drayton. "Of course she saw it. We all did."

Theodosia turned away from Delaine and gazed toward the rocky shore where Oliver Dixon's body still lay. The paramedics had arrived with a bustle, looking very official and snappy in their bright blue uniforms. They'd brought oxygen canisters, defibrillating equipment, IV needles, and bags of saline. Though they'd been working on Oliver Dixon for some time now, Theodosia knew there wasn't a single thing the paramedics could pull out of their bag of tricks that would make a whit of difference. The situation was completely out of their hands. Oliver Dixon was with his maker now.

Of course, the Charleston police had also arrived on the heels of the paramedics. Squealing tires had bumped up and over curbs, chewing across soft turf and leaving tire treads in their wake. In many spots, grass and newly sprouted flowers had been completely torn up.

Theodosia put her head in her hands and tried to shut out the low buzz of the crowd as the police began asking questions. She rubbed her eyes hard, then looked back at the minor furor that was still taking place over Oliver Dixon's body. One of the paramedics, the husky one, had inserted a tube down the poor man's throat and was pumping a plastic bag furiously.

Two men, obviously police, detached themselves from a cluster of onlookers and joined the paramedics.

Theodosia squinted, trying to protect her eyes from the glare of sun on water, and tried to sort out what exactly was going on between the paramedics and the police. When one of the policemen turned sideways, Theodosia realized with a start that she recognized that ample silhouette.

It was Burt Tidwell.

Theodosia sighed. Burt Tidwell had to be one of the most arrogant, cantankerous detectives on the entire Charleston police force. She'd run up against Tidwell last fall when a guest at one of the Lamplighter Tours had been poisoned. He'd been the investigating detective, obtuse in his questioning, brash in his demeanor.

At the same time, Tidwell was a star player. He was the Tiger Woods of detectives.

Theodosia watched as Tidwell took command of the scene. His physical presence loomed large, his manner was beyond take-charge, veering toward overbearing. The paramedics, finally resigned to the fact that all their heroic efforts were in vain, quit what they were doing and stepped back. It was no longer their show. Now it was Tidwell's.

Finally, Theodosia could stand it no more.

"Where will you be taking him?" Theodosia plucked at the sleeve of Tidwell's tweed jacket. It was just like Tidwell to be wearing wool on the first really hot day. On the other hand, Tidwell wasn't the kind of man who concerned himself with matters of fashion. His was a more focused existence. Two things seemed to hold Tidwell's interest; crime and food. And not necessarily in that order.

Tidwell's bullet-shaped head swiveled on his broad shoulders until he was staring straight at Theodosia. His lower lip drooped, and his bushy eyebrows spread across his domed forehead like an errant caterpillar. Only his hooded eyes, clear and sharp, reflecting keen intelligence, registered recognition.

"You," he finally growled.

"You'll have to step back, miss." A uniformed officer with a name tag that read Tandy grabbed Theodosia by the elbow and began to apply pressure, attempting to pull her back. He was instantly halted by Tidwell's angry gaze.

"Leave her alone," Tidwell growled. His voice rumbled from his ample stomach like a boiler starting up.

Startled, Officer Tandy released Theodosia's arm and stepped back. "Yes sir," he said politely.

Tidwell eyed Theodosia. He took in her wet skirt and slippers, registered her obvious distress. "Probably not to the hospital," Tidwell said quietly as he watched one of the paramedics begin to pull a sheet up over Oliver Dixon's body. "This poor devil is most assuredly dead."

Once again, Theodosia took in the mud and bloodstains. Then her eyes strayed to something she hadn't noticed before. Pieces of the exploded pistol lay scattered about. An embossed grip sat on wet sand a few feet from where they were standing. Another piece of twisted gray metal was nestled in a crack between two nearby rocks.

"But then, you knew that, didn't you?" Tidwell gazed at her pleasantly. "The paramedics said you were first on the scene. They said you were the first one to reach him." Tidwell had a maddening way of phrasing questions as statements.

"Yes, I guess I was," said Theodosia. It suddenly occurred to her that she might be experiencing a mild case of shock. It wasn't every day that someone was killed right before her very eyes.

"I believe I am correct in stating that the unfortunate Mr. Dixon was killed instantly when the pistol misfired," said Tidwell. He gazed across Charleston Harbor, his eyes seeming to search for something on the distant shore. "Hell of a thing, these old pistols," he murmured. "Thing works

fine for years, decades it would seem in this case. Then one
day . . . *ker-bang*." Tidwell's hands flew into the air in a
gesture that seemed to communicate a randomness of fate.

"Sir." Officer Tandy handed a pair of latex gloves to
Tidwell.

Wordlessly, Tidwell accepted the gloves, then worked
the tight rubber over his chubby hands. He leaned down
and began collecting the remnants of the pistol.

As Theodosia watched him, her normally unlined brow
suddenly puckered into a frown. "You're going to have
those pieces examined by a ballistics expert, aren't you?"
she asked.

Burt Tidwell's hooded eyes blinked slowly, like a rep-
tile contemplating its prey.

Tidwell dropped two pieces of the pistol into a plastic
bag, handed the task off to Tandy, who hovered nearby.
Then he hooked a large paw under Theodosia's elbow and
began leading her away. Theodosia was aware of pressure
on her arm and the crunch of tiny white seashells under-
foot. And two hundred sets of eyes watching her.

When they were a good forty paces from the shore and
Oliver Dixon's body, they stopped under a giant live oak
tree and faced each other. Spanish moss waved in lacy,
gray green banners above them. Warm, languid breezes off
the bay caressed Theodosia's face, reminding her it was
still Sunday afternoon: But the day no longer felt glorious.

"Tell me." Tidwell cocked an eye toward her. "Are you
always filled with such suspicion and unbridled skepti-
cism?"

"Of course not," said Theodosia defensively. *Lord,* she
thought, *here we go again. Burt Tidwell has to be the most
obstinate, obtuse cuss that ever roamed the face of this
earth.*

Last October, during the Lamplighter Tour, Tidwell had
kept them all on pins and needles for weeks with his suspicions and vexing accusations when Bethany Shepherd,

one of Haley's friends who filled in occasionally at the tea shop, had come under scrutiny. Of course, Tidwell had been unapologetic, even after Theodosia had been the one to discover that it was Samantha Rabathan and not Bethany who had perpetrated the deadly deed.

That death in the garden of the Avis Melbourne Home had appeared accidental, too. Now Theodosia had learned to be a bit more skeptical and exercise a modicum of caution.

She also knew Tidwell could be an irritant or an ally. Today, she wasn't sure which one he'd be. That coin was still up in the air.

"Miss Browning," began Tidwell, "I have already spoken with one of the yacht club's board members. He is an attorney of note and is of the opinion that this was simply an unfortunate accident."

"Did he tell you where the pistol is usually kept?" pressed Theodosia.

"I presume at the yacht club," replied Tidwell. His smile was the kind tolerant adults often reserve for children. "Where it has always been kept under lock and key."

"Which club?" asked Theodosia.

There was a sharp intake of breath as Tidwell hesitated. *Aha,* Theodosia thought to herself, *he doesn't know.*

"There are two yacht clubs," Theodosia informed Tidwell. She hesitated a moment before she continued. "And they are rivals."

CHAPTER 3

TEAKETTLES CHIRPED and hissed, and the aroma of freshly brewed teas permeated the air: a delicately fruited Nilgiri, a sweet Assam, and a spicy black Yunnan from southwest China. Sunlight streamed in through the antique panes, bathing the interior of the tea shop in warm light and lending a glow to the wooden floors and battered hickory tables that were, somehow, just the right backdrop for the dazzling array of teapots that ranged from Cordon Bleu white porcelain to fanciful hand-painted floral ceramics.

Haley had been up early as usual, working wonders in the oversized professional oven they'd managed to squeeze into the back of the shop. Now benne wafers, blueberry scones, and lemon and sour cream muffins cooled on wooden racks. When the tea shop's double doors were propped open, as they so often were, Drayton swore the tantalizing aromas could be enjoyed up and down the entire length of Church Street.

By nine A.M., the day's first customers, shopkeepers from Robillard Booksellers, Cabbage Patch Needlepoint

Shop, and other nearby businesses, had already stopped by for their cup of tea and breakfast sweet. All had pressed Theodosia, Drayton, and Haley for details on the terrible events of yesterday, shaking their heads with regret, murmuring about the dreadful turn of events, and wasn't it a shame about the young widow, Doe.

Then there was a lull before the next wave of customers arrived. These were usually regulars from the historic district, who were wont to stop by for tea and a quiet perusal of the morning's newspaper as well as tourists who arrived via horse-drawn carriages and colorful jitneys.

It was during this lull that Theodosia, Drayton, and Haley had gathered around one of the round tables to sip tea and rehash yesterday's tragic events. They'd been joined by Miss Dimple, their elderly bookkeeper, who'd dropped by to pick up last week's receipts.

"And the pistol just exploded?" asked Miss Dimple with awe as the story unfolded once more for her benefit.

"With a cataclysmic crash," said Drayton. "Then the poor man simply collapsed. But then, what else would you expect? I'm sure he was killed instantly."

"And nobody did anything," added Haley, "except Theodosia. She ran over and checked the poor man out. Oh, and that nice antique dealer, Giovanni Loard, called the paramedics."

"Good girl," said Miss Dimple, glancing at Theodosia approvingly. "But you must still feel a bit shaken up."

"A little," admitted Theodosia. "It was a terrible accident."

Miss Dimple leaned back in her chair and took a sip of Assam. "Are they sure it was an accident?" she asked.

Haley frowned and gave an involuntary shudder. "Miss Dimple," she said, "you just gave me chills."

"What makes you say that, Miss Dimple?" asked Theodosia.

"Well," she said slowly, "it seems like they've been

using that old pistol for as long as I can remember. When I was a little girl, back in the forties, my daddy used to take us down to White Point Gardens to watch sailboat races. Not just the Isle of Palms race, either. Lots of different races. They used that same old pistol back then, and there was never a problem. Not until now, anyway."

"That's what Burt Tidwell said, too," remarked Theodosia. "But he said you could never tell about those old things. One day they just backfire."

Mrs. Dimple smiled, apologetic that her idle speculation had caused Haley such consternation. "Well then, you *see*. An expert like that, he's probably right."

"I think Theodosia wants to solve another mystery," piped up Haley.

"Haley," Theodosia protested, "I've got better things to do than run around Charleston investigating what was undoubtedly an accidental death."

Drayton peered over his half glasses owlishly and studied Theodosia. "Oh you *do*," he said. "I can tell by the look on your face."

Theodosia's bright eyes flashed. "I'm merely curious, as I'm sure you all are. It isn't every day someone as prominent as Oliver Dixon dies right before our very eyes."

"Before four hundred eyes," added Haley. "If someone had murder in mind, it was cleverly done."

"What do you mean?" asked Drayton.

"Too many witnesses is what she means," said Theodosia. "With so many sets of eyes, you'll get endless versions of the story, none of which will jibe."

"Now it's you girls who are giving me chills," said Miss Dimple, who had set down her pencil and closed the black leather ledger she'd been peering into.

"But does that really track?" asked Drayton. "Oliver Dixon was fairly well liked, right? He wasn't a scoundrel or a carpetbagger or anything like that."

Theodosia slid her teacup across the table, allowing Drayton to pour her a second cup of Nilgiri. "Delaine was saying something about Oliver Dixon launching a high-tech company," she said.

"Oh, I read about that in the business section," said Haley.

"Since when do you read the business section?" demanded Drayton.

"Since I decided to pursue an MBA," said Haley. "I want to run my own business someday. Like Theodosia." She smiled companionably at Theodosia.

"Haley, I think you're already a whiz at business," said Theodosia. "But tell us about this new company of Oliver Dixon's. And don't interrupt, Drayton."

"Yes, dear." Drayton hunched his shoulders forward, assuming a henpecked attitude, and they all giggled.

"Oliver Dixon had just swung a pile of venture capital money to launch a new company called Grapevine," said Haley. "You know, as in 'heard it on the grapevine.' Anyway, Grapevine is set to manufacture expansion modules for PDAs."

"Pray tell, what is a PDA?" asked Drayton.

"Personal digital assistant," explained Haley. She reached into her apron pocket and produced a palm-sized gizmo that looked like a cross between a cell phone and a miniature computer screen. "See, I've got one. Mine's a Palm Pilot. I keep notes and phone numbers and recipes and stuff on it. It even interfaces with my computer at home. According to *Business Week*, PDAs are the hottest thing. The world is going wireless, and PDAs are the newest techie trend."

"I don't like to hear that," shuddered Drayton. He was a self-proclaimed Luddite who strove to avoid all things technological. Drayton lived in a 160-year-old house that had once been owned by a Civil War surgeon, and he prided himself on maintaining his home in a historically accurate fashion. Drayton may have bowed to convention by having a telephone installed, but he drew the line at cable TV.

"Anyway," said Haley, "Oliver Dixon received his venture capital from a guy by the name of Booth Crowley. Grapevine was going to produce revolutionary new pager and remote modules that would make certain PDAs even more versatile."

"Oh my," said Miss Dimple. She was suddenly following the conversation with great interest.

"What?" asked Theodosia.

"Booth Crowley is a very astute businessman," said Miss Dimple. "Apparently he doesn't let a penny escape his grasp unless he's got a carefully worded contract that his lawyers have put under a microscope. Mr. Dauphine, God rest his soul, was on the Arts Association committee with Booth Crowley and told me the man was *extremely* mindful of how funds were dispersed."

Mr. Dauphine had been Miss Dimple's longtime employer. He had owned the Peregrine Building next door and had passed away last fall, while they were in the middle of trying to solve the mystery of the poisoning at the Lamplighter Tour.

Theodosia nodded. She'd heard about Booth Crowley. Certainly nothing bad, but his business dealings bordered on legendary. He was a very powerful man in Charleston. Besides heading Cherry Tree Investments, one of Charleston's premier venture capital firms, Booth Crowley sat on the board of directors of the Charleston Symphony Orchestra, the Gibbes Museum of Art, and Charleston Memorial Hospital. He was certainly a force to be reckoned with.

The bell over the door tinkled merrily, and a dozen people suddenly poured into the shop. Haley and Drayton instantly popped up from their seats and swept toward them, intent on getting their visitors seated, settled, and served.

Theodosia watched with keen approval as Haley adroitly addressed the group.

"How many? Three of you?" Haley asked. "Why don't you ladies take this nice table by the window. There's lots of sunshine today."

Drayton was just as charming. "Party of five?" he asked. "You'll like this round table over here. I could even put several teapots on the lazy Susan and do a tea tasting, if you'd like. Now, I'll be just two shakes, and then I'll be back with tea and some complimentary biscuits."

And the rest of the day was off and running at the Indigo Tea Shop.

"I'll be back on Wednesday, dear." Miss Dimple put a plump hand on Theodosia's arm.

"Thank you, Miss Dimple. I'm so glad you've been able to help out here at the tea shop. Now that Bethany's got a job at the museum in Columbia, we've been woefully shorthanded."

"It's you who deserves the thanks," said Miss Dimple. "Not everyone would take a chance on a creaky old book-keeper. Seems like the trend these days is to hire young."

"Trends don't concern us here at the tea shop," said Theodosia warmly. "People do."

"Bless you, dear," said Miss Dimple. And she toddled out the door, a barely five-foot-tall, plump little elf of a woman who was still sharp as a tack when it came to tabulating a column of numbers.

CHAPTER 4

❦

"*THEODOSIA.*" DRAYTON HAD a teapot filled with jasmine tea in one hand and a teapot of Ceylon silver
tips in the other. "As soon as we get our customers taken
care of, I need to speak with you."

Theodosia glanced out over the tables. Their customers
had already settled in and were munching benne wafers
and casting admiring glances at the shelves that held cozy
displays of tea tins, jellies, china teapots, and tea candles.

"What's up?" she asked.

He cocked his head to one side and gave a conspiratorial roll of his eyes. "The *mystery* tea," he told her in a qua-
vering, theatrical voice.

Theodosia grinned. Drayton was certainly in his ele-
ment planning all his special-event teas. But this mystery
tea had really seemed to capture his imagination. It would
appear that Drayton, the straitlaced history buff and Heritage Society parliamentarian, had a playful side, after all.

Anyway, Theodosia decided, Drayton certainly had an
astute business side. His mystery tea was already shaping
up as a success. Counting the two calls they'd received

earlier this morning, they now had twelve confirmed reservations for Saturday night. And Drayton had audaciously put a price of forty-five dollars per person on the event.

"Okay, Drayton," she said, "I'll be in my office."

Theodosia disappeared behind the panels of heavy green velvet that separated the tea shop from the back area, where the tiny kitchen and her even tinier office were located.

Sitting at her antique wooden desk, thumbing through a catalog from Woods & Winston, one of her suppliers, Theodosia had a hard time keeping her mind on carafes and French tea presses. Her thoughts kept returning to yesterday afternoon, to Oliver Dixon's demise and to her subsequent conversation with Burt Tidwell.

She had taunted Tidwell a bit with her crack about rival yacht clubs. She'd been testing him, trying to ascertain what his suspicions had been, for she knew for a fact that, Burt Tidwell being Burt Tidwell, he'd certainly harbor a few thoughts of his own.

But had she really thought that members from one yacht club would plot against another? No, not really. She knew the Charleston Yacht Club and the Compass Key Yacht Club competed against each other all the time. And relations had always been friendly between the clubs. Besides the Isle of Palms race, they also ran the Intercoastal Regatta and some kind of event in fall that was curiously dubbed the Bourbon Cup.

What she *was* interested in knowing more about was Oliver Dixon and his new start-up company, Grapevine.

Then there was the obviously intoxicated Ford Cantrell, who had staged a somewhat ugly scene in front of Oliver Dixon and Giovanni Loard. What had that been about?

Haley had mentioned something earlier about her looking for a mystery to solve. Perhaps she had found her mystery.

"Knock, knock," announced Drayton as he pushed his way into her office, tea tray in hand. "Thought you might like to try a cup of this new Japanese Sencha. It's first flush, you know, and really quite rare," he said as he set the lacquer tray down on her desk.

Theodosia nodded expectantly. Any time you were able to get the first picking of a tea, you were in for a special treat. The new, young shoots were always so tender and flavorful.

Drayton perched on the overstuffed chair across from her desk, the one they'd dubbed "the tuffet," and fussed with the *tetsubin,* or traditional iron teapot. Moments earlier, he'd used a bamboo whisk to whip the powdered green tea, along with a dollop of hot water, into a gentle froth. Then he'd poured more hot water over the mixture, water that had been heated until it was just this side of boiling.

Now Drayton poured a small amount of the bright green tea into two teacups. Like the tea, the teacups were Japanese, tiny ceramic cups with a decorative crackle glaze that held about two ounces.

Savoring the heavenly aroma, Theodosia took a sip and let the tea work its way across her tongue. It was full-bodied and fresh, with a soothing aftertaste. Green tea was usually an acquired taste, although once a tea drinker became captivated by it, green tea soon found a place in his tea-drinking lexicon. It was a tea rich in fluoride and was reputed to boost the immune system. In a pinch, green tea could also be used on a compress to soothe insect bites or bee stings.

"Splendid," exclaimed Theodosia. "How much of this tea did we order?"

Drayton favored her with a lopsided grin. "Just the one tin. It's priced sky high, a lot more than most of our customers are used to paying. What say we keep it for our own private little stash?"

"Okay by me," agreed Theodosia. "Now, what's up with this mystery tea?" Drayton had worked out the concept on his own, distributed posters up and down Church Street and in many of the bed-and-breakfasts. But, so far, no one at the tea shop had been privy to his exact agenda.

Drayton whipped out his black notebook and balanced his reading glasses on the tip of his nose. "Twelve customers have signed up so far, and we have room for, oh, maybe ten more. We'll begin with caviar on toast points and serve Indian *chai* with a twist of lemon in oversized martini glasses. Then, as the program proceeds, we shall . . ." He glanced up to find a look of delight on Theodosia's face. "Oh," he said. "You like?"

"I like it very much," she replied. "What else?"

Drayton snapped his notebook shut. "No, all I really wanted was to gauge your initial reaction. And I'm extremely heartened by what I just saw. Now you'll have to wait until Saturday night to find out the rest."

"Drayton!" Theodosia protested with a laugh. "That's not fair!"

He shrugged. "I guess that's why they call it a mystery tea."

"But it sounds so charming," she argued. "At least the snippet you shared with me is. And you certainly can't do it . . . I mean, you *shouldn't* do it all by yourself. You'll need help."

Drayton shook his head firmly as a Cheshire cat grin creased his face. "Nice try," he told her. "Now I've got to get back out there and give Haley a hand." He took a final sip of tea and set his teacup back down. "Oh, and Theodosia, can you figure out what to do with the leftovers from yesterday? They're absolutely jamming the refrigerator, and I'm going to need space for my . . ." He dropped his voice. ". . . *mystery* goodies."

After he had gone, Theodosia leaned back in her chair, a wry smile playing at her lips. *All right, Drayton,* she thought, *I'll go along with your little game. We'll just wait and see what excitement you've cooked up for Saturday night.*

She took another sip of Sencha tea and thought for a moment about the dilemma inside the refrigerator. Drayton was certainly correct; there were packages of finger sandwiches that had been in the hamper from yesterday, and now they'd been crammed into the refrigerator. What could she do, aside from tossing them out and wasting perfectly good food?

I know, she decided, *I'll pack everything up and take it to the senior citizen home with me. After all, I'm going there tonight with Earl Grey.*

Her heart melted at the thought of Earl Grey, the dog she'd dubbed her Dalbrador. Part dalmatian, part Labrador, Theodosia had found the dog cowering in her back alley two years ago. Hungry and lost, the poor creature had been rummaging through trash cans in the midst of a rainstorm, trying to find a morsel of food. Theodosia had taken the pup in, cared for him, and opened her heart to him.

And Earl Grey had returned her kindness in so many ways. He'd turned out to be a remarkable companion animal. One who was personable and gentle and a perfect roommate for her in the little apartment upstairs. Earl Grey had taken to obedience training extremely well, delighted to learn the essentials of being a well-mannered pooch. He'd also shown a keen aptitude for work as a therapy dog.

Attending special therapy dog classes, Earl Grey had learned how to walk beside a wheelchair, how to gently greet people, and to graciously accept old hands patting him with exuberance. When one elderly woman, with tears streaming down her face and a mumbled story about a long-remembered pet dog, threw her frail arms about Earl Grey's neck, he calmly allowed her to sob her heart out on his strong, furry shoulder.

Upon graduation from therapy dog classes, Earl Grey had received his Therapy Dog International certification and was awarded a spiffy blue nylon vest that sported his official TDI patch and allowed him entry to the O'Doud Senior Home two nights every month.

"Hey." Haley stood in the doorway. "What's the joke between you and Drayton? He looks like a cat that just swallowed a canary."

Theodosia waved a hand. "It's the mystery tea thing."

"Oh, that," said Haley. "He's driving me crazy, too. Gosh, I almost forgot why I came in here. You've got a phone call. Jory Davis. Line two."

Theodosia grabbed for the phone. "Hello?"

"Theodosia?" came a familiar voice.

"What happened?" she asked. "Where were you? Your boat never finished the race."

"You wouldn't believe it," said Jory Davis. "When we got out of the shelter of the harbor, just past Sullivan's Island, the wind was so strong it blew out our genoa sail. We had to scrub the race and pull in at the Isle of Palms. By the time we found a place to moor the boat and hitched a ride back to Charleston, it was after ten. But we *did* hear all about Oliver Dixon. Poor fellow, what a terrible way to go. Kind of shakes you up. One day he's glad-handing at the clubhouse, and the next day he's gone. Do they have a handle yet on how the accident happened? Anybody examined that old pistol? I mean, it *was* an accident, right?"

That's funny, thought Theodosia. Jory Davis was the second person she'd spoken with who'd made a casual, questioning remark about whether it had been an accident or not. Correction, make that the third person. She, herself, had implied the same thing to Tidwell yesterday.

"Apparently, the pistol just exploded," said Theodosia.

"Wow," breathed Jory Davis. "Talk about a bad day at Black Rock for the Dixons."

"What do you mean?" she asked, her radar suddenly perking up.

"Oliver Dixon's two sons, Brock and Quaid, were supposed to be in the race with us, but they got disqualified."

"Why was that?" asked Theodosia.

"They had an illegal rudder on their boat. They're claiming that Billy Manolo, the guy who does maintenance on some of the boats at the yacht club, tampered with it. Frankly, I think those guys probably sanded the rudder down themselves in an attempt to streamline it. Anyway," continued Jory, "I don't want to trash those guys after their father just died so tragically."

"No, of course not," murmured Theodosia.

"And I didn't want to call you last night and risk waking you up. Especially in light of the kind of day you probably had. I understand you were the first person to reach Oliver Dixon's body."

"Yes," she said.

"That's pretty tough, kiddo. You doing okay?"

"I think so," said Theodosia. "I can't help thinking about Doe, however. I mean, they'd only been married something like nine weeks."

"It's a tragedy," said Jory. "I saw Doe and Oliver together at Emilio's Restaurant a week or so ago, and they were absolutely gaga over each other. Of course, the saving grace in all this is that Doe is still young. She'll be a lot more resilient and able to bounce back."

"Bounce back," repeated Theodosia absently. "Yes."

"But, listen," Jory continued, "I didn't call to rehash this misfortune. People have probably been stopping by the tea shop all morning to do that. I really called to tell you I'm flying to New York this afternoon."

"New York!" Theodosia exclaimed. She'd been hoping she could get together with Jory Davis and coax a little information from him. Being a longtime yacht club member, he'd undoubtedly have an inside track. And with his keen lawyer's perception, he might just notice if something seemed a little out of alignment. He could also fill her in on that historic old pistol they supposedly kept under lock and key at the yacht club clubhouse. Well, all that might have to wait.

"Our firm is representing some fast-food franchises who really got hosed by the parent corporation," he said. "I've got to depose witnesses, then file papers for a class action suit. Listen, I'll be staying at the Waldorf. If you need me for anything, anything at all, just leave a message at the desk, okay?"

"Okay. Good luck." Theodosia hung up the phone, feeling slightly out of sorts. Gazing at the wall that faced her desk, her eyes scanned the montage of framed photos, opera programs, tea labels, and other memorabilia that hung there.

There was a photo of Earl Grey taken when she'd first found him, all ribs and scruffy fur. There was her dad posed jauntily on his sailboat. That had been taken just a year before he passed away. Another photo, one of her favorites, showed her mom and dad at Cane Ridge Plantation. That photo had been taken back in the early sixties, right after they'd gotten married. They looked so young and hopeful and so very much in love, with their arms entwined around each other. Six years after that photo had been taken, she had been born. Her mother had lived only eight more years.

Heaving a giant sigh, Theodosia told herself not to feel sad but to feel lucky. She had known unconditional love and support from her parents. Her parents' ultimate gift to her had been to fix firmly in her mind the notion that she could accomplish anything she set her mind to.

And she had.

Stop being a goose, she scolded herself, *just because Jory Davis is taking off for New York. You can always give him a buzz. He said as much, didn't he? And you've got lots of other friends and plenty of pressing business to keep you busy.*

Haley had accused her of wanting to solve another mystery. *Is that true?* she wondered. Is that why she felt so unsettled and restless? And did she really believe Oliver Dixon's death had been anything other than a terrible, unfortunate accident?

Theodosia let the idea tumble around in her brain as she reached for one of the catalogs and slowly thumbed through it, contemplating all manner of teapots and trivets.

CHAPTER 5

❧❧❧

A FURRY BROWN muzzle poked over the metal rails of
the bed.

"Hello doggy." A tiny, birdlike woman reached out and
gently rested her blue-veined hand on Earl Grey's forehead. He snuggled to her touch, and the old lady squealed
with delight.

"You're a good doggy to come visit me," she told him.
"A very good doggy."

Standing ten steps back, allowing Earl Grey the free-
dom he needed to interact with the residents, Theodosia
beamed. This was what it was all about. Affording older
folks the joy of touch and connection with an animal that
demanded nothing of them, yet offered a warm, furry presence that inexplicably seemed to render a calming effect.

Tonight, Earl Grey and Theodosia had spent most of
their time visiting the rooms of residents who were bedrid-
den. Earl Grey, who was often exuberant when chasing a
ball tossed by one of the residents down the wide hallways,
seemed to understand that these types of visits required
considerably more restraint. And Theodosia was pleased

that Earl Grey had conducted himself with a great deal of doggy decorum.

"Theodosia? Can you bring Earl Grey into the TV room?" Suzette Ellison, one of the night nurses who had worked at the O'Doud Senior Home for more than fifteen years, stood in the doorway.

"What's up, Suzette? Another liver brownie cake for Earl Grey?"

Suzette grinned. "What else? But this is a special occasion. Your anniversary. It's been two years since you and that nice dog of yours have been coming here, and some of our ladies and gentlemen want to thank you."

"Surprise!" The group called out in unison as Theodosia and Earl Grey walked into the room.

Theodosia threw her hands up in surprise, and Earl Grey, immediately homing in on the liver brownie cake that rested on a low table in the center of the room, shook his head in anticipation and let out a sharp *woof*.

"Happy anniversary, Earl!" one of the ladies called out with exuberance. "Thanks for always making us smile."

Suzette had laid out all the sandwiches Theodosia had brought with her on a long table and rustled up a bowl of punch. The residents wasted no time in helping themselves to snacks, and the room suddenly buzzed with the makings of a party.

Theodosia grabbed a cup of punch for herself and wandered among the residents. They smiled and nodded at her, but Earl Grey was, of course, the real star. He was the one they wanted to talk to and pet. He was the one they looked forward to seeing.

"This is a lovely picnic you brought, Miss Browning."

Theodosia smiled down at an elderly man in a wheelchair. Freckles covered his bald head, and deep wrinkles cut into his face, but his eyes shone bright with interest.

"Glad you're enjoying it," she said.

"Kind of different from yesterday afternoon, eh?" said the old man.

Surprised, Theodosia sank down on one knee so she was eye level with him. He smiled at her then, a kind, knowing smile that suddenly took years off his tired, lined face.

"Oh yes," he told her as he wagged a finger, "I heard all about the accident from my son. He was there."

"Your son was in White Point Gardens yesterday?" asked Theodosia.

"Yup," said the old man. "Course, he didn't just phone me out of the blue and tell me. I read about it in the newspaper this morning. Then I called him so I could get the real poop. My son used to race Lasers with the yacht club," he explained.

The old man stopped abruptly, as if all this talking had been a considerable effort for him.

"Would you like something to drink?" asked Theodosia. She thrust her cup of punch toward him. "Here, take mine."

The old man eagerly grasped her drink and helped himself to several good swallows. "Good," he croaked. Setting the empty cup aside on a nearby table, the old man stuck out a withered hand. "I'm Winston Lazerby."

"Theodosia Browning," she said, shaking his hand. "And your son is . . . ?"

"Thomas Lazerby. He's a cardiologist at Charleston Mercy Medical. You know, a heart doctor." Winston Lazerby thumped his own skinny chest as if to demonstrate his son's specialty. "The minute I saw that article about Oliver Dixon," Winston Lazerby continued, "I thought of the feud."

Tiny hairs on the back of Theodosia's neck rose imperceptibly. "What do you mean, Mr. Lazerby?" she asked.

"The Dixon-Cantrell feud," Winston Lazerby said, staring at Theodosia intently. "Those two families have been going at it for almost seventy years."

Theodosia glanced around quickly. No one seemed to be paying the two of them a bit of attention. *Good,* she thought. "Tell me more, Mr. Lazerby," she urged him.

The old man leaned forward. "They been fighting with each other ever since the thirties, when Letitia Dixon up and ran off with Sam Cantrell."

"This Letitia Dixon, how was she related to Oliver Dixon?"

Winston Lazerby thought for a moment. "Aunt," he said. "Letitia would've been Oliver's mother's sister."

"And Sam Cantrell?" asked Theodosia.

Winston Lazerby nodded. "Related to all them Cantrells. Don't know the full story there. But I do know Sam was a smooth-talkin' feller, and Letitia was a young gal, eighteen years old at most, and wilder 'n seven devils."

"What happened to them?" asked Theodosia, intrigued. "Where did they run off to?"

"Nobody knows," replied Winston Lazerby. "There was rumors that Letitia ended up in Portland, Oregon, and died of rheumatic fever a few years later. But I personally think they was just rumors. People always think the worst when something like that happens."

"And there's still bad blood between the two families?" said Theodosia.

Winston Lazerby nodded knowingly. "Very bad blood."

"So that might explain why Ford Cantrell was so hot under the collar in front of Oliver Dixon and Giovanni Loard," murmured Theodosia.

"Giovanni Loard," giggled the old man suddenly. "Ain't that a fancy new name. Fellow's Christian name was George Lord. Guess he figured calling himself Giovanni would play better with the tourists. Or adding an *a* to his last name. Folks might mistake him for a real Southern gentleman."

"Do you know what the Dixons and Cantrells have been fighting over recently?" asked Theodosia.

"You name it, they probably fight over it," said Winston Lazerby. "Those two families have wrangled over business, over real estate, over *women*." He shook his head. "Crazy."

Theodosia glanced up and saw that many of the residents had begun to move off toward their rooms. It was eight-thirty and getting late for these older folk.

"Mr. Lazerby, could we talk again sometime?" Theodosia asked.

"Sure," he agreed. "Come on over any time. You know where I live." He gave her a wink.

Warm breezes caressed her face and carried delicious scents for Earl Grey's inquisitive nose as Theodosia sped home through the night, the windows of her Jeep Cherokee rolled down. She'd purchased the Jeep two years ago against the advice of Drayton and had immediately fallen in love with it.

When summer's heat and humidity hit full bore, wrapping Charleston in its smothering grip, Theodosia loved nothing better than to escape to the low country. Crashing down shady, narrow roads that were lush and overgrown with twining vines, she'd maneuver long-forgotten trails, confident in her Jeep's nimbleness and four-wheel drive. There were old rice dikes to bump over and moss-covered mounds that were remnants of old, abandoned phosphate mines. In the tangle of sun-dappled woods and myriad meandering streams guarded by live oaks, those grand sentinels of the South, Theodosia would find cool refuge and tranquility.

Tonight, however, Winston Lazerby's words weighed heavily on her mind. As she flipped a left turn onto Beau-

fain Street, past R. Pratt Antiques and Campbell's Architectural Supply, Theodosia wondered if he had been correct in his recollection, wondered if perhaps there really
was something to Mr. Lazerby's story concerning a Dixon-
Cantrell feud.

Well, she decided, as she pulled the Jeep in close to the
rear of her little building and eased into her parking spot,
there's only one way to find out. Do a little research.

Above the tea shop, Theodosia had created a cozy little
abode for herself. Filled with a mélange of antiques and
choice hand-me-downs, it was an airy little apartment with
windows that not only pushed open to catch the harbor
breezes but also afforded a spectacular view up and down
Church Street and across Meeting Street toward The Battery.

While Earl Grey padded off to cuddle up on his bed, an
oversized chintz cushion tucked into the corner of her bedroom, Theodosia fixed herself a cup of Orange Elixir tea.
One of Drayton's custom blends, Orange Elixir wasn't really a tea per se, since it was not derived from *Camellia
sinensis,* the tea plant. Rather, it was a delicious infusion of
orange peel, hibiscus, gingko, and linden blossoms. Perfect for stimulating the mind but not the nerves.

Sitting down at her spinet desk, Theodosia turned on
her iMac and clicked on Netscape Navigator. When the
site came up, she typed *"Charleston Post and Courier"*
into the search engine.

She took a sip of the flavorful fruit and herb drink and
waited, hoping she'd be able to peruse their newspaper
morgue.

No, the *Post and Courier* was archived back only to
1996. Theodosia tapped her fingers on the keyboard. What
else could she try? The Heritage Society? Why not?
They'd been around for well over a century, and their mission was to preserve written records as well as historic
buildings and objects.

Theodosia typed "www.charlestonheritagesociety.org" into the browser. Within seconds, the Heritage Society's home page offered up a colorful photo montage of historical buildings and a menu with a dizzying array of choices.

Theodosia studied that menu, then clicked on "Historical Records."

Another menu spun out before her listing "Deeds," "Marriages," "Maps and Plans," "Military," "Civil War," "Ships' Logs," and "City Planning."

No, she told herself, *the last thing I want to do is rummage, hit or miss, through hundreds of individual documents.*

Theodosia scrolled to the bottom of the page and clicked on "Search." Now she could type in the name *Cantrell* and, if it was mentioned somewhere on the Heritage Society's Web site, the search engine would pull it up as a hit.

Five hits came up, each with a one-line descriptor. The first three were duds as far as Theodosia was concerned, since they all dealt with someone named Cora Cantrell, who'd been a schoolteacher in the town of Eutaville during the late 1800s.

Clicking on the fourth hit, Theo pulled up an article about the defunct Cantrell Canal that had been used by barges laden with indigo, cotton, and rice.

The fifth hit was far more enlightening. This was a newspaper clipping from the *Colton Telegraph*, a defunct newspaper from a now-defunct village. The article chronicled an altercation that had taken place in 1892 between one Jeb Cantrell and one Stuart Dixon. During a duel in the woods near Pamlico Hill Plantation, Jeb Cantrell had shot Stuart Dixon to death.

Were these two duelists the long-dead ancestors of Ford Cantrell and Oliver Dixon?

Had to be.

So this duel was perhaps the kindling that had sparked

the nasty Dixon-Cantrell feud. Not a scandal concerning runaways from the two families like Winston Lazerby had thought. That had come later.

Historical dueling had always sounded so romantic, mused Theodosia. And yet, the heads of these two families had tragically fought each another over some point of honor. And one had been mortally wounded.

Theodosia lifted her eyes from the computer screen and stared across her living room at the moody seascape painting that hung above her fireplace.

She thought about how history had taught so many cruel lessons, one of them being that families, tribes, and often countries are rarely able to surmount a blood feud. Rather, the feud perpetuates itself, growing like a foul mushroom in the dank recess of a forest, feeding off decay.

Even when descendants are unclear about circumstances that led to the feud or had never personally known the ancestors who'd first spilled blood, these terrible blood feuds seemed to persist. An eye for an eye, a tooth for a tooth.

Theodosia stretched both arms over her head until she felt the tension in her shoulders ease. Then she placed her hands at the base of her neck and rubbed gently. If the Dixon-Cantrell feud *was* still going on—and hostility certainly seemed to have been roiling inside Ford Cantrell yesterday afternoon—then the whole situation certainly bore looking into.

Shouldn't Ford Cantrell be questioned? Not so much to ask him flat out if he'd somehow engineered an exploding pistol but to perhaps eliminate him as a suspect?

Theodosia rose swiftly from her chair, walked to a pine cabinet that displayed a small, tasty collection of Wedgewood, and pulled open one of the narrow drawers. Thumbing through a brown leather card case, Theodosia found Burt Tidwell's business card. She held it between her thumb and index finger as she continued to turn her question over in her mind.

Finally, she carried the card back to her computer, sat down, and composed a short E-mail message to Burt Tidwell. It was both an invitation and a request to stop by the Indigo Tea Shop tomorrow to discuss an important concern.

She paused for a moment, wondering if she was doing the right thing. Then she clicked "Send."

CHAPTER 6

❦

"*MARIAGE FRÈRES TEAS*," Theodosia told her three guests, "are blended in France. This particular tea, Mirabelle, is a Chinese black tea scented with the tiny but exquisite mirabelle plum that grows in northern France. Hence the mildly sweet aroma."

It was Drayton, for the most part, who conducted tea tastings. But this group of women, all women of a certain age and residents of the historic district, had specifically requested Theodosia's assistance. The three had met her while serving on a committee for Charleston's Garden Fest Tour and had been enthralled with Theodosia's knowledge of tea, her vibrancy, and her sweet nature.

That was just fine with Drayton this morning. Working as a backup for Haley, he'd been holding down the fort at the little table nearest the counter where the old cash register and various sweetgrass baskets filled with tea tins and tea goodies sat. Working diligently, he'd been able to put the finishing touches on all his ideas for summer teas.

"Need any help?" he asked Haley as she brushed past him with a second plate of apple tartlets for a group of five giggling tea shop regulars who seemed to be enjoying their morning tea immensely.

"Oh please," said Haley as she put a hand on her hip and tossed her head. "This is child's play."

Haley was incredibly task oriented and competitive, and once she'd decided to handle the morning's customers single-handedly, it was woe to anyone who tried to interfere.

"Just checking," Drayton assured her. "I wouldn't *dream* of interfering."

"Oh Drayton," she commented dryly, "I love your oratorical excess, but not as much as you love my cranberry scones." It was a pointed reference to the fact that Drayton had already consumed two of the giant pastries.

"When you get to be my age, you don't have to watch your girlish figure quite so much," quipped Drayton.

Drayton swiveled his head suddenly as Theodosia's group of ladies rose from their chairs and headed his way. He got to his feet immediately and stepped deftly around the counter to face them. "Ladies," he greeted them.

"I am in need of a tea press," said a lady in a yellow straw hat.

"And I have several marvelous ones to show you," replied Drayton as he plucked samples off the shelf and placed them on the counter.

The other two ladies immediately picked up sweetgrass baskets and began to coo over them. "These are wonderful," exclaimed one. "I had a sweetgrass basket that I used for years as a summer handbag. When it got tattered and worn, my granddaughter begged me to give it to her. She said they have some of these baskets on display at the Smithsonian."

"Indeed, they do," proclaimed Drayton. "A collection of South Carolina sweetgrass baskets resides in the Smithsonian's permanent collection, a fitting tribute to our lowcountry craftspeople."

Drayton held up one of the elegant, woven baskets that had been resting on the countertop. "These," he said enticingly, "were made from a sweetgrass crop cultivated on Johns Island. Would any of you ladies care to take one home?"

Two heads nodded, and Drayton beamed.

"You're a natural-born salesman, Drayton," Theodosia told him with unabashed admiration as she sat down across from him. Even though they'd been together almost three years, she was still slightly in awe of Drayton's prodigious sales talent. True, she had huckstered food products and computer peripherals on a national scale when she'd been in the advertising business. But selling one-on-one was still slightly disconcerting to her. She tended not to *sell* an item per se but, instead, let the item speak for itself.

Theodosia reached a hand across the table and tapped the black leather-bound ledger that Drayton had come to regard as his bible. It contained most of his tea-tasting notes and all of his ideas for tea blends, special events, and tea promotions.

"You've been working on the summer teas," Theodosia said with appropriate seriousness.

Drayton nodded.

"Your White Point Green was certainly a hit at the picnic, so we'll want to package that for sale," Theodosia said.

Drayton nodded again. "I agree. And I came up with one more iced tea." He paused. "I call it Audubon Herbal, a tribute to our nearby Audubon Swamp Garden."

Theodosia nodded. "Where John Audubon chronicled South Carolina's waterbirds."

"Right. The tea's a scant amount of black tea with hibiscus, lemongrass, and chamomile added. Mild, refreshing, not too stimulating."

Theodosia's eyes sparkled. "I like it. The tea and the tribute. What else?"

"Two more teas that veer decidedly toward the exotic," said Drayton. Then he added hastily, "But we've seen time and again that people *like* exotic teas."

"You won't get any argument from me, Drayton."

"The first one I call Ashley River Royal. It's a Ceylonese black tea with a pear essence."

"You're right, it *is* exotic."

"No, *this* one's the coup de grâce. Swan Lake Iris Gardens. Again, an homage to the elegant gardens that are home to . . . what? Seven species of swans? And you know how much everyone enjoys visiting the gardens in spring when the Dutch and Japanese iris are blooming."

"Of course," said Theodosia. "And what's the blend?"

"Four different teas with a top note of smoky lopsang."

"Drayton, you're not just going to capture the hearts of tea lovers, you're going to endear yourself to bird lovers and gardeners, too. And in Charleston, that's just about everyone."

"I know," smiled Drayton.

"Hey," interrupted Haley, "we're not going to package this stuff ourselves, are we? Remember last fall when we did holiday teas? My back gets sore just *thinking* about it."

"No, we'll have Gallagher's Food Service handle all that," said Drayton. "Frankly, I thought it was fun when we all worked together, but apparently no one else shared my enthusiasm. You all seemed to have mutiny on your minds."

"Last fall we had an extra pair of hands," said Haley. "But now that Bethany's moved to Columbia, who else could we shanghai? Miss Dimple?"

"Now *she's* a sport," said Drayton. "I bet she wouldn't complain half as much as you did."

"Drayton, don't you dare ask poor Miss Dimple to package tea," laughed Theodosia.

"One more thing," said Drayton, closing his book and getting up. "New packaging." He reached around to the back of the counter and pulled out a shiny, dark blue box with a rounded top that folded over. "Indigo blue boxes," said Drayton.

"They're the exact same color as the gift paper we use!" Theodosia squealed with delight. "Aren't you clever. Where did you find them?"

"Supplier in San Francisco," said Drayton. "We can have Gallagher's package the tea in our regular foil bags, then pop those bags into the blue boxes. From there we just need to add a label. I took the liberty of getting samples of gold foil labels from our printer. All you have to do is pick a label style and a typeface," said Drayton. "Then it's a done deal."

"Easy enough," said Theodosia.

"Don't look now," said Haley under her breath, "but that boorish cop just came in. Wonder what he wants?"

"I invited him," said Theodosia.

"You *invited* him?" Haley was stunned.

"Run and put together a nice pastry sampler, will you, Haley? And Drayton, could you do a fresh pot of tea? Maybe that Dunsandle Estate?"

"Of course, Theo," agreed Drayton. Then he turned to Haley. "Are you rooted to the floor, dear girl? Kindly fetch the pastries Theodosia requested."

"Okay," Haley agreed grudgingly. "But you know I can't stand that guy. He almost drove Bethany to a nervous breakdown with all his questions and nasty innuendos. He's a bully, pure and simple."

"He's a detective first grade," corrected Drayton under his breath. "Now the pastries, please?"

"Right," said Haley.

"Detective Tidwell," Theodosia greeted him warmly. "Sit here by the window."

"Nice to see you again, Miss Browning," said Tidwell as he lowered his bulk into a wooden captain's chair. "Good of you to drop me a note, even if it was of the electronic version."

He gave a cheery smile that Theodosia knew contained very little cheer. Tidwell's chitchat and tiny pleasantries were opening salvos that could be a steel-jawed trap for the unsuspecting.

"I wanted to talk to you about Oliver Dixon," said Theodosia.

"You mean Oliver Dixon's death," corrected Burt Tidwell.

"Since you put it that way, yes," agreed Theodosia.

She sat quietly as Haley placed teacups, plates, knives, and spoons in front of each of them, then Drayton followed with a steaming pot of tea. Theodosia poured some of the sweet elixir into Tidwell's cup and smiled with quiet satisfaction as his nose twitched. Then Haley delivered her plate of baked goods, and Tidwell brightened considerably.

"Oh my, this *is* lovely," he said as he scooped a raspberry scone onto his plate. "Is there, perchance, some jelly to accompany this sweet?"

But Haley was already back at the table with a plate of butter, pitcher of clotted cream, and various jars of jelly.

"Detective Tidwell," began Theodosia, "have you learned anything more about the pistol that killed Oliver Dixon?"

Tidwell sliced a sliver of butter and applied it to his pastry.

"Some," he said. "The pistol was American made, manufactured in the mid-1800s to Army specifications, and used as a side arm by officers. Stock is curly maple and there's an acorn design on the trigger guard. Graceful lines but a crude weapon. It was really only effective at close range."

But effective enough to mortally wound Oliver Dixon, Theodosia thought to herself.

"By the way," Tidwell said, "the pistol *was* kept at Oliver Dixon's yacht club. In friendly territory. So it's doubtful anyone would have tampered with it."

"Who loaded the pistol?" asked Theodosia.

"Fellow by the name of Bob Brewster. Been doing it for years. Apparently, you take a pinch of gunpowder and twist it inside a little piece of paper. Not unlike a tea bag," Tidwell told her. "Then you place the little packet in the barrel. Brewster's just sick about it, by the way."

"But Oliver Dixon *could* have had an enemy there," said Theodosia.

Tidwell stroked his ample chin. "Most people I've spoken with were highly complimentary of Oliver Dixon. He was a past commodore and had contributed a considerable amount of funds for the betterment of the place. He paid to have the boat piers reinforced and a clubhouse fireplace installed." Tidwell pulled a spiral notebook from his breast pocket and glanced at it. It was the same kind of notebook children purchased from the five-and-dime store. "Oh, and Oliver Dixon underwrote a sailing program last summer for inner-city youth. Kids Can Sail, or something like that."

"Dixon was known for his philanthropy?" asked Theodosia.

"And for being an all-around good guy," replied Tidwell. He smiled at her, then helped himself to an almond scone. "Lovely," he muttered under his breath.

He's not given me an ounce of useful information, thought Theodosia. *But then, did I really think he would?* She sighed inwardly. Conversations with Tidwell were always of the cat-and-mouse variety.

"You realize," she began, "there is a long-standing feud between the Dixons and the Cantrells." She watched him as her words sank in. He gave her nothing.

"The feud dates back to the 1880s," she said. "The heads of the two families fought a duel to the death."

"Mm-hm." Tidwell took another bite from his pastry, but Theodosia knew she had his attention.

"Sometime during the thirties, Oliver Dixon's aunt ran off with a Cantrell. Apparently, the two families have been openly hostile toward each other ever since."

"So you suspect young Ford Cantrell?" Tidwell's bright eyes were riveted on her.

"If I had a suspect in mind," Theodosia said slowly, "that would imply I believed a criminal act had been committed. And I have no proof of that."

"Aha," said Tidwell, "so this conversation is simply neighborly gossip."

Theodosia stared at him unhappily.

Seeing her displeasure, Tidwell's eyes lost their merriment, and he suddenly turned serious. "Yes, I have heard rumblings about this so-called Dixon-Cantrell feud. Although you seem to have gained the upper hand as far as specific details."

Though large in girth, Tidwell's words could be spare and pared down when he wanted them to be.

"Do you know much about antique pistols?" she asked him.

He looked thoughtful. "Not really. Obviously, our ballistics people are taking a look at it, but their forte, as one might imagine, really lies in modern weapons."

But I know an expert, thought Theodosia. *And I just might take a chance on talking to him.*

Tidwell seemed to contemplate helping himself to a third pastry, then thought better of it. "Ah well." He struggled to his feet, brushed a fine sheen of granulated sugar from his jacket lapels. "Time to be off. Thank you for your kind invitation and the lovely tea."

And he was out the door, just like that.

Theodosia gathered up the dirty dishes and carried them

into the back of the tea shop. "Drayton," she called over her shoulder, "is Timothy Neville in town? The symphony was invited to perform in Savannah. Do you know if he's back?"

"He's back." Drayton popped his head through the curtains. "I spoke with Timothy yesterday."

"Oh," was all Theodosia said. Contemplating a visit with Timothy Neville and actually *talking* to Timothy Neville were two different things.

"Do you think he still hates me for suspecting him of poisoning that real estate developer?" she asked.

"Nonsense," said Drayton. "Timothy Neville doesn't hate you; he hates everyone. Timothy has always been an equal-opportunity curmudgeon. Don't give his ill humor a second thought."

CHAPTER 7

❧❧❧

TIMOTHY NEVILLE WAS going to celebrate his eightieth birthday next month. But he wasn't about to spill the beans to the wags in the historic district. No sir, his DOB had long been a hot topic of conversation, and he wasn't going to spoil the fun now. Some folks put him at eighty-five; others kindly deducted ten years.

What did it matter?

He was in excellent physical condition except for a touch of arthritis in his hands. And that came from playing the violin these many years and bothered him only when the temperature dipped below fifty degrees.

Fact was, he had outlived two of his doctors. Now he rarely even bothered with doctors. He had Henry, his butler, take his blood pressure twice a day, and he swallowed a regimen of supplements that included ginkgo biloba, coenzyme 10, choline, and vitamins B_1, B_6, C, and E.

True, he had made a few concessions in his diet, switching from predominantly red meat to fish and from bourbon to wine. He still smoked an Arturo Fuente cigar occasionally but, more and more, that was becoming a rare treat.

Genetics. Timothy Neville chalked it all up to genetics.
His mother had lived to ninety and had taken to her bed
only on the day prior to her death. Her ancestors, most of
whom dated back to the original Huguenots who fled reli-
gious persecution in France during the mid-1600s, had
been a determined and hardy lot. They had endured the
hardships of an ocean voyage, worked tirelessly to help
colonize Charles Town, fought off the greedy English
crown, then managed to survive the War Between the
States. Today, his ancestors were numbered among the
founding fathers of Charleston and considered social aris-
tocracy.

Timothy Neville smiled to himself as he studied the
landscape painting he held in his hands. It had been
painted in the late thirties by Alice Ravenel Huger Smith,
a watercolorist famed for her moody renditions of low-
country rice plantations. The piece had sustained some
damage. One corner had been gnawed by insects, and a
brown splotch of water damage shot through the sky. The
painting hadn't been preserved in acid-free paper, either,
so it was slightly faded. It would take considerable conser-
vation skills to restore the little watercolor, but the piece
was well worth it. Huger Smiths were few and far between
these days, and most people who held one in their posses-
sion preferred to sell it at auction in New York rather than
donate it to a museum.

"Mr. Neville? There's someone to see you?" Claire, one
of the secretaries, hovered in the doorway.

Timothy didn't look up. "Who, please?"

"Theodosia Browning?" *Claire has a way of making
everything sound like a question. Why is that?* he wondered. He'd heard other young women speak in that same
maddening way. Were they too insecure to spit out a simple declarative statement?

It didn't matter. Timothy knew he was merely stalling
for time, letting the idea that Theodosia Browning had

come to call upon him ruminate in his mind. There was certainly nothing wrong in allowing her a brief cool-your-heels period in the anteroom. After all, she had harbored suspicions about him being involved in the death of that real estate developer last fall and had helped herself to a merry snoop in his home during a music recital. Since that incident, he felt that she had been more cool and aloof with him than he with her. Embarrassment? Remorse over her actions? Had to be.

"Show her in," Timothy said finally.

Theodosia Browning entered his office in a whisper of silk. He heard the slight rustle of the fabric, could detect a pleasant, slightly floral scent about her. He wondered if it was perfume or tea.

Timothy laid the painting down on the table in front of him and turned to face her. He did not make any indication for her to take a chair.

She smiled at him, looking, he decided, rather pretty in her aqua silk slacks and jacket with that mass of curly auburn hair framing her head like a friendly Medusa.

"Mr. Neville . . ." began Theodosia.

"Call me Timothy," he said in his clipped, no-nonsense manner. "We are well acquainted with each other, are we not?"

Theodosia flinched slightly, and her cheeks flared pink from embarrassment.

"Timothy, then," said Theodosia. She was beginning to regret her impulsiveness at coming here. Timothy Neville had clearly not forgotten her actions of a few months ago. She swallowed hard, determined to get through this. "You're an expert in antique weaponry," she began. "Guns, pistols, the like. Would you be able to help me understand how a pistol might explode on its own?"

"Snooping again, are we Miss Browning?" Timothy Neville favored her with a remote smile.

"One could call it investigating, Mr. Neville," she

replied. *To heck with calling him Timothy,* Theodosia decided. Addressing him as Mr. Neville was far more preferable. The formality kept him at arm's length, which was probably where she should keep this strange little man.

"One could," Timothy replied. "But then one would have to be a duly sworn investigator. I don't recall that you are."

Theodosia ignored Timothy's remark. "My interest is in Oliver Dixon's death . . . the terrible accident that befell him. You are—"

"Yes, of course I'm aware of what took place," murmured Timothy. "Terrible tragedy. He was a fine fellow." Timothy's bright eyes bore into her. "And you think because I have a collection of antique weapons that I know about exploding pistols and the like, is that it?"

"I rather thought you might be able to offer some type of explanation," said Theodosia.

"An explanation for an accident," said Timothy slowly. "I'm not sure I follow your logic. Or that I see there's any logic to follow."

"But if it wasn't accidental, then . . ." She stopped abruptly. "You're not going to help me, are you?" said Theodosia. This conversation wasn't going the way she'd hoped. She knew her feelings of regret for snooping on Timothy were a huge obstacle for her to overcome. That and the fact that Timothy Neville's brilliance made her feel like a plodding schoolchild.

Timothy Neville shrugged imperceptibly.

"Well, it might interest you," said Theodosia out of frustration, "that I have discovered a few clues of my own on the Heritage Society's Web site."

Timothy just stared at her.

"That's right," Theodosia continued. "Thanks to old newspaper clippings that reside on *your* Web site, I've discovered a few things about the Dixon-Cantrell feud."

"Good for you," said Timothy. He hadn't meant to

sound flippant and harsh, but it came out that way. He knew he was a crusty old man, prone to caustic remarks and pronouncements, and he regretted his sarcastic tone instantly.

But his words cut Theodosia to the quick and made her spin on her heel.

It's definitely time to leave, she decided. *Timothy Neville is not going to give me one iota of cooperation.*

She had already retreated through the doorway when Timothy began to speak. "Miss Browning, if I were to hazard a guess, I'd say you might possibly have the right church but are looking in the wrong pew." His words, meant to appease, tumbled out in a rush. He'd also spoken so softly that Theodosia was barely able to register all his words. It had been like listening to a faulty record or tape and catching only fragments.

"What?" Theodosia asked, unsure of what he was trying to tell her.

But Timothy Neville had turned back to his painting.

CHAPTER 8

✦❈✦

"*DID YOU FIND* out what you wanted?" Drayton asked. After Theodosia returned to the tea shop, he had waited the better part of an hour before approaching her. She'd retired to her office immediately, and he'd heard her tapping away on her laptop computer. Probably working on some marketing ideas. Between the shop and the Web site and the specialty teas and her new idea for tea bath products, Theodosia was awfully busy. And a little distracted, too. "You were gone long enough," Drayton added.

Theodosia leaned back in her chair and exhaled slowly. "The meeting with Timothy didn't last all that long. But I was so darned upset afterward that I had to take a cool-down stroll behind Saint Philip's."

The cemetery behind Saint Philip's was one of those hidden places in Charleston, a spot not too many tourists found their way to. Filled with fountains and sculpture and fascinating old tombstones, it was a quiet, restful place where one could usually find solace.

"Timothy said something to upset you?" asked Drayton.

He knew Timothy was old and crusty, but he also knew the man could be handled. Of course, you had to use kid gloves.

"Timothy Neville hates me," declared Theodosia. "I'm sure of it. He gave me that hard-eyed, calculating look that just seems to pierce right through you. I know all of you folks on the board at the Heritage Society think he does a masterful job, raising money and helping save old buildings by securing landmark status for them, but I don't see him as anything but rude and dismissive." She put her elbows on her desk and dropped her chin in her hands. "That's it," she said. "It's as simple as that. He hates me."

"Theodosia, I think you're being paranoid," said Drayton.

"I'm not. He really is an abominable little man."

"Who can also be quite charming," argued Drayton. "Besides, if Timothy hated you, he wouldn't have invited you to his Garden Fest party."

Charleston's annual Garden Fest started next week, a weeklong event where more than three dozen backyard gardens in the historic district were open for public viewing. Many would-be garden enthusiasts had been working on their gardens for years, adding fountains and cultivating prize flowers in an attempt to get on the venue. But it was a select number that were chosen every year. And it was a great honor. Of course, Timothy Neville's courtyard garden at the rear of his enormous Georgian-style mansion on Archdale Street topped the list.

"He didn't invite me," said Theodosia, "he invited *you*."

"Yes, but your name went back on the RSVP, as you had agreed to accompany me."

Theodosia wrinkled her nose. "Do I have to go?"

Drayton looked stern. "Of course you do. I certainly can't cancel at this late date. Not very gentlemanly. Plus it's an important event."

"Okay," Theodosia sighed. She stuck her legs out straight and kicked off her loafers. They were exquisitely thin leather and perfectly matched her aqua silk outfit. Delaine, her fashion guardian angel, had seen to that. "I just hope Timothy doesn't toss me out on my ear."

"Timothy didn't give you any information at all?" Drayton prodded gently. "That's not like him. He might toy with you a bit, but Timothy is generally flattered when asked to lend his expertise."

Picking up a fat black pen, Theodosia began to make doodles on the art pad that sat front and center on her desk.

Drayton decided it might be advantageous to change the subject. "You've been working on your bath teas."

"Yes."

"Any ideas?"

Theodosia brightened. "Actually, lots. What would you think of an entire line of bath products? Tea bags for the bath, so to speak. So many green teas are excellent for relaxing sore muscles, and herbals like lavender, jasmine, calendula blossoms, and rose petals are soothing to the skin. The bath care market, especially those products with natural ingredients, is taking off like crazy, and I think soothing tea products would fit right in."

"So do I," agreed Drayton.

They batted ideas back and forth for the better part of an hour, Theodosia taking notes like mad, finally switching to her laptop computer because, she contended, she could get the ideas down faster.

At five o'clock, Haley came in.

"I'm going to lock up, okay?" said Haley.

"Sure, fine," waved Theodosia, completely out of her funk now. "Have a terrific evening."

"You, too," said Haley. "Bye, Drayton."

"Good night," he called.

Theodosia and Drayton sat quietly for a moment, listening as Haley snapped off lights, then exited the front door, locking it behind her. The only light on in the tea shop was the glowing Tiffany lamp that sat on Theodosia's desk.

"Drayton," said Theodosia slowly, "Timothy Neville *did* say something to me."

He stared at her patiently.

"Timothy mumbled something about 'right church, wrong pew.' I think he was referring to the Dixon-Cantrell feud. You've heard about that?"

Drayton nodded. "Dribs and drabs over the years."

"That's what I was talking to Detective Tidwell about today."

"That's kind of what Haley and I figured. You think Ford Cantrell . . . ?"

Theodosia shrugged. "Maybe . . . You saw how irate he was at the picnic."

"Howling mad," agreed Drayton.

"Of course, Timothy could have been trying to send me off in the wrong direction, too," said Theodosia.

"That doesn't sound like Timothy," said Drayton. "He usually prides himself on being rather insightful and precise."

They stared at each other for a moment.

"So," said Drayton, *"are* you going to keep investigating?"

Theodosia's blue eyes were as lovely and unpredictable as the nearby Atlantic. "Count on it," she told him.

CHAPTER 9

❦

"*I*SN'T IT A cunning little piece? See how the light catches the gray green glaze? I'm so hoping it was crafted by one of the Edgefield potters."

Theodosia carefully placed hot blueberry muffins on her serving tray and listened to that voice. She knew that voice. At least she *thought* she did.

Parting the curtains and stepping out into the tea shop, she was mildly surprised to find Giovanni Loard, cradling a teapot in his hands and talking animatedly with Drayton.

"Yes," Drayton was saying, "the Edgefield provenance is correct, and I'd definitely date it to the early nineteenth century."

Theodosia noted that Drayton had allowed his glasses to slip halfway down his nose and was speaking in what Haley called his Heritage Society voice. Timothy Neville may have loved to be called upon to lend his expertise, but Drayton wasn't far behind.

"Good morning," Theodosia greeted the two men after she'd dropped off pastry baskets at the various tables.

Drayton smiled absently while Giovanni Loard jumped up from his chair and eagerly took her hand.

"Miss Browning, so nice to see you again," Giovanni gushed. "And so lovely to finally visit your tea shop."

"Delighted to have you," she replied. "My condolences again on the death of your cousin."

Giovanni's smile crumpled. "Thank you. It's been a difficult time for all of us. Especially Doe. Thank goodness for small kindnesses from people like you."

"Look at this," said Drayton, delivering a sturdy little ceramic into Theodosia's hands.

"Your absolutely brilliant colleague here has been kind enough to take a look at this teapot," said Giovanni. "He's quite sure it's an Edgefield."

Edgefield pottery came from a rich supply of heavy clay found in Edgefield County, northwest of Charleston and located along the Savannah River. In the 1800s, Edgefield potters had crafted pitchers, storage jars, bowls, and teapots as well as little jars with faces molded into them.

"Lovely," said Theodosia as she turned the little clay vessel over in her hands. "These things are getting hard to find. Did you just pick this up for sale in your shop?"

"Oh, no," said Giovanni, "it was one of Doe and Oliver's wedding gifts. Poor girl can't bear to even look at any of these objects now. It breaks her heart to have them in the house. She's kindly asked me to handle the sale of several pieces for her."

"I'm sure she's utterly shattered," said Theodosia, even though she found it strange and almost improper for Doe to be selling off wedding presents so soon after Oliver Dixon's death. For goodness sake, the man's funeral wasn't until tomorrow!

"There hasn't been any forward progress in determining what happened to Oliver," Giovanni said with a long face. "Everyone's clucking about what a terrible accident it was.

But, of course, I suspect the pistol was tampered with. So does Doe."

"The police are investigating, are they not?" said Drayton.

"Yes," said Giovanni slowly. "And I have asked them to take a rather hard look at Ford Cantrell. He's a rotten egg, that one." Giovanni shifted an earnest gaze at Theodosia. "Thank you again for your quick action at the picnic."

Theodosia waved a hand. She would have done the same for anyone.

"Let me keep this teapot for a day or two," offered Drayton, "and I'll consult with an acquaintance of mine. He collects Edgefield pieces and might be able to provide us with some idea on price."

"That would be wonderful," murmured Giovanni Loard. His face eased into a smile as Haley approached their table, bearing a pot of tea. "Hello," he greeted her.

"Ah, here's the tea now," said Drayton. "Thank you, Haley." He poured cups of munnar tea for Giovanni, Theodosia, and himself.

But Haley didn't budge, and Giovanni continued to smile warmly at her.

"Giovanni Loard, this is Haley Parker," said Theodosia.

"Pleased to meet you," said Haley. "Could I offer you a sweet? I have some lemon tarts I just took out of the oven."

"That would be lovely," smiled Giovanni, and Haley dashed off to fetch the pastries.

"Pretty girl," remarked Giovanni as he took a sip of tea. "Oh, this is excellent," he exclaimed. "And I know nothing about tea. I couldn't tell you if this was Japanese or Chinese."

"Actually," said Theodosia, "it's from India."

"You see, what did I tell you," said Giovanni. "Oh my!" he exclaimed as Haley returned and set a plate of pastries in front of him. "You all are just bowling me over with your care and hospitality! I can't believe I didn't find my way to your tea shop sooner."

"You recently purchased a house nearby, didn't you?" asked Theodosia. She'd recalled that Delaine had said something to her about it.

"Yes," said Giovanni. "Over on Legare. It's one of those old Victorian single houses. You know . . . charm, carved balustrades, and absolutely *everything* in desperate need of a repair? I'd have to characterize it as a money pit so far, but I'm holding out hope that I'll be able to return it to classic status someday."

"I'm familiar with that particular row of houses," said Drayton. "Most of them have lovely gardens."

Giovanni nodded eagerly. "The garden has been my saving grace. The brick patio, small fountain, and statuary are in almost perfect condition. All I really had to do was update a few plantings. Don't laugh," Giovanni said in a conspiratorial tone, "but my garden is actually included in next week's Garden Fest."

"That's wonderful," exclaimed Drayton. Besides historical restoration, Drayton was also passionate about gardening. He had cultivated an elegant garden in his small backyard and had even ventured recently toward becoming a bonsai master. "But I didn't realize you were a member of the garden club, much less that your garden was on this year's tour."

"My garden *open house* is Friday evening," said Giovanni, "the night after Timothy Neville's big kickoff party. I'd be honored if you all would drop by."

"I think Giovanni Loard wants to date Haley," said Drayton afterward.

Haley blushed all the way down to her toes. "No way," she said. "He's just a nice guy. A gentleman."

"Do you really think so?" said Theodosia. She had remained fairly quiet during Giovanni Loard's visit. Everything that had seemed charming about him during their

initial encounter last Sunday now seemed a trifle forced.
On the other hand, he might have been nervous being
thrust in among the three of them. Their chattiness *could*
be a little overpowering.

"Does it seem strange to you that Doe is selling her
wedding presents?" Theodosia asked Haley as she stacked
jars of DuBose Bees honey and Dundee's Devonshire
cream on the shelves.

"It's tacky," agreed Haley. "And I'm beginning to suspect that Doe is a bit of a social climber. Why else would
she have married someone so much older? I think Delaine
was probably right about the money part."

Is Doe just an out-and-out fortune hunter? Theodosia
wondered to herself. *Is that the bottom line?*

Doe appeared harmless enough, more youthful than
anything. A pretty young woman who had fallen in love
with an older man. Then again, her husband had just been
killed and, Oliver's sons not withstanding, Doe stood
squarely in line to inherit a good deal of his money. Which
suggested she could also be regarded as a suspect.

Theodosia had been turning the idea of attending Oliver
Dixon's funeral over in her head. She had pretty much
made up her mind to go.

Why not? she asked herself. Oliver Dixon had lived in
the historic district, and that made him a neighbor. Going
to his funeral would be a neighborly thing to do.

And, of course, she'd been present at the time of Oliver
Dixon's demise. True, she'd merely played a walk-on role,
but that was more than most folks had done that terrible afternoon in White Point Gardens.

"Is this a good time?" Miss Dimple hovered in the doorway to Theodosia's office. "I can come back a little later if
you'd like. No problem."

"Oh, Miss Dimple," said Theodosia, pulling herself out

of her thoughts. "I really was lost in thought there for a moment. Come in."

"I brought you the spreadsheet for last month," Miss Dimple said, smiling at Theodosia. "Things are looking fairly good, even with start-up costs on the Web site."

"Miss Dimple," said Theodosia, a germ of an idea flickering in her brain, "you're an accountant. Is there some way to run a check on a company's finances without them finding out?"

"We could run a D and B. You know, a Dun and Bradstreet."

"Is that fairly easy to do?"

"I used to do it all the time for Mr. Dauphine. Now I understand it can be done even faster over the Internet."

"The Internet? Really?" Theodosia beamed. Here was territory she was familiar with. "Terrific suggestion. Let's do it."

CHAPTER 10

❧

"*HAVE YOU HEARD* the news?" Delaine Dish swept through the front door of the tea shop and planted herself at a table with all the aplomb of a Romanoff grand duchess.

"What news is that, Delaine?" Theodosia asked with a slightly resigned air. They had been frantically busy over lunch and had run out of sandwiches. Haley had bravely saved the day by whipping together a dozen fruit and cheese plates and tucking in mini stacks of water biscuits. Those fruit and cheese plates had seemed to do the trick for the folks who came in late, but Theodosia was still trying to catch her breath and wasn't completely sure she could fully cope with Delaine and her accompanying histrionics today.

"Remember that nasty man at the picnic?" asked Delaine. She whipped out a gold compact and lipstick. "Ford Cantrell?" Now she gave her lipstick a good twist and aimed it at her lips, confident she had everyone's attention. "I heard he was taken in for questioning," she murmured in an offhand manner as she held her mouth rigid and applied her signature pink.

Dropping her makeup into her handbag, Delaine aimed a dazzling smile at Theodosia and Drayton. "Isn't that something?" she asked, as though she were somehow acutely involved.

"Well, I can't say that I'm surprised," said Drayton. He grabbed a freshly made pot of tea, teacups, and what remained of his lunch, set it all down on Delaine's table, then eased himself into a chair across from her. "Whew, after the busy lunch we had, I'm almost done in," he declared. "I'm getting too old for this."

"Nonsense," said Delaine. "You're a man in his prime. Barely middle-aged."

"That's right, Drayton's planning to live to a hundred and twenty," said Haley as she brushed past him.

"Oh, shush," said Delaine. "Don't go getting Drayton all upset. I happen to know he's got another birthday coming up."

"Don't *you* have another birthday coming up, too, Delaine?" asked Haley.

"Good heavens no," she said. "That's a long way off yet." She eyed the fruit and cheese plate Drayton was picking at. "Do you have another one of those sweet little luncheon plates?" she asked Haley.

"Sure," Haley grinned. "Hang on." And she scampered into the small kitchen to fix a plate for Delaine.

"How did you hear about Ford Cantrell?" asked Theodosia.

"Oh, honey, the news is all up and down Church Street. Monica Fischer told me this morning when she stopped by the shop. Then I ran into Dundy Baldwin on the street. Anyway, that Cantrell boy embarrassed us all at the picnic, picking an argument with Oliver Dixon and that handsome cousin of his."

"Do you know what they were arguing about?" asked Theodosia.

"I don't know," said Delaine, waving a hand dismissively, "some silly thing. Fishing, I think. Did you know that Ford Cantrell's great-uncle ran off with Oliver Dixon's aunt a long time ago?" Delaine arched her eyebrows with disapproval. "People *still* talk about that."

"Do they really?" asked Drayton. "It's been an awfully long time, and Charleston has had some rousing good scandals since then."

Delaine leaned forward in anticipation. "Has something else happened I should know about?"

"One fruit and cheese plate, madam." Haley placed a pink and white bone china plate piled with slices of Camembert, cheddar cheese, grapes, and apple slices in front of Delaine. "Oh, and I was checking E-mails before and printed out this stuff for you," Haley continued. She thrust a handful of sheets at Theodosia. "I think they're for you. Some kind of financial profile on Grapevine?" She gave Theodosia a questioning glance.

"Grapevine?" piped up Delaine. "Isn't that the company Oliver Dixon started? Whatever would you want with *financial* information? Are you planning a little merger and acquisition we don't know about, Theodosia?"

"Try this tea, Delaine," offered Drayton. "It's a lovely Darjeeling."

"Why, thank you, Drayton." Delaine favored him with a dazzling smile as he carefully served her, then she speared a small piece of cheese on her plate and nibbled it delicately. "Oh, this Camembert is *heavenly,* simply *melts* in your mouth. I don't even want to *think* about butterfat content!"

"Theodosia, I am *so* sorry," said Haley. She shifted nervously from one foot to the other, and her face betrayed her anguish. "Mentioning that E-mail in front of Delaine like that . . . I just didn't think!"

"It's not your fault. You were just trying to be helpful," said Theodosia as she slid a stack of papers into her attaché case. She wasn't pleased about the incident either, but what could she do? Haley was usually very careful and discreet. This had been a slipup. It was just too bad the slipup had occurred in front of Delaine Dish.

On the other hand, Drayton had rushed in to distract Delaine by offering her a cup of Darjeeling. Maybe he had been successful. She'd just have to wait and see.

"I feel like such a jerk," said Haley.

"Don't," said Theodosia. "It could've happened to any one of us."

"You really think so? No, you're just saying that."

"Haley," said Theodosia. "Enough. Don't make yourself crazy over this."

"I was trying to save you some time by printing out E-mails, and I'd just been skimming this article," replied Haley. She held up a section of the *Charleston Post and Courier* for Theodosia to see.

"Which article is that?"

"Well, it's not really an article," amended Haley. "It's mostly photos from the picnic last Sunday. The Oliver Dixon thing has been in the forefront the last couple of days, so I guess the *Post and Courier* just now got around to covering the sailboat race. It's more society gabbing than news. Who was there, what friends were visiting from out of town, that kind of thing."

Theodosia took the page from Haley and scanned the article. Haley was right; it was soft news, society fluff. "That's right," said Theodosia, "they had one of their photographers there to cover the picnic, didn't they?"

"Yes. Seemed like he took gobs of pictures. Course, they only printed but three of them."

Theodosia stared at Haley intently. "I sure wish I could take a look at the rest of those photos."

"You do?"

Theodosia put a hand to her cheek and stroked it absently, thinking. "The photos might, you know, *chronicle* what happened," she said slowly. "From what Tidwell says, nobody seemed to see anything out of the ordinary. And nobody's completely sure how many people handled the pistol once it was removed from its rosewood box."

Haley was suddenly grinning like a little elf. "Let me try to make up for my little faux pas," she exclaimed. "Let me see if I can get my friend Jimmy Cardavan to get us a look at the photos. He's a copy intern there."

"Really?" asked Theodosia. "How would we do that? Go down there? I have to run out to a Spoleto marketing meeting right now, but maybe we could swing by afterward."

Haley's grin stretched wider. "I've got a better idea. Let me E-mail Jimmy and see if he's got access to the *Post and Courier*'s intranet. If so, he can pull the photos up from their site and send them to us in a pdf format. That way you could look at the photos on your computer and print the ones that interest you. That is, if one or another *does* interest you."

"Haley, you're a genius," declared Theodosia.

CHAPTER II

S*POLETO FESTIVAL USA* was Charleston's big arts festival, an annual gala event highlighting dance, opera, theater, music, art, and even literary presentations. Beginning each Memorial Day, Spoleto ran for an action-packed two weeks, launching an invasion of visiting directors, dance troupes, and theater companies that comingled with Charleston's already-strong arts scene and created a rich fusion of performance, visual, and literary arts.

Theodosia had served on Spoleto's marketing committee for six years. Originally, she'd been "volunteered" by her boss, but after the first year had found the experience so rewarding and enjoyable that she'd stayed on, even after she left the advertising agency.

This year, she'd produced a fast-paced thirty-second TV commercial, using snippets of footage from past events set to a jazz track. Then she negotiated favorable rates with the five commercial TV stations in Charleston, some of the TV stations in Columbia and Greenville, and those in Savannah and Augusta, Georgia, as well. The idea being that

Spoleto's appeal would extend to arts-minded folk in neighboring cities and states as well as those in Charleston.

Now, as Theodosia meandered the broad corridors of the Gibbes Museum of Art, she decided to treat herself to a side trip into a couple of the smaller galleries. She'd arrived about ten minutes early and was, after all, heading in the general direction of the conference room where the marketing committee was scheduled to meet.

In the Asian Gallery, Theodosia studied the exquisite collection of Japanese wood-block prints. Many were by revered masters such as Hiroshige and Hokusai, but there were contemporary prints, too, by new masters such as Mitsuaki and Eiichi. These were artists who played with color, technique, and style, and sought to push the boundaries of Japanese printmaking. Fascinating, she thought, what a lovely, hazy feel they had, almost like twilight in the low country.

Glancing at her watch, Theodosia saw it was almost three o'clock. Hustling out of the Asian Gallery, she turned right and headed down the main corridor. At the entrance to the museum's administrative offices, she paused to shut off her cell phone, a small courtesy that she wished more people would observe. When she glanced up, a woman was staring at her, a woman with washed-out blue eyes and a frizzle of red hair shot with strands of gray.

"Do you have a moment?" the woman asked in a low voice.

"Pardon?" Theodosia stared quizzically at the woman.

The woman cocked her head to one side. "I'm Lizbeth Cantrell," she announced bluntly. "And you're Theodosia Browning."

"Yes, hello," said Theodosia, completely taken aback.

"I saw your name on the marketing committee list," announced Lizbeth Cantrell as she stuck out her hand. "I was just here for a meeting, too. I'm on the ticket committee."

Theodosia accepted Lizbeth Cantrell's hand as she

studied her. *What is this all about?* she wondered. Had Lizbeth Cantrell somehow gotten wind of the fact that she'd
done a little investigating into the Dixon-Cantrell feud?
No, couldn't be. That would lead back to Tidwell, and Tidwell would never divulge a source of information. You'd
have to handcuff the man and beat it out of him. Then what
did Lizbeth Cantrell want?

As Lizbeth Cantrell shuffled her feet and ducked her
head, Theodosia realized the woman had to be at least six
feet tall. Long-boned and angular, she had a face that
seemed all cheekbone and jaw.

"Can we talk privately?" Lizbeth Cantrell asked.

"Of course," agreed Theodosia, finding herself all the
more curious about this casual encounter that had no doubt
been staged.

When they'd retreated to one of the conference rooms
and pulled the double doors closed behind them, Theodosia studied Lizbeth Cantrell. All the qualities that made
her brother, Ford Cantrell, tall and good-looking seemed to
work against Lizbeth Cantrell. She was obviously older
than her brother and appeared far more subdued and faded,
as though her red hair had somehow leached all color and
emotion from her.

Truth be known, Lizbeth Cantrell was a woman who
was both plain and plainspoken, at her happiest when she
was whelping a litter of puppies or crashing through the
woods atop a good horse.

"You're a smart woman," began Lizbeth Cantrell. "A
businesswoman. That makes you a breed apart from a lot
of ladies."

"Thank you . . . I think," said Theodosia. "But what
do—"

Lizbeth Cantrell held up a hand. "This isn't easy for
me," she said. "I'm not used to asking for help."

"You want my help?" said Theodosia. This conversation was getting stranger by the minute, she decided.

"I know you were at White Point Gardens last Sunday when Oliver Dixon was shot," said Lizbeth Cantrell. "And I also hear that you know how to track down a murderer."

"I think you've got me confused with someone else," said Theodosia.

"No, I don't," said Lizbeth Cantrell firmly. "Your aunt Libby told me all about you. Last fall, the police thought maybe the girl who worked in your tea shop was responsible for the death of that man at the Lamplighter Tour. But you stood behind her. You figured it all out."

Realization was not dawning quickly for Theodosia. "My aunt Libby told you . . . ? Excuse me, exactly what are you asking me to do?"

"I want you to help clear my brother's name," said Lizbeth Cantrell. "He didn't tamper with that old pistol. Folks just think he might have because he acts so crazy most of the time. And because he collects guns and likes to hunt. But I know Ford is a good man, an honest man. He's no killer."

Let's not be so hasty, thought Theodosia. It was, after all, Ford and Lizbeth's great-great-grandfather, Jeb Cantrell, who shot Stuart Dixon to death back in 1892 and set the Dixon-Cantrell feud in motion.

On the other hand, even though Ford Cantrell had looked awfully suspicious at first, Theodosia wasn't so sure blame should be laid entirely at his feet. Doe was fast earning a place on her list of suspects, too. And Oliver Dixon's two sons, Brock and Quaid, bore looking into as well.

"Can you help me?" asked Lizbeth Cantrell. Her pale eyes transfixed Theodosia with their intensity. "I know you're a good lady. A smart lady."

"You live at Pamlico Hill Plantation," said Theodosia. "A few miles down the road from my aunt Libby's."

"That's right." Suddenly, a ghost of a smile played on

Lizbeth Cantrell's plain face, bringing with it a softness and quiet animation that hadn't been visible earlier.

"I know you, don't I?" said Theodosia. Somewhere, in the depths of her memory, a faint recollection stirred.

"Yes, ma'am, you do," Lizbeth replied.

Theodosia stared at Lizbeth as though she were a distant shadow and tried to conjure up the memory. "You were there when my . . . my mother died," she finally said.

"Yes," Lizbeth replied softly. "You were just a little bug of a thing back then, couldn't have been more than seven or eight years old."

The flashback of that long-ago summer rushed at Theodosia in a Technicolor whirl and exploded in her brain. And along with it, came a wash of memories. The oppressive heat, her father's hopeful whispering, her heartbreaking sadness.

"My mother helped take care of your mother," explained Lizbeth. "And sometimes I came along."

"You came along," said Theodosia, as though she were in a trance. "You were older than I, and you took me swimming on hot days."

"That's right," said Lizbeth. "We went to Carpenter's Pond." Her smile was gentle, and she waited patiently as Theodosia's brain processed everything.

"Yes, I remember you," said Theodosia slowly. Her initial shock now over with, she was able to look back and slowly replay the memory. Her mother's last summer on this earth, spent at Cane Ridge Plantation in the low-country. Her mother had wanted more than anything to be able to watch sunlight play across the marsh grass, to gaze upon pink sunsets over shadowy, peaceful pine groves. And, finally, to be laid to rest in the old family cemetery there. Theodosia stretched one hand out tentatively, touched Lizbeth's sleeve. "You were so kind."

"You were so sad."

The conference room's double doors rattled noisily.

"I got to go," Lizbeth said as she began to gather up her purse and notebook. "I think your meeting's about to start." She paused and gave Theodosia a look filled with longing. "Will you help?" she asked.

The door burst open, and a half-dozen people crowded into the room. They swarmed around the table, paying little heed to Lizbeth and Theodosia, totally unaware of the highly charged atmosphere that seemed to permeate the room.

Theodosia dropped her arms to her sides and nodded. "I'll try," she said. She didn't know exactly what she was promising. Or why. But how could she not?

Lizbeth blinked back tears. "Thank you," she said simply.

CHAPTER 12

❦

𝒜 POT OF lentil soup simmered on the back burner; popovers baked golden and fluffy in the oven. Although Theodosia's upstairs apartment was not overly large, it possessed that rare trait so often lacking in many newer apartments: style. Aubasson rugs in faded blue and cinnamon covered the floors. French doors gave the appearance of a living and dining room that flowed together flawlessly, while cove ceilings gave the rooms a cozy, architectural ambiance. Draperies and sofa were done in muted English chintz and prints.

Earlier, Drayton had gone next door to Robillard Booksellers and borrowed one of their oversized magnifying glasses on the pretext of trying to decipher some old Chinese tea labels. Now Theodosia held the magnifying glass in her hand as she sat at her dining room table, studying the black and white printouts. They'd been transmitted electronically just as Haley had promised, sliding, as if by magic, from her laser printer.

The photos were interesting in that they did, indeed, chronicle the events of that Sunday afternoon. Here were photos of sailboats jostling in the harbor at the beginning of the race. Then photos of the two dozen or so boats, sails filled with wind, setting off toward the Atlantic. The photographer had then concentrated on shots of the crowd. There were photos of people talking, people shaking hands, people hugging and exchanging air kisses. Delaine was in a couple shots; Drayton showed up in a few as well.

Here was Billy Manolo standing next to the table that held the rosewood box containing the pistol. And the commodore in the ill-fitting jacket with all the gold braid.

Theodosia shuffled through the printouts. They were interesting but a little disappointing at the same time. She hadn't expected anything to jump right out at her; that would've been too easy. But she felt the rumblings of a low-level vibe that told her there must be *something* to be learned.

That hope spun dizzyingly in her head as Theodosia decided to shift her attention to the Dun & Bradstreet report that had arrived so speedily this afternoon. There were just four pages, but they contained what looked like a good assessment of Grapevine: a rundown on its products and the company's growth potential. Just as Haley had mentioned a few days ago, Grapevine had started production on a number of different expansion modules for PDAs. Although competition was stiff in this area, the report seemed to indicate that Grapevine had done its homework and was about to launch a very viable product.

Theodosia finally took a break when the oven timer buzzed. Ambling out into the kitchen, she slid her hand into a padded mitt and pulled the popovers from the oven. They were perfect. Golden brown and heroically puffed. Haley's recipes were the best. They always turned out.

After pouring the lentil soup into a mug, Theodosia carried everything back to the dining room table on a tray, sliding the printouts out of the way before she set her food down. Earl Grey was immediately at her elbow, giving a gentle nudge, lobbying for a bite of popover.

"Leftovers when I'm finished," she told him, and he assumed that worried look dogs often get.

Theodosia had finished her soup and was plowing through the printouts a second time, when she stopped to study the single photo of Oliver Dixon lying facedown, half in, half out of the water.

The photographer must have snapped the shot just moments before she reached down to check for a pulse, because the tip of her right hand was slightly visible. They hadn't printed that photo in the paper because it was, undoubtedly, too gruesome, but they'd retained it in their collection of shots from that day.

Closing her eyes, Theodosia tried to recall her impression of that single, defining moment. She had a strong, visceral recollection of the hot, pungent aroma of exploded gunpowder, chill water lapping at her ankles, and a sense of unreality, of feeling numb, as she stared at Oliver Dixon's still body.

What had Tidwell told her about loading the old pistol? Theodosia searched her memory. Oh yes, Tidwell had said you put a pinch of gunpowder on a little piece of paper and twist it. Kind of like creating a miniature tea bag.

Theodosia held the magnifying glass to the printout. It was extremely grainy and hard to discern any real detail. She could just make out the back of poor Oliver Dixon's head, dark against a lighter background.

Theodosia sighed. There just didn't seem to be anything here.

CHAPTER 13

❧❧❧

APRIL HERALDS SPRING in Charleston. Flickers and cat-birds warble and tweet, flitting among spreading live oaks, searching out twigs and moss for building nests. Days become warmer and more languid and, ever so gradually, the tempo of Charleston, never moving at breakneck speed anyway, begins to slow.

On this extraordinarily fine morning, the fresh Charleston air was ripe and redolent with the scent of magnolias, azaleas, and top notes of dogwood.

But no one took notice.

Instead, mourners walked in somber groups of twos and threes into the yawning double doors of Saint Philip's Church. Overhead, the bells in the steeple clanged loudly.

There is no joy in those bells, thought Theodosia as she walked alongside Drayton. There were so many times when those bells had rung out in exaltation. Easter Sunday, Christmas Eve, weddings, christenings. There were times when they tolled respectfully. But today, the bells clanged mournfully, announcing to all in the surrounding historic district that one of God's poor souls was being laid to rest.

Choosing seats toward the back of the church, Theodosia and Drayton sat quietly, observing the other mourners. Most seemed lost in their own private thoughts, as is so often the case when attending a funeral.

Marveling at the soaring interior of Saint Philip's, Theodosia was reminded that it had been designed by the renowned architect Joseph Nyde. Nyde had greatly admired the neoclassical arches of Saint Martin-in-the-Fields church in London and had transferred those airy, sculptural designs to Saint Philip's.

With a mixture of majesty and pathos, the opening notes from Mozart's *Requiem* swelled from the pipe organ, and everyone shuffled to their feet. Then the funeral procession began.

Six men, all wearing black suits, white shirts, and black ties, and walking in perfect cadence, rolled Oliver Dixon's bronze casket down the wide center aisle. A good ten steps behind the casket and its catafalque, head bowed, hands clasped tightly, Doe Belvedere Dixon, Oliver's wife of nine weeks, solemnly followed her husband's body. Oliver Dixon's two grown sons, Brock and Quaid, followed directly behind her.

In her black, tailored suit and matching beret, her blond hair pulled back in a severe French twist, Doe looked heartbreakingly young.

"The girl looks fetching, absolutely fetching," murmured Drayton as she passed by them. "How can a woman look so good at a funeral?"

"She's young," said Theodosia as the choir suddenly cut in, their voices rising in a litany of Latin verse, "and blessed with good skin."

Reverend Jonathan, the church's longtime pastor, stepped forward to deliver his eulogy. Then a half-dozen other men also took the podium. They spoke glowingly of Oliver Dixon's accomplishments, of his service to the community, of his impeccable reputation.

As the service grew longer, Theodosia's mind drifted.

Staring at the backs of Brock and Quaid, Oliver Dixon's two sons, she wondered if their disqualification from the race was in any way related to this.

She recalled the strange walk-on scene Ford Cantrell had staged at the picnic. Wondered what his feelings would be today. *Had he shown up here today?* She ventured a look around. *No, probably not.*

Theodosia thought about the printouts she studied last night, the ones she'd hoped might be helpful. The final printout, the one where Oliver Dixon's upper body was silhouetted against a somewhat stark background, seemed burned in her memory.

Theodosia shifted on the hard pew, crossed her legs.

Stark background.

Theodosia suddenly sat up straight, uncrossed her legs. What *was* that background, anyway? Rocks perhaps? Or wet sand? She searched her memory.

It had to be her tablecloth.

Her tablecloth. The idea came zooming at her like a Roman candle. And on the heels of that came the realization that whatever residue might still be left on the tablecloth—gunpowder, exploded bits of metal, or even blood—it could just offer up some semblance of a clue.

A clue. A genuine clue. Wouldn't that be interesting?

As the final musical tribute came to a crashing conclusion, Theodosia managed to catch herself. She'd been about to break out in a smile, albeit one tinged with grim satisfaction.

Goodness, she thought, struggling to maintain decorum, *I've got to be careful. People will think I'm an absolute ghoul. Smiling at a funeral!*

"Let's go," Theodosia whispered to Drayton as she bounded to her feet.

"Yes, let's do express our condolences," said Drayton.

They waited in line a good twenty minutes, watching as

Doe Belvedere Dixon hugged, kissed, and clutched the hands of the various mourners. She seemed to converse with them in an easy, gracious manner, accepting all their kind words.

"Does she seem slightly vivacious to you?" asked Drayton, studying her carefully. "Do you have the feeling she's a bit like Scarlett O'Hara, wearing rouge to her own husband's funeral?"

"I think the poor girl was simply blessed with good looks," said Theodosia. "She seems heartbroken."

"You're right," amended Drayton. "I should be ashamed."

"Should be," whispered Theodosia and aimed an elbow toward Drayton's ribs. She, too, had been watching Doe carefully, getting the feeling, more and more, that Doe might be wearing her mourning much the same as she would another beauty pageant title.

Finally, Theodosia and Drayton were at the head of the line, clasping hands with Brock and Quaid, Oliver Dixon's two sons. "So sorry," she and Drayton murmured to them in hushed tones. "You have our condolences."

Then Theodosia was eye to eye with Doe.

Drayton's right, she suddenly realized. The girl looked appropriately sad and subdued but, at the same time, she seemed to be playing a role. The role of grieving widow.

"My deepest sympathy," said Theodosia as she grasped Doe's hand.

"Thank you." Doe's eyes remained downcast, her long eyelashes swept dramatically against pink cheeks. Theodosia idly wondered if they were extensions. Eyelash extensions were a big thing these days. First had come hair, now eyelashes. These days, it seemed like a girl could improve on almost anything if she wanted to. And had enough money.

"As you may know," said Theodosia, "I was the first to reach him."

Doe's eyes flicked up and stared directly into Theodosia's eyes. Her gaze didn't waver. "Thank you," she whispered. "How very kind of you."

Theodosia was aware of Drayton gently crowding her. It felt like he was beginning to radiate disapproval. She knew it was one thing to speculate on Doe's veracity, another to push her a bit. Still, Theodosia persisted.

"Anyone would have done the same," Theodosia assured her. "Such a terrible thing . . . the pistol . . ."

Doe had begun to look slightly perturbed. "Yes . . ." she stammered.

"After all, your husband was an avid hunter, was he not? He was extremely familiar with guns?"

"Yes, I suppose . . . as a member of the Chessen Hunt Club he . . . I'm sorry, I don't see wha—"

"Shush," said Theodosia, patting the girl's hand. "If there's anything Drayton or I can do, please don't hesitate to call."

"That was expressing condolences?" hissed Drayton when they were out of earshot. "You just about browbeat the poor girl. She didn't know what to think." They walked a few steps farther. "I assume you were testing the water, so to speak? Trying to ascertain if Oliver Dixon knew anything about guns?"

"Drayton . . ." Theodosia grabbed his sleeve and pulled him out of the stream of people passing by. "I think Oliver Dixon was set up."

He pursed his lips and gazed at her with speculation. "Set up. You mean—"

"Someone *caused* that pistol to misfire," Theodosia said excitedly.

"You know, I really don't like where you're going with this," Drayton said irritably.

"Hear me out," said Theodosia. If someone tampered with that pistol, and I've really come to believe that's exactly what happened, then hard evidence might also exist. Like explosives or—"

"Hard evidence," said Drayton with a quizzical frown. "Hard evidence *where*?"

"On the tablecloth," said Theodosia.

Drayton just stared at her.

"One of my tablecloths was on the table that Oliver Dixon fell onto. He tumbled onto the table, then slid down into a heap. Remember?"

Drayton hesitated a moment, trying to fix the scene in his mind. "Yes, I do. You're right," he replied finally.

"So there could be particles of gunpowder or explosives or whatever still clinging to that tablecloth," prompted Theodosia.

"Oh," said Drayton. Then, "*Oh,* I see what you mean!"

"Now, if I could only figure out what happened to that darned tablecloth," said Theodosia. "In all the hubbub and commotion, I'm not entirely sure where it ended up." She stared out the open doors of the church toward the street.

"I have it," said Drayton.

She whirled toward him in surprise. "*You* have it?"

"I'm almost certain I do. At least I have a vague recollection of untangling it and packing it up with the other things."

"So where is the tablecloth now?"

"Probably still in the trunk of my car. I was going to drop all the dirty linens at Chase's Laundry yesterday, then I got busy with the Heritage Society. I received a call that someone had brought in this old, wooden joggling board . . . you know, they were used for crossing ditches on rice plantations? They're so terribly rare now and I—"

"Drayton . . ."

"Yes?"

"I'm so *glad* you have your priorities straight," Theodosia said as they strolled out into the sunlight. "Because you very nicely *preserved* what could amount to *evidence*."

Suddenly, Theodosia's smile froze on her face and she stopped dead in her tracks. "Oh rats. That's Burt Tidwell over there."

Drayton frowned. "Why do you suppose *he's* here?"

"Why do you think?" she said, squinting across the way at him.

"Investigating?" squeaked Drayton. "Looking for suspects?"

"Same as us," said Theodosia. She bit her lip, debating whether or not she should go over and talk to him.

"Well, are you going to talk to him?" Drayton asked finally.

She hesitated a moment, then made up her mind. "Why not? Let's both waltz over there and see if we can push his buttons before he starts to push ours."

"All right," agreed Drayton. "But nothing about the—"

Theodosia held an index finger to her lips. "Mum's the word," she cautioned.

They strolled over to where a bank of memorial wreaths was displayed. Theodosia decided that Oliver Dixon must have been extremely well liked and respected to have garnered a church full of flower arrangements as well as a huge assortment of memorial wreaths that had spilled outside.

Burt Tidwell was studying one of the wreaths. "Look at this," he said to them. "Wild grape vine entwined with lilies, the flower symbolizing resurrection. So very touching." Tidwell inclined his head slightly. He'd captured Theodosia in his peripheral vision; now his eyes bore into her. "Miss Browning, how do. And here's Mr. Conneley, too."

"Hello," said Drayton pleasantly.

"You took Ford Cantrell in for questioning," said Theodosia without preamble.

Tidwell favored her with a faint smile. "My dear Miss Browning, you seem somewhat surprised. I thought you'd be absolutely *delighted* that I followed up on your so-called *tip*." Tidwell pronounced the word tip as though he were discussing odiferous compost in a garden.

Theodosia turned her attention to the memorial wreaths as Burt Tidwell rocked back on his heels, enormously pleased with himself. Here was a lovely floral wreath from the Heritage Society, she noted. And here was . . . Well, wasn't this one a surprise!

"You might also be interested to know," Tidwell prattled on, "that we discovered Ford Cantrell has a rather extensive gun collection. And that our Mr. Cantrell has recently turned his old plantation into a sort of hunting preserve."

Tidwell suddenly had her attention once again. "What kind of hunting?" Theodosia asked.

"He claims to be appealing to all manner of wealthy sportsmen, promising prizes of deer, turkey, quail, and wild boar," answered Tidwell.

"My aunt Libby has lived out that way for the better part of half a century," said Theodosia, "and the wildest critters she's ever encountered have been possum and porcupines." She paused. "And once, when I was a kid, we ran across a dead alligator. But I don't suppose that really counts."

"No one ever characterized Ford Cantrell as being an honest man," said Tidwell.

"Or hunters as being terribly bright," added Theodosia with a wry smile.

Their conversation was suddenly interrupted by loud voices.

"What are you doing here?" came an angry scream.

Theodosia, Drayton, Burt Tidwell, and about forty other people turned to watch the beginnings of a shouting match on the lawn of Saint Philip's.

"Who on earth is that?" asked Theodosia. She didn't know his name, but she recognized the angry man with the flopping white hair, florid complexion, and hand-tailored pinstripe suit as the very same man from the yacht race. The commodore in the tight jacket swathed in gold braid.

"That's Booth Crowley," Tidwell told her.

"*That's* Booth Crowley?" said Theodosia, stunned. Booth Crowley had been the one who'd been beckoning to Oliver Dixon that fateful Sunday. Booth Crowley had handed him the pistol.

And just look at who he's yelling at, she thought. *Billy Manolo, the worker from the yacht club who asked to borrow the tablecloth. Wasn't this a strange little tableau?*

."Hey buddy, cool your jets," Billy Manolo cautioned. Lean, dark-complected, and a head taller than Booth Crowley, Billy stood poised on the balls of his feet, glowering back and looking as dangerous as a jungle cat.

Still, Booth Crowley persisted in his tirade.

"Is there some *reason* you're here?" Booth Crowley thundered. "Don't you think you've caused *enough* problems?"

"Hey man, you're crazy." Billy Manolo curled his lip scornfully and waved one hand dismissively at Booth Crowley. "Take it easy, or you'll put yourself into cardiac arrest."

Indeed, thought Theodosia. Judging from Booth Crowley's beet-red face and frantic antics, it looked as though he might go into cardiac arrest at any moment. She wasn't sure she'd ever seen anyone quite so worked up. Booth Crowley was putting on a rather amazing show. And in front of the church at that.

"Do you know the fellow Crowley's yelling at?" asked Drayton, mildly amused by the whole spectacle.

"That's Billy Manolo," replied Theodosia.

Drayton's eyebrows shot sky high. "You *do* know him?"

"Met him," said Theodosia. "He apparently works at the yacht club, taking care of the boats and doing odd jobs, I guess."

The three of them watched Billy Manolo stalk off while Booth Crowley continued to rage at no one in particular.

"So that's the Booth Crowley who's a major donor to the symphony *and* the art museum *and* the hospital," commented Drayton. "He doesn't *look* like a mover and a shaker. Well, maybe shaking mad."

"Ssh, Drayton, he's heading this way," cautioned Theodosia.

Booth Crowley looked like a furnace that had been stoked too high. He strode across the green lawn purposefully, both arms pumping furiously at his sides, his nostrils flared, his mouth gaping for air.

"You . . . Tidwell," Booth Crowley hollered. "A word with you."

Tidwell stood silently, a look of benign amusement on his jowly face.

Booth Crowley came puffing over to Tidwell. "I want you to keep an eye on that one." Booth Crowley gestured wildly at the empty street behind him. "Billy Manolo. Works at the yacht club. Things have been missing. Manager had to dress him down last week, threatened to fire him if things don't improve. Boy is a hoodlum. No good."

Theodosia stifled a grin and wondered if Booth Crowley's sentence structures were always this staccato and devoid of nouns and prepositions. A strange man. With a strange way of talking, too.

Drayton put a hand on Theodosia's arm and began to steer her away from Tidwell and Booth Crowley. Crowley had eased back on the throttle a bit but was still sputtering. Tidwell was nodding mildly, listening to him but not really favoring Booth Crowley with his complete and undivided attention.

"Exit, stage left," Drayton murmured under his breath.

"I agree," said Theodosia. "But first . . ." Theodosia turned her focus on the bank of memorial wreaths she'd been studying earlier. *Where is that wreath?* she wondered. There was one composed of only greenery and purple leaves that had caught her eye earlier. *Ah, here it is.* She reached out and plucked a cluster of leaves from it even as Drayton propelled her away from one of the strangest memorial services she'd ever witnessed.

"What are you up to with that?" he asked.

Theodosia fingered the snippet of leaves. "They're from the wreath that was sent by Lizbeth Cantrell."

"Good Lord, you're not serious. She sent a wreath and her brother is the prime murder suspect?"

"I promised to help her," said Theodosia.

Drayton peered at her. "You did?" He shook his head. "You never fail to amaze me."

"Do you know what this is? The greenery, I mean."

Drayton pulled his half glasses from his jacket pocket and slid them onto his nose. "Coltsfoot," he declared. "I'm awfully sure it's coltsfoot."

"What a strange thing to use for a memorial wreath. It's not all that attractive," Theodosia mused. "Maybe that's why Lizbeth chose it. She was making a statement. Or anti-statement."

"It's more likely she chose it for the symbolism," said Drayton.

Now it was Theodosia's turn to give Drayton a strange look. "What symbolism might that be?"

"Coltsfoot represents justice," said Drayton.

"Justice," repeated Theodosia, now highly intrigued by Lizbeth Cantrell's use of symbolism.

"It seems to me that more and more people are paying attention to certain symbols or talismans," said Drayton. "I think it's a symptom of unsettled times."

"I think you may be right," said Theodosia.

CHAPTER 14

❧

"WHAT DO YOU think this could be?" asked Theodosia. They had waited until late in the afternoon when the tea shop was finally empty before they brought out the tablecloth. Drayton had fished it out of the trunk of his Volvo, and now they were staring at the stains and splotches that traced irregular patterns across what had once been pristine linen.

"Yuck," said Haley. "It's blood. What else would it be?"

"No, look here." Theodosia scratched at a brownish gray stain with her fingernail. "It could be powder marks," she said. "Gunpowder."

"Perhaps," said Drayton with a frown. Using the borrowed magnifying glass, he studied the tablecloth carefully. "What about some variety of seaweed?" he proposed. "One end of it did end up dragging in Charleston Harbor. Isn't there some kind of microorganism that might have washed over it and caused this mottled effect?

"You mean like plankton?" asked Haley. She had quizzed the two of them at length about the funeral, then listened with rapt attention as they told their story of the raging Booth Crowley and the disdainful Billy Manolo.

"Well, it *could* be," replied Drayton, not entirely convinced by his own theory.

"What about schmutz?" countered Haley.

They both stared at her.

"You know," said Haley. "Dirt, pollution, oil . . . schmutz."

"Should the EPA ever offer you a position," Drayton told her, "I'd advise you to turn them down."

"All right, smarty, what do you think it is?" she said. "The darn thing slid onto the ground, some poor guy bled all over it, and then it knocked around in your trunk for a few days. Anything could have gotten on it."

"Whatever's on this tablecloth is from the picnic and not my trunk," replied Drayton. "But, like Theodosia, I'm getting more and more fascinated." He favored Theodosia with a serious look. "I do think you're on to something." He pulled a handkerchief from his pocket and cleaned his glasses. "You're still adamantly against mentioning anything about this to Tidwell?"

"Absolutely," said Theodosia. "I'm sure he's running his own investigation. For all we know, he could have an entire team of forensic experts poring over Oliver Dixon's clothing right now." She gave a sharp nod, as if to punctuate her sentence, then momentarily shifted her attention from the tablecloth to the printouts of the picnic photos. She had laid them out on the table earlier and was now sifting through them, still hoping to piece together some answers.

Haley picked up one of the printouts. "Who's this guy?" she asked.

Drayton peered at the photo. "That's Billy Manolo, the fellow we saw getting chewed out this morning by Booth Crowley."

"Hmm," mused Haley. "He looks kind of tough. You know, work-with-your-bare-hands kind of tough."

"He's the one who set up the table and borrowed the tablecloth," said Theodosia.

"So he handled the box with the pistol in it," said Haley.

Theodosia thought about it. "Probably. Then again, several people did. Booth Crowley, the fellow Bob Brewster, who Tidwell told us did the actual loading of the gun, and probably a few people at the clubhouse."

"How about Oliver Dixon's two sons, Brock and Quaid?" said Drayton.

"You don't think they wanted to do away with their own father, do you?" asked Haley.

"I don't know," said Theodosia slowly. Brock and Quaid didn't seem like viable suspects, certainly not as viable as Doe. On the other hand, Billy Manolo could be in the running, too. He had, after all, been seen handling the box that contained the mysterious exploding pistol.

Could he have tampered with the pistol? she wondered. Billy certainly would have had easy access. He worked at the clubhouse and did maintenance on the boats. It's possible he could have resented Oliver Dixon for any number of reasons. They could have had an argument or some misunderstanding. Of course, the big question was, why had Billy Manolo shown up at Oliver Dixon's funeral at all? Had he come to gloat? Or simply to mourn?

Theodosia reached out with both hands, pulled all the printouts to her, tamped them into one neat stack like a deck of playing cards.

One thing she knew for certain. She had to get this tablecloth analyzed.

"Theodosia," said Drayton in a cautionary tone, "if this should lead to something more, I don't want you to put yourself in harm's way. A man has been killed. What we all took to be an accident, what the *police* took to be an accident, could just be a clever charade."

"Maybe I need to speak with Timothy Neville again," said Theodosia.

"He knows more about antique pistols than anyone I know," agreed Drayton.

And so does Ford Cantrell, interestingly enough, thought Theodosia.

"Hey, give me that!" Haley suddenly snatched the tablecloth from where it lay balled up on the table. "Turn those printouts over," she ordered as she suddenly caught sight of a familiar face outside the window. "Delaine is heading for the door!" Haley warned as she scrambled for the back room.

Theodosia flipped the printouts facedown in a mad rush and flutter as Delaine Dish pushed through the door of the Indigo Tea Shop.

"Theodosia, Drayton, I'm so glad you're both still here, I have the most wonderful news," she gushed.

"What's that, Delaine?" said Theodosia. She put a hand to her chest to calm her beating heart.

"Alicia Abbot's seal point Siamese had kittens a few weeks ago, and she's giving me one!"

"That's wonderful, Delaine." Theodosia knew that when Delaine's ancient calico cat, Calvin, died almost a year ago, Delaine had been bereft. It had taken her a long time to get over Calvin's death.

"What are you going to call him? Or is it a her?" asked Haley as she emerged from the back, empty-handed now.

"It's a little boy kitty," smiled Delaine. "And I haven't settled on a name yet. Maybe Calvin II?"

"Catchy," said Haley.

"Or Calvin Deux," added Drayton, giving Haley a cautionary look as he scooped up the printouts and headed for Theodosia's office in back.

"Maybe I'll just call him Deux," said Delaine. "I don't know. What do you think, Theodosia? You were in advertising. You used to come up with names for all those products. And you dream up such wonderful names for all your teas." Delaine moved across the tea shop and peered at a row of silver tea canisters. She began reading off labels. "Copper River Cranberry, Tea Thymes, Lemon Zest, Black Frost . . ."

So that's what this is all about, thought Theodosia. *Naming her cat.*

"Let me think about it," said Theodosia. "I'll knock it around with Drayton, too. He's really good at that kind of thing," she added, noting that Haley had to clap a hand over her mouth to stifle a chuckle.

But Delaine wasn't ready to leave just yet. She hung around the tea shop, finally forcing Haley to offer her a cup of tea and a shortbread cookie.

"It's nice you can be gone from your store so long," said Haley.

"Oh, Janine's taking care of things. Besides, business is slow today. I think it's fixing to storm. The sky was so blue this morning, and now it's starting to cloud up." She wrinkled her nose. "I hope it's not going to rain. My hair will frizz."

"Mine, too," remarked Haley, patting her stick-straight brown locks.

"Theo, you went to the service this morning, right?"

"Yes, Delaine."

"Heard anything more about that awful Cantrell fellow?"

"Just that he's turned his plantation into a hunting preserve."

"A *hunting* preserve? That sounds awful," said Delaine. "Killing poor, defenseless animals." She shuddered. "That's a terrible thing. Makes a person upset just hearing about it."

Theodosia smiled sympathetically, but she also knew that many Southerners grew up with a shotgun clutched in their hot little hands. Shooting varmints was a rite of passage in the South. She'd certainly done it herself and, while she no longer chose to hunt, she wasn't about to condemn those who did.

"Besides," said Delaine, still outraged at Ford Cantrell's new enterprise, "isn't that a concept at odds with itself? Hunting and *preserve*?"

"Like educational TV," said Haley. "No such thing, really."

"Or army intelligence," added Delaine, with a giggle. "Oh, ladies, I could sit here and chat for hours, but I really have to get back to the store now."

"Bye, Delaine," said Theodosia.

"Whew," said Haley after she'd left. "That lady can really take it out of you."

CHAPTER 15

RAIN SPATTERED DOWN in oversized droplets, drumming on roofs and turning city streets and sidewalks into miniature levees. Colorful horse-drawn carriages that plied the markets, antique district, and historic sites were abandoned as tourists sought shelter by the droves in shops and cafés.

From the steamed-up confines of her car, Theodosia punched in the phone number for the tea shop.

Drayton picked up on the second ring. "Indigo Tea Shop, Drayton speaking."

"Drayton? It's Theodosia. How are things going?" Theodosia had decided she'd better check in and make sure everything was running smoothly at the tea shop. Now she held her cell phone up to her ear while she drove one-handed through the pelting rain. It wasn't easy. Her defrosters didn't seem to be doing the job, the Jeep's windshield was hopelessly fogged, and traffic was in a nasty snarl.

"We're busy," said Drayton. "Lots of tourists trying to

wait out the storm, but nothing we can't handle. Where are you? Better yet, are you coming in?"

But Theodosia had one thing on her mind. "Drayton, remember Haley's schmutz?" she asked excitedly.

"The tablecloth," Drayton said with an edge to his voice. "Oh dear, I was afraid that's what your little errand was about." He sighed disapprovingly. "What exactly did you do with the ghastly thing?"

"Remember Professor Morrow?"

"Morrow . . . Morrow . . . the botany professor at the University of Charleston?"

"That's the one."

"As I recall, you spoke quite highly of him when you took his classes. Back when you were still a tea initiate."

"He's agreed to analyze the tablecloth," said Theodosia. There was a note of triumph in her voice.

"What has poor Morrow gotten himself into?" asked Drayton. "Did you persuade him to turn his botany lab into a crime lab?"

"No, but he's got the same electron microscopes and apparatus for analyzing bits of metal or soil samples that a crime lab does. Let's just say I'm curious about whether what's on that tablecloth is animal, vegetable, or mineral."

"And poor, unsuspecting Professor Morrow has agreed to do this for you?"

"Yes, of course."

"Let's hope he doesn't lose his tenure over this," said Drayton.

"That's being a trifle overdramatic, don't you think?"

"Overdramatic, my dear Theodosia, is looking for murder at every twist and turn."

"Drayton, I knew this call would cheer me up. Oh, would you look at that!"

"Theodosia, please tell me you didn't sideswipe someone," Drayton cried with alarm.

"Hang on a minute." There was silence for a few moments, then Theodosia came back on the line. "You know where George Street crosses King Street?"

"Yes," said Drayton. "Of course."

"I just passed Loard Antiquarian Shop. I'm going to run in. Pay Giovanni Loard a surprise visit. Do a little snooping."

"*Then* you'll be back?"

"Yes . . . no . . . I don't know."

"Well, when you see Giovanni, tell him my friend authenticated the teapot. Definitely an Edgefield, estimated worth between eight and twelve hundred."

"Okay, Drayton. Bye."

Theodosia came around the block again, swerved across a lane of traffic, and headed, nose first, into a vacant parking space. It was pure impulse that had made her decide to stop in and pay Giovanni Loard a visit. And luck, she noted, that the rain had let up slightly, allowing her a chance to make a mad dash from her Jeep to the antique shop.

Loard Antiquarian Shop was one of over three-dozen antique shops in a two-block area. Situated on the first floor of a three-story Italianate red-brick building, the large front display window was filled with seventeenth- and eighteenth-century English furniture as well as a tasty selection of majolica, pewter, and antique clocks. The name, Loard Antiquarian Shop, was painted prominently on the window in ornate gold script.

Giovanni Loard looked up hopefully as the bell over the front door rang merrily. He had been touting the merits of an antique brass spyglass to a woman from West Ashley for almost half an hour now, and she still showed no hint of wanting to buy. The woman had come in searching for a "fun" anniversary gift for her stockbroker husband and had alternately been captivated by an antique clock, a carved wooden box and, finally, the brass spyglass.

Business had been slow lately, and the brass spyglass, purchased at an estate sale in Summerville for 85 dollars, would yield a tasty profit with its new price tag of 450 dollars.

When Giovanni recognized Theodosia, a smile creased his handsome face.

"Miss Browning," he called out. "Be with you in a moment."

Giovanni turned back to the lady from West Ashley. "Perhaps you want to think it over." He reached for the brass spyglass, but the woman, sensing another customer behind her, a customer who perhaps might be interested in the very same piece, suddenly made up her mind.

"I'll take it," she declared. "It's perfect."

Giovanni nodded. "An excellent choice, ma'am. I'm sure your husband will be thoroughly delighted."

Giovanni accepted the woman's MasterCard and zipped it through his machine. *What luck,* he thought to himself, *that Theodosia Browning walked in when she did.* So often, customers were pushed into purchasing when it became apparent they would no longer enjoy a shopkeeper's undivided attention.

While Giovanni finished up with his customer, Theodosia wandered about the shop. She paused to admire a small collection of Coalport porcelain and a tray of vintage watches. It was a nice enough shop, she decided, but the inventory seemed a trifle thin. *Hard times?* she wondered. *Or just an owner who preferred a few tasty items to the usual overdone pastiche of furniture, silver, rugs, candlesticks, and porcelains?* On the other hand, in a town that was almost wall-to-wall antique shops, it must be awfully hard to remain competitive.

"Hello again." Giovanni Loard turned his hundred-watt smile on Theodosia once he'd shown his customer to the door.

"I was just driving past and spotted your sign," said

Theodosia. "I decided this was the day to come in and look at those paintings I've heard so much about."

"For that special wall," he said.

"Exactly," said Theodosia, smiling back at him and wondering why she suddenly felt like she was playing a role in a drawing room comedy.

Giovanni Loard beckoned with an index finger. "Back here," he told her. "In my office."

Theodosia followed him obediently to the back of the store, waited as he unlatched a door, then stepped into a small wood-paneled office.

"Wow," was all she said.

The office was relatively small, perhaps twelve by fifteen feet, but its walls were covered with gleaming oil paintings. There were portraits, landscapes, seascapes, and still lifes. Some were dreamy and ethereal, others were incredibly realistic. All were exceedingly well done.

"What a lovely collection. Why don't you have some of these paintings on display in your shop?" she asked.

He shrugged with what seemed feigned indifference. "Once in a while I do," he said, and reached forward to straighten a small landscape painting that was slightly crooked. "But mostly, I keep them in here to admire for myself. And to save the very best pieces for special customers.

"This one . . ." Giovanni extended an arm pointed toward a small gem of a portrait. "This one reminds me of you."

Theodosia gazed at the painting, mindful of Giovanni's gaze upon her. The painting was of a woman in a full-skirted, corseted dress reclining on a chaise. The style invoked the antebellum period and the predominant colors were muted pinks and purples, with alabaster skin tones.

"It's beautiful," said Theodosia. The painting was a beauty, but there was an ethereal quality about it that was oddly disquieting.

"Thank you for coming to the funeral yesterday," Giovanni said, changing the subject abruptly. "I saw you during the service, but with everyone milling about afterward, we never did get a chance to say hello."

"How is Doe holding up?" asked Theodosia.

"Better than expected," replied Giovanni. "Her friends and family are being very supportive, and she's a brave girl, although I have to say, she's feeling a tremendous amount of frustration about the ineptitude and total inactivity of the police. They've gone absolutely nowhere in their investigation."

"Is there somewhere to go?" asked Theodosia.

Giovanni lifted an eyebrow. "They took Ford Cantrell in for questioning."

"I take it you're fairly convinced that Ford Cantrell somehow tampered with the pistol?" said Theodosia.

"Yes, I am," said Giovanni. "I simply don't believe it was an accident."

"Could someone else have tampered with it?"

Giovanni frowned as though the idea had never occurred to him. "I can't think of another soul who would have wanted to harm Oliver Dixon."

"Oliver Dixon was heavily involved in a new start-up company," said Theodosia. "There could have been someone who did not want him to succeed."

"I see what you mean," said Giovanni. "Oliver was a truly brilliant and gifted man. The ideas he was bringing to Grapevine would have helped revolutionize how people use PDAs." He paused. "Or so I'm told. I, unfortunately, function at a relatively low technology level. The fax machine is about the most I can manage," he added ruefully.

"But it sounds like there was a tremendous amount at stake," said Theodosia. "Competition in business has been known to trigger volatile deeds. A fearful competitor, angry supplier, skittish investor . . . any one of them could have resented Oliver Dixon mightily."

"Highly doubtful," said Giovanni. "As you may or may not know, Booth Crowley was Grapevine's major under-writer, and he's known to have an impeccable reputation around here."

"I'm sure he does," said Theodosia, wondering if Giovanni had also witnessed Booth Crowley's over-the-top display of anger yesterday. "However," she continued, "that doesn't mean someone didn't have it in personally for Oliver Dixon."

Giovanni's face clouded. "I suppose you could be right," he conceded.

"Too bad about the disturbance yesterday."

"Pardon?" said Giovanni. He'd turned his gaze toward the painting he'd indicated had reminded him so much of Theodosia.

"At the funeral. The somewhat ugly scene between Booth Crowley and a fellow named Billy Manolo. Do you know him? Billy, I mean?"

"No, not really. Well, only by reputation. Fellow does odd jobs at the yacht club, I believe."

"Do you think he could have had a grudge against Oliver Dixon?"

"I don't see how he could have," said Giovanni in a condescending tone. "I mean, the man was hired help. They didn't exactly mix on the same social level."

That's precisely the reason why Billy Manolo might carry a grudge, Theodosia thought to herself.

Giovanni drew a deep breath, let it out, concentrated on trying to refocus his energy and his smile. "Shall I hold the painting for you?" he asked brightly.

"No, I don't think so," said Theodosia.

CHAPTER 16

❧

"*I'VE BEEN WATCHING* the weather channel, and it looks like there's a storm moving in," said Jory Davis.

"There is," agreed Theodosia. After five days in New York, Jory had finally phoned her. "It's been raining all day, and everything just seems to be building in intensity. Something's definitely brewing out in the mid-Atlantic. I spoke with Drayton earlier, and he's worried sick that all the flowers will get blown about and smashed. Which means next week's Garden Fest will be an absolute bust."

Theodosia was cozied up in her apartment above the tea shop. Even though it was Friday evening, it was far too rainy and miserable to contemplate going out anywhere.

"I'm worried about my boat," said Jory. "Eldon Cook, one of my sailing buddies, went over to the Isle of Palms a couple days ago and brought it back, so it's moored at the yacht club now. But if there's an even worse storm blowing in . . ."

"What can I do to help?" offered Theodosia.

"Could you stop by my office and pick up the second set of keys? I know Eldon locked up the boat, so if you

could take the keys to the yacht club and give them to Billy
Manolo—"

"Billy Manolo?"

"Yeah," said Jory, "he works there. He's a kind of
handyman."

"I know who he is," replied Theodosia. "I met him yesterday morning. Well, I didn't actually meet him, I saw
him. At Oliver Dixon's funeral."

"Of course," said Jory. "I'd completely forgotten that
the funeral was yesterday. How was it?"

"Sad," said Theodosia. "But nicely done. A lot of his
friends stood up and said some wonderful things about
him."

"That's good," said Jory. "Oliver deserved it."

"So take the keys to Billy and have him do what?" continued Theodosia.

"Secure the boat, turn on the bilge pump. Probably
check to make sure the sails are stored properly. Your basic
hurricane preparedness."

"You trust this guy to do this?"

"Yeah. Sure I do. It's his job to do this kind of stuff."
Jory paused. "Is there some problem, Theo? Something I
don't know about?"

"No, of course not. Don't worry about a thing," said
Theodosia. "I'll take care of everything. How are things on
your end? How are the depositions going?"

Jory sighed. "Slow."

Theodosia hung up the phone and peered out her
kitchen window as rain thudded heavily on the roof and
sloshed noisily down drain spouts. She could barely make
out the little garden apartment across the cobblestone alley
where Haley lived, so strong was the downpour.

Shuddering, she buttoned the top button of her chenille
sweater. Charleston was usually engulfed in warm weather
by now, and everyone was enjoying a lovely, languid

spring before the buildup of summer's oppressive heat and humidity. But this was a whole different story: nasty weather and a chill Atlantic breeze that seemed to whip right through you.

The teakettle on the stove began its high-pitched, wavering whistle, and Theodosia quickly snatched it from the back burner. Pouring boiling water over a teaspoon of Darjeeling, she let it steep for three minutes in the tiny one-cup teapot. It was funny, she thought, the biggest enemies of tea were air, light, heat, and dampness. And, so often, Charleston's climate offered up abundant helpings of all of these!

Theodosia retreated to her living room and stretched out on the couch. Earl Grey, already well into his evening nap, lifted his head a few inches, eyed her sleepily, and settled back down.

As Theodosia sipped her tea, she thought about Lizbeth Cantrell, the woman who had implored her for help just a few days ago.

She still didn't know why she'd promised Lizbeth that she'd try to clear Ford Cantrell's name. After all, she was the one who'd been suspicious of Ford in the first place.

She supposed it was the connection between Lizbeth Cantrell and her mother that had triggered her answer. The bittersweet flood of memories had been a strange, slightly mind-altering experience.

And, deep down, she knew that she also felt beholden to Lizbeth. In the South, with its curious code of honor, when you were beholden to someone, you helped them out when they needed you. No questions asked.

But what would she do if she couldn't keep her promise to Lizbeth?

What if more investigating proved that Ford Cantrell really had tampered with that old pistol? Ford was, after all, the one with an extensive gun collection. So he had expertise when it came to antique weapons. And the man had recently turned his plantation into a hunting preserve. She wasn't exactly sure what that proved, but it was the kind of thing that could carry nasty implications in court.

But Lizbeth had seemed utterly convinced of her brother's innocence. Then again, Lizbeth was a believer in signs and portents. Like the wreath of coltsfoot. What was it supposed to symbolize again? Oh, yes, justice.

And exactly what justice had Lizbeth been making reference to? Theodosia wondered. *Justice for her brother, Ford Cantrell? Or the type of justice that might have already been meted out against Oliver Dixon?*

Theodosia stared at the bone china cup that held her tea. She had begun collecting individual coffee, tea, and demitasse cups long before she'd opened the tea shop. She'd found that when she set her table for a dinner party, it was fun to arrange it with mismatched pieces, pairing, for example, a Limoges plate with a Lilique cup and saucer.

Now the information she'd managed to collect so far on the people surrounding Oliver Dixon also seemed like mismatched pieces. But unlike the eclectic table settings her guests often raved over, none of these pieces seemed to fit together.

Theodosia stood, stretched, and tried to shake off the chill. She'd been avoiding turning on the heat—it seemed kind of silly to still be using heat in April—but her apartment felt like it was growing colder by the minute.

Relenting, Theodosia walked across the room and flipped the lever on the thermostat. She was immediately rewarded by an electrical hum followed by a small puff of warm air.

Okay, she asked herself, *what am I missing?* She stood, staring at the droplets of water that streamed down the outside of the windows, reminding her of tears. Like Doe's tears for her dead husband, Oliver Dixon?

She believed fervently that Oliver Dixon was more than just the victim; he was also the linchpin in all this. If she could figure out why someone wanted Oliver out of the way, she could establish motive.

And when you found motive, you usually found the murderer.

Theodosia went to her computer and sat down. She had looked at the financial and start-up information on Oliver Dixon's new company, Grapevine, and nothing seemed particularly out of the ordinary. They'd spent a lot of money on research and development, but that was fairly typical. And because Grapevine was a start-up high-tech company, their burn rate, or rate of spending for the first few months, had been high but certainly not unexpected.

She wondered what the media had written about Grapevine. Haley had quoted from an article in the business section of the *Post and Courier*. But, from the rah-rah sound of it, the article had probably been reedited from a press release that the company itself had prepared. That was usually how those things worked. Lord knows, over the years she herself had written enough press releases that got turned into newspaper articles or sidebars in trade publications.

But what had the hard-nosed business analysts said about Grapevine? The techie guys from Forrester or the business mavens at Arthur Andersen? Or even the reviewers at some of the vertical trade pubs?

Easy enough to check, she thought, as she clicked on Netscape and typed in the key word "Grapevine."

Forty-seven thousand hits came up for Grapevine, everything from rock bands to a restaurant in Napa Valley. *Oops. Definitely got to narrow the search,* Theodosia decided.

Now she added the term PDA to the search parameter. That yielded sixty-three hits. Far more manageable.

Theodosia scanned down her new list of hits, searching for a company profile, analyst's report, anything that might give her an outsider's snapshot view of Grapevine.

She clicked open an article from *Technology Voyage*, a well-respected publication that reported on new products and trends in E-commerce and provided top-line analyses of various new high-tech companies. She had actually placed advertising in *Technology Voyage* and met with its editors when she worked on the Avanti account, a company that manufactured semiconductors.

The *Technology Voyage* article was titled "PDAs on the Fast Track." It began with a good overview of the PDA market. Sales were erupting, topping three billion dollars with projections of more than six billion dollars by next year. And just as Haley had said, PDAs were touted as portable, pocket-sized devices that let you magically keep track of appointments, addresses, phone numbers, to-do lists, and personal notes. More full-featured PDAs could even be used to send and receive E-mail, surf the Internet, or support digital cameras.

The article went on to list the various PDA manufacturers, manufacturers of PDA applications, chips and inner workings, and PDA wireless service and content providers.

According to the article, Grapevine was a manufacturer of flash memory cards, thirty-two and sixty-four-megabyte SD cards for storing data in those PDAs that used the Palm operating system.

Wow, thought Theodosia. *What with working on computers, setting up a Web site, and trading stocks on-line, I'm fairly well versed in technology, but this is getting slightly complicated!*

The article went on to list the burgeoning number of PDA manufacturers that included such companies as Casio, IBM, Hewlett-Packard, Royal, Compaq, and Handspring, and briefly detailed Microsoft's competing operating system, Pocket PC.

Theodosia put two fingers to her forehead, kneaded gently at the beginnings of a techno headache. Better to quit while she was ahead? She scanned the rest of the arti-

cle quickly, then became caught up again. As she read the
"Editors Choice" thumbnail sketches of several different
PDAs, she wondered how she'd ever gotten along without
a Blackberry to deliver wireless E-mails. Then she
changed her mind in favor of an Ericsson that boasted
handwriting and voice recognition. And finally, Theodosia
decided the daVinci, with its tiny folding keyboard, had to
be the slickest thing yet.

Would one of these minicomputers work for her? Perhaps so. A whizbang PDA might help her keep better track
of all manner of things. Tea party commitments, shopping
lists and—she pulled her face into a wry grin—a list of
murder suspects? She shook her head. Time to give it a
rest. She was starting to obsess, and that wasn't good. That
wasn't good at all.

CHAPTER 17

"*H*ALEY, WHERE ARE the tea candles?" barked Drayton.
"Top shelf," she called from the kitchen.

"Not the colored ones, I want the beeswax candles in the little Chinese blue and white containers." Drayton stood behind the counter, frowning, studying the floor-to-ceiling shelves.

"Bottom shelf," came Haley's voice again. "On the left."

Mumbling to himself, Drayton bent down and began pulling rolls of blue tissue paper, small blue shopping bags, and corrugated gift boxes from the cupboard in a mad rush to find his candles.

"Stop it." Haley, ever vigilant and slightly phobic about tidiness, appeared behind him and admonished him sharply. "You're getting everything all catawampus."

She knelt down. "Better let me do it," she said in a kinder tone. Opening the cupboard door on the far left, she pulled out the candles Drayton had been searching for. "Here," she said as she put two boxes into his outstretched hands. "Candles. Far *left*."

"Thank you," Drayton said sheepishly. "Guess I really am in a twitter today."

"You got that right," Haley grumped as she stuffed everything back into the cupboard. "Good thing this mystery tea thing isn't a weekly event. I'd be a wreck. We'd all be a wreck."

"Who's a wreck?" asked Theodosia as she let herself in the front door.

"Drayton is," joked Haley. "In his sublime paranoia to keep everything a secret, he's ending up doing most of the prep work himself. Although he has *deigned* to allow me to bake a few of his menu items," she added with a wicked grin.

"Like what?" asked Theodosia. "I'm in the dark as much as you are," she explained as she slipped off her light coat and shook raindrops from it.

"Oh, let's see," said Haley. "*Cannelles de Bordeaux, croquets aux pignons*, and *fougasse*. Which is really just pastry, cookies, and breads. Except when you say it in French, it sounds exquisite. Of course, anything said in French sounds exquisite. A case in point: *boudin noir*."

"What's that?" asked Theodosia.

"Blood sausage," replied Haley.

Drayton rolled his eyes. "A bit bizarre for one of my teas," he declared as his eyes went to his watch, a classic Piaget that seemed to perpetually run a few minutes late. "Haley, it's almost nine. Better unlock the door."

"Theodosia already did," Haley shot back, then threw Theodosia a questioning glance. "You did, didn't you?" she whispered.

Theodosia gave a quick nod.

"I heard that, Haley," said Drayton.

"I don't know how many customers we'll have today," said Theodosia. "It's still raining like crazy out there."

"Oh, there'll be a few brave souls who'll come out to tromp the historic district," said Drayton. "And when they find their way to us, there's a good chance they'll be hungry."

"And cold," added Haley as she gave a little shiver.

"Right," agreed Drayton. "Which is why you better get back there and finish your baking," said Drayton.

"You don't need me to help out here? Set tables and things?"

"I'll set the tables and brew the teas, you just tend to baking."

"Okay," Haley agreed happily.

Standing at the cash register, fussing with an arrangement of tea canisters, Theodosia was aware, once again, of how much she loved their mix of personalities and the easy bantering that went on among the three of them. Anyone else walking in might think they were being slightly argumentative, but she knew it was the unrestrained familiarity that was usually reserved just for family members. Yes, they joked and pushed one another at times, but at the first sign that someone was feeling slightly overwhelmed or even provoked, they rallied to that person's defense.

The door flew open, and cold, moist air rushed in. A bulky man in a nondescript gray raincoat lowered his umbrella and peered at them.

"Detective Tidwell," Theodosia greeted him as she closed the door quickly and ushered him to a table. "You're out and about early. And on a Saturday yet."

"Tea?" offered Drayton as he approached Tidwell with a freshly brewed pot of Kandoli Garden Assam.

Tidwell lowered himself into a chair and nodded. "Thank you. Yes."

Drayton poured a cup of tea, then stroked his chin thoughtfully. "Perhaps I'm being presumptuous, Detective Tidwell, but you look like a man who might possibly be in need of a Devonshire split."

Tidwell's beady eyes gleamed with anticipation. "Pray tell, what is a Devonshire split?"

"A traditional little English sweet bun that we serve with strawberry jam. Of course, if we were in England's lake country, we would also serve it with clotted cream."

"Pretend that we are," Tidwell said. "Especially in light of this hideous wet weather."

Slipping into the chair across from Tidwell, Theodosia studied the man carefully. Tidwell had obviously come here bearing some type of information. Would he be forthright in telling her what was on his mind? Of course not. That wasn't Tidwell's style. He preferred to play his own maddening little games.

But today Tidwell surprised Theodosia. For, once his pastry and accompaniments arrived, he became quite talkative.

"We've finished most of our ballistics tests," he told her. "Regretfully, nothing's jumped out at us." Tidwell sliced his Devonshire split in half, peered at it expectantly. "At first we thought the bullets in the pistol might have been dumdums."

"What exactly are dumdums?" asked Theodosia. She'd heard the term before, but had no idea what dumdums really were.

"A nasty little trick that originated in India," said Tidwell as he lathered clotted cream onto his pastry. "Put succinctly, dumdums are expanding bullets. When they impact something, they expand."

"And you thought these tricky little bullets might have impacted Oliver Dixon's head?" she said.

"Well, not exactly," said Tidwell. "The pistol would have to have been pointed directly at him for that to occur. And from everything we know, from interviews with fairly reliable people, Oliver Dixon was holding the pistol at shoulder level and pointing it up into the air. If it had been loaded with dumdums, they could have exploded and dealt a fatal wound, but something would've been needed to make them explode."

"So your tests revealed nothing," said Theodosia.

Tidwell took a sip of tea and set his tea cup down with a gentle clink. "Let's just say our tests were inconclusive."

"What about Oliver Dixon's jacket?" asked Theodosia. "I would imagine you ran forensic tests on that?"

Tidwell sighed. "Spatters of blood, type B positive, which is somewhat rare, maybe only ten percent of the population. Definitely belonging to Oliver Dixon, though; we checked it against his medical records. On the sleeves and jacket front, residue from Charleston Harbor showing a high nutrient concentration and a low N-P ratio. And a small amount of imbedded dirt. Probably from the shore."

Theodosia thought about the blood-spattered, dirt-smeared linen tablecloth that now resided in Professor Morrow's botany lab. "Probably," she agreed, trying to keep any sign of nervousness from her voice. If Tidwell knew what she was up to, she'd be in deep trouble, and the tablecloth would undoubtedly be confiscated by the police.

They both fell silent as the front door opened with a whoosh and two couples, obviously tourists, pushed their way in.

"Can we get some coffee and muffins?" asked one of the men. He wore a yellow slicker and spoke with a Mid-westerner's flat accent.

Theodosia was up and out of her chair in a heartbeat. "How about tea and blackberry scones?" she invited. "Or a plate of lemon tarts?"

"Tea," mused the man. He turned to the rest of his party, who were all nodding agreeably, pulling off wet outerwear and settling into chairs. "Why not," he said, "as long as it's hot and strong."

Tidwell sat at his table, happily sipping tea and eating his pastry while Theodosia and Drayton quickly served the new customers.

Like many tourists who wandered into the Indigo Tea

Shop, they seemed eager to embrace what would be a new experience for them.

On the other hand, Theodosia had to remind herself that, after water, tea was the most popular drink in the world, a much-loved, long-established beverage that had been around almost 5,000 years. Sipped, savored, or tossed back hastily, the peoples of the world consumed more than 700 billion cups of tea in a single year.

"Detective Tidwell." Theodosia put her hands on the back of one of the creaky, wooden chairs and leaned toward him. "Do you remember the fellow who was involved in the terrible scene at Oliver Dixon's funeral the day before yesterday?"

"You mean Booth Crowley?" he asked.

"No, I mean Billy Manolo," she said. *Do not allow him to fluster you*, she cautioned herself. *The man is obstinate only because he relishes it as great sport.*

"You realize that Billy Manolo works at the yacht club," she said. "He had access to the pistol."

"Of course he did," said Tidwell. "In fact, his fingertips were found on the rosewood box that the pistol was kept in."

"What do you make of that?" asked Theodosia.

Tidwell shrugged. "A half-dozen other sets of fingerprints were also found on that box."

"Was Ford Cantrell's among them?" she asked.

"Do you really think Ford Cantrell would be foolish enough to leave his prints on the box if, in fact, he tampered with the pistol?" asked Tidwell. He picked up a silver spoon, scooped up yet another lump of sugar, and plunked it into his teacup.

Theodosia stared at Tidwell. *He has a unique talent for deflecting questions*, she decided. *And answering questions with another question designed to throw you slightly off track.*

"I take it you have elevated Billy Manolo to suspect status?" said Tidwell.

"The notion of Billy as suspect is not without basis," said Theodosia.

Tidwell shook his great head slowly. "Doubtful. Highly doubtful. Billy Manolo seems like a troublemaker, I'll grant you that. And he has a past history of being involved in petty thievery and nefarious dealings. But is our Billy cool enough, calculating enough, to plan and execute a murder? In front of two hundred people? I hardly see even a flash of that type of required brilliance. I fear Billy Manolo exhibits only limited capacity."

Theodosia knew what was coming and steeled herself for it. She had sent Tidwell careening down this path, and she regretted it mightily. To make matters worse, her commitment to Lizbeth Cantrell felt pitifully hollow, as though there wasn't a prayer in the world that her brother's name could be cleared.

"Ford Cantrell, on the other hand, is a man with a grudge," continued Tidwell. "A man who manufacturers his own munitions. Yes," Tidwell reiterated when he saw Theodosia's eyes go large, "Ford Cantrell makes a hobby of packing gunpowder into his own cartridges. If anyone knew how to rig that old pistol to explode, it would be someone with the critical knowledge that Ford Cantrell possesses. I am confident of a forthcoming arrest."

CHAPTER 18

❖❖❖

A LONE TERN RODE the crazed thermals, wheeling high above the yacht club where J-24s, Columbias, and San Jose 25s creaked up against silvered wooden pilings and tugged at their moorings as they pitched about in the roiling sea. The only sound, save the howling wind, was a sputtering bilge pump, somewhere out on the end of the long main pier.

Nobody home, thought Theodosia as she cinched her trench coat tighter about her and stepped onto the pier. In some places, the weather-beaten boards had two-inch gaps between them, so she had to really watch her footing. There didn't appear to be anybody on this long, wet pier today, and the water looked cold and unforgiving. A misstep was unthinkable.

She'd first tried the door to the clubhouse and found that locked. Even pounding on the door and punching the doorbell hadn't roused anyone. It was conceivable no one was here at all, that Billy Manolo didn't work on Saturday or hadn't come in because of bad weather or might be planning to show up later.

Theodosia did hold out a faint hope that someone might be hunkered down on the sailboat at the far end of the pier where the bilge pump sounded so noisily. It could be Billy Manolo, she mused, pumping out a leaky boat, working down below, trying to elude the wind's nasty bite.

Halfway to the end of the pier, Theodosia gazed out toward Charleston Harbor. Only two ships were visible through the gray mist. One appeared to be a commercial fishing vessel; the other looked like a Coast Guard cutter, probably from the nearby Coast Guard station located just down from The Battery at the mouth of the Ashley River. It certainly was a far cry from almost a week ago, when the harbor had been dotted with boats, when the promise of spring had hung in the air.

"Anybody there?" She reached the end of the pier and saw that the pump was running full tilt, pouring a steady spew of frothy green water from a twenty-five-foot Santana into the harbor. She stepped down to the smaller pier that ran parallel to the moored boat. These side piers weren't anchored by deep pilings like the main pier. Instead, they floated on top of barrels. Now, with the wind whipping in from the Atlantic at a good ten knots, the smaller, auxiliary pier pitched about precariously.

"Billy?" Theodosia called, fighting the rising panic that was beginning to build inside her as the small pier bobbed like an errant cork.

Get a grip, she admonished herself as she extended both arms out to her sides for better balance, then picked her way carefully back to the safety of the main pier. *You've walked up and down piers your whole life. This is no time to get spooked.*

Jory Davis's boat was moored at slip 112, more than halfway back in the direction of the clubhouse, with side piers that were considerably more stable since they were sheltered. Theodosia walked out to *Rubicon,* the J-24 that he loved to pilot around Charleston Harbor and up and down the Intracoastal Waterway, put her hands on the side hull, and clambered aboard. Standing in the cockpit, she felt the rhythm of the boat, heard the noisy overhead clank of halyards against the mast. She leaned forward, stuck the key in the lock for the hatch, and turned it. Grabbing the handle, she braced herself and tugged it open.

Theodosia peered down into the boat. Jory had been right. *Rubicon* was seriously taking on water. At least three inches of green seawater had managed to seep inside and was sloshing around.

She searched for a bilge pump, found one, then wasn't exactly sure how to connect the darn thing and get it started.

No, she finally told herself, *leave well enough alone.* The best thing to do was follow Jory's advice. Find Billy Manolo and have him take care of this.

Still crouched on the deck, Theodosia searched for a clue that might tell her how to get in touch with the elusive Billy Manolo.

Flipping open one of the small storage bins, she found a clear plastic pouch that contained the boat's user manual and a clutch of maps. Following her hunch, she unsnapped the pouch and rummaged through the papers.

On the inside cover of the user manual was a hand-written list of names. The fourth one down was Billy M. There was a phone number listed and an address: 115 Concannon.

Could this be Billy Manolo? The yacht club's Billy Manolo? Had to be.

CHAPTER 19

❦

UPRIVER, ON THE west bank of the Cooper River, sits
the now-defunct Charleston Naval Base. Decommissioned some ten years ago, it is technically situated in
North Charleston, an incorporated city of its own and the
third-largest city in South Carolina.

With sailors and officers gone, the economy forever
changed, real estate had become more affordable, zoning
more forgiving.

Theodosia drove slowly down Ardmore Street, searching each street sign for the cross street, Concannon. Here
was an older part of Charleston, but not the part that
showed up in glossy four-color brochures sent out by the
Convention & Visitors Bureau. Instead, these small, wood-frame houses looked tired and battered, many in dire need
of a coat of paint. Yards were small, often with more bare
patches than tended lawn. Those places that were better
kept were often surrounded by metal fences.

Just past a tire recycling plant, Theodosia found Concannon Street. She made a leap of faith, put the Jeep into a
right turn, and searched for numbers on the houses.

She had guessed correctly. Here was 215, here 211. Billy's home at 115 Concannon was in the next block.

A vacant, weed-filled lot bordered Billy Manolo's house, a one-story home that was little more than a cottage. Once-white paint had been ground off from years of wind, rain, and high humidity, and now the weathered wood glowed with an interesting patina. As Theodosia strode up the walk, she noted that, aside from the paint, everything else appeared sturdy and fairly well kept.

Grasping a black wrought-iron handrail, she mounted the single cement step and rang the doorbell.

Nothing.

She hit the doorbell again, held it in longer this time, and waited. Still no one came to the door. Perplexed, Theodosia stood for a moment, let her eyes wander to an overgrown hedge of dogwood, then to a small brick walkway that led around the side of the house.

Why not? she decided, as she crossed wet grass and started around the house.

It was like tumbling into another world.

Sections of beautifully ornate wrought-iron fences and grilles danced before her eyes. Elegant scrolls, whimsical corn motifs, and curling ivy adorned each piece. Wrought-iron pieces that had been completed leaned up against wood fences and the back of Billy Manolo's house. Other pieces, still raw from the welder's torch and awaiting mortises and hand finishing, were stacked in piles and seemed to occupy every square foot of the small backyard.

Sparks arced from a welder's torch in the dim recess of a sagging, dilapidated garage that appeared slightly larger than the house.

Billy Manolo lifted his welder's helmet and glared at Theodosia as blue flame licked from his torch. "What do you want?" he asked. His voice carried the same nervous hostility he'd exhibited the other day at Oliver Dixon's funeral.

Still in a state of delighted amazement, Theodosia peered past him, her eyes fixing on even more of the beautifully crafted metalwork. Most was stacked in hodgepodge piles, a few smaller pieces hung from the ceiling.

"These are wonderful," she said.

Billy Manolo shrugged as he flicked the switch on his oxyacetylene torch. "Yeah," was all he said.

"You made all these?" she asked.

Billy grunted in the affirmative. His welder's helmet quivered atop his head like the beak of a giant condor.

"They're beautifully done. Do you do a lot of restoration work?" Theodosia knew that Charleston homes, especially those in and around the historic district, were always in need of additions or repairs.

"Who wants to know?" Billy Manolo demanded.

"Sorry." She colored slightly. "I'm Theodosia Browning. We met at the picnic last Sunday? You borrowed the tablecloth from me." She moved toward him to offer her hand and almost tripped on a stack of metal bars.

"Careful," Billy cautioned. "Last thing I need around here is some fool woman falling on her face." He stared at her. "How come you came here?" he asked abruptly. "I don't keep no pictures here. You got to go to Popple Hill for that."

"Popple Hill?" said Theodosia. She had no idea what Popple Hill was or what Billy was even talking about.

"The design folks," Billy explained impatiently as though she were an idiot child. "Go talk to them. They'll figure out size and design and all. I just make the stuff." Billy Manolo shook his head as though she were a buzzing mayfly that was irritating him. He leaned forward, slid a grimy hand into a leather glove that lay atop his forge. There was a hiss of air and immediately flame shot from his welder's torch again.

"I see," said Theodosia, averting her eyes and making a mental note to ask around and find out just who these Popple Hill designers were. "Actually, I just came from the yacht club," she explained. "Jory Davis in slip one twelve wanted me to give you these." She reached into her purse, grabbed the keys, and dangled them at Billy. "The keys for *Rubicon*."

Billy Manolo sighed, switched the torch off again.

"He wants you to turn on the bilge pump," said Theodosia, this time putting a tinge of authority into her voice. "He's stuck out of town on business, and he's afraid his boat is taking on water. Actually, it is taking on water. I was just there."

Billy Manolo pulled the welder's helmet from his head and strode toward her. He reached out and snatched the keys from her outstretched hand and stared stolidly at her.

"Great," she answered, a little too heartily. She gazed about the backyard, realizing full well that Billy Manolo was an ironworker by trade, that he'd probably made some of the gates, grills, and balcony railings that adorned many of Charleston's finer homes.

And along with that realization came the sudden understanding that Billy Manolo, with his knowledge of metals and stress points and such, could easily have been the one who had tampered with the old pistol. Billy Manolo, whose fingerprints had certainly turned up on the rosewood box that the old pistol had been housed in.

"Look," Theodosia said, caught somewhere between losing her patience at Billy's rudeness and a small insinuation of fear, "the very least you can do is be civil."

He tilted his head slightly, gave her a surly, one-eyed glance. "Why should I?"

Theodosia lost it. "You might want to seriously consider working on your people skills," she told him. "Because should you be questioned by the Charleston police, and the possibility is not unlikely, the inhospitable attitude you have just shown toward me will not play well with them."

Billy Manolo snorted disdainfully. "Police," he spat out. "They don't know nothin'."

"They are not unaware of your little public to-do with Booth Crowley two days ago," said Theodosia.

"Booth Crowley has a lot to hide," snarled Billy.

"From what I hear, Billy, *you* might have a few things to hide," Theodosia shot back. She was fishing, to be sure, but her words were more effective than she'd ever thought possible.

Stung by her innuendo, Billy bent down, picked up an iron rod, and glared at her dangerously. "Get lost, lady, before you find yourself floating facedown in Charleston Harbor!"

CHAPTER 20

DOZENS OF SMALL white candles flickered on every table, countertop, shelf, nook, and cranny of the Indigo Tea Shop. Muted paisley tablecloths were draped elegantly across the wooden tables, and the overhead brass chandelier had been dimmed to impart a moody aura.

"It looks like someone unleashed a crazed voodoo priestess in here," declared Haley.

"What?" Drayton's usually well-modulated voice rose in a high-pitched squawk. "It's *supposed* to look mysterious. I'm trying to create an atmosphere that's conducive to an evening of high drama and new experiences in the realm of tea."

"And it does," Theodosia assured him. "It's very atmospheric. Haley," she cautioned the young girl, "ease up on Drayton, will you? He's got a lot on his mind."

Haley's needling banter was usually welcome in the tea shop and easily parried by the often erudite Drayton, but tonight Drayton did seem a little discombobulated.

Haley sidled up to Drayton and gave him a reassuring tap on the shoulder. "Okay. It's cool."

"You *do* think the shop has a certain dramatic, stage-setting appearance, don't you?" Drayton peered anxiously at Theodosia.

"It's perfect," declared Theodosia. "Our guests will be thrilled." She gazed at the lineup of Barotine teapots borrowed from one of Drayton's antique dealer friends. The fanciful little green and brown glazed teapots were adorned with shells, twining vines, and snail-like shapes, and lent to the aura of mystery.

Then there were the centerpieces. Here again, Drayton had gotten a few choice antique pieces on loan and let Hattie Boatwright at Floradora run wild with them. An antique ceramic frog peeked from behind clusters of purple hydrangeas, a bronze sculpture of a wood nymph was surrounded by plum blossoms, a jade statue of the Buddha sat amid an artful arrangement of reeds and grasses.

"You've managed to instill elegance as well as a hint of mystery in our little tea shop," praised Theodosia, "and I, for one, can't wait to see what's going to happen tonight!"

Truth be told, Theodosia wasn't exactly sure what was going to take place, but she had complete confidence in Drayton and knew that, whatever menu and program unfolded, he'd pull it off with great style and aplomb. Besides, while she'd been out this afternoon, getting drenched at the yacht club and then insulted by Billy Manolo, four more people had called, begging for last-minute reservations. That meant they'd had to slip in extra chairs at a few of the tables.

As Theodosia laid out silverware and linen napkins, Haley placed tiny gold mesh bags at each place setting.

"What are those?" asked Theodosia.

"Favors," said Haley. "Drayton had me wrap tiny bricks of pressed tea in gold fabric, then tie them with ribbons."

"Drayton's really going all out," said Theodosia, pleased at such attention to detail.

"You don't know the half of it," whispered Haley. She

glanced around to make sure Drayton was in the back of the shop. "He's got five actors from the Charleston Little Theater Group coming in tonight. They're going to do a kind of one-act play while they help serve tea and goodies. And, of course, they'll drop clues as they go along. At some point in the evening, one of them will have a mysterious and fatal accident, and the audience has to figure out who perpetrated the dastardly deed!"

"You mean like Mr. Mustard in the library with the candlestick?" asked Theodosia.

"Something very close to it," said Haley.

Drayton emerged from the back room, carrying a tray full of teacups. "Listen," he instructed, one finger aimed at the ceiling.

Theodosia and Haley stopped what they were doing and listened to gentle drumming on the roof.

"It started raining again," said Drayton. "Sets the mood perfectly, don't you think?"

"Quoth the raven . . . nevermore," giggled Haley.

Halfway through Drayton's mystery tea, Theodosia found herself perched on the wooden stool behind the counter, utterly charmed and fascinated by what was taking place before her. True to Haley's prediction, five members from the Charleston Little Theater Group, all amateurs and friends of Drayton, had shown up. Upon serving the first course, a hot and sour green tea soup, they immediately launched into a fast-paced, drawing room type play that, except for the murder, bordered heavily on comedy and kept their guests in stitches.

The audience had been swept up in the drama from the outset. Chuckling in all the right places, oohing and ahing as tiny candles sputtered out at strategic times during the play, gasping when Drayton suddenly doused the overhead lights and the "murder" took place.

Theodosia had been delighted that Delaine Dish had

shown up with her friend Brooke Carter Crockett, who owned Heart's Desire, a nearby jewelry shop that specialized in high-end estate jewelry. Miss Dimple had brought her brother, Stanley, a roly-poly fellow who, except for being bald as a cue ball, was the spitting image of Miss Dimple. Plus there were tea shop regulars and lots of friends from the historic district. In all, twenty-five guests sat in the flickering candlelight, enjoying the mystery tea.

And they'd had a couple surprise guests, too: Lizbeth Cantrell and her aunt Millicent.

Theodosia hadn't expected to see Lizbeth Cantrell so soon, and especially not tonight. But the ladies had slipped in at the last moment, Lizbeth nodding knowingly to Theodosia, then found their seats and settled back comfortably to enjoy the play.

The actors, down to four now, were serving the main course, chicken satays with a spicy sauce of Sencha tea and ginger, and playing their roles rather broadly. Theodosia had her money on the Theodore character as the murderer. He was a pompous patriarch who certainly *looked* like he could whack someone on the head with a bronze nymph. (Now she knew why Drayton had gone to all that trouble with table centerpieces!)

On the other hand, you never could tell when it came to spotting suspects. First impressions weren't always that reliable. Look how she'd pinned her suspicions on Ford Cantrell. He'd certainly appeared to be the perfect suspect, and now she wasn't sure at all.

But Theodosia did know one thing for sure. She was going to get to the bottom of Oliver Dixon's murder. If she discovered the real killer and was able to clear Ford Cantrell, she'd have done a great kindness for Lizbeth Cantrell. On the other hand, if Ford Cantrell wasn't the innocent man his sister professed him to be . . . well, then at least the truth would be out. And knowing the truth was always better than not knowing at all.

Loud clapping and shouts of "Bravo!" brought Theodosia out of her musings and back to the here and now. Drayton was extending a hand toward the four remaining actors as they took a collective bow and then struck exaggerated poses.

"I present to you, the suspects," announced Drayton, obviously pleased with the crowd's reaction. "As they have dropped bold clues and broad hints throughout the evening, we shall now pass ballots around the table so *you* can be both judge and jury and hopefully solve our murder mystery."

The guests' voices rose in excited murmurs as the amateur actors, obviously still relishing their roles, walked among the tables, passing out paper and pens.

"And," added Drayton, "while you ponder the identity of the perpetrator of the crime, we shall be serving our final course, tea sorbet with miniature almond cakes."

"What's the prize for solving the mystery?" called Delaine.

"Haley, care to do the honors?" asked Drayton.

Haley stepped to the front of the tea shop and cleared her throat. "The winner or winners, should there be a tie, will receive a gift basket filled with teas and a half-dozen mystery books."

"Perfect!" exclaimed Miss Dimple. "Then you can have your very own mystery tea . . . any time you want."

"But our evening is far from drawing to a close," said Drayton. "After dessert, we shall be offering tastings on a number of select estate teas." He paused dramatically. "And we have a special guest with us, Madame Hildegarde. Using her fine gift of divination, Madame Hildegarde will read your tea leaves."

There was a spatter of applause, and then chairs slid back as people stood up to stretch their legs, move about the tea shop, and visit with friends at other tables.

Lizbeth Cantrell wasted no time in coming over to speak with Theodosia.

"I don't know if you've ever met my aunt," said Lizbeth Cantrell. "Millicent Cantrell, meet Theodosia Browning."

Theodosia shook hands with the diminutive woman who also had a no-nonsense air about her and gray hair that must have also been red at one time.

"Hello," Theodosia greeted her. "I hope you've enjoyed the evening so far."

Millicent Cantrell smiled up at Theodosia. "I've never been to a mystery tea before. Went to a mystery dinner once at the Hancock Inn over in Columbia, but everything was terribly overdone and not very good."

Theodosia smiled at the old woman, even as she wondered if Millicent Cantrell was referring to the play or the cooking.

Millicent Cantrell's hand groped for Theodosia's. "You're a real dear to help us."

Theodosia searched out Lizbeth Cantrell's eyes.

Lizbeth met her gaze. "I told her you had pledged to help clear my brother's name."

"Pledged, well, that might be . . ." began Theodosia, feeling slightly overwhelmed. These ladies seemed to have pinned all their hopes on her. It suddenly felt like an overwhelming responsibility.

"You're a good girl, just like your momma," Millicent Cantrell told her as tears sparkled in her old eyes.

"And she's smart," added Lizbeth. "Theodosia's not thrown off by the occasional red herring, to use an old English fox hunting term."

"Isn't this cozy? I had no idea you all knew each other." Delaine Dish had slipped across the room and now raised a thin, penciled brow at Theodosia. She seemed to be waiting expectantly for some sort of explanation. Theodosia wondered how much Delaine had overheard.

"Hello, Delaine," said Lizbeth pleasantly. "Nice to see

you again. Theodosia and I are getting pretty excited about the upcoming Spoleto Festival. She and I are both serving on committees."

"Spoleto," purred Delaine. "Yes, that does happen soon, doesn't it?"

"It's my third year on the ticket committee," said Lizbeth smoothly.

"The ticket committee," said Delaine in her maddening, parrotlike manner. "Sounds terribly interesting."

"It is," said Lizbeth, ignoring the fact that Delaine's comments, delivered in a bored, flat tone, implied it wasn't interesting at all. "As you probably know, tickets for the various Spoleto arts events are sold in packages."

"Mn-hm." Delaine leaned in close and narrowed her eyes.

"And our committee works out the various pairings." Lizbeth ducked her head and grinned, and Theodosia could see that she was having a little fun with Delaine now. "Actually," continued Lizbeth, "it's kind of like seating guests at a dinner party. You try to pair the interesting ones with the shy ones. In this case, we pair the real blockbuster events with some of the events that people might perceive as sleepers but are, of course, really quite stimulating."

"What a quaint analogy," murmured Delaine.

"Delaine, come have your tea leaves read." Drayton appeared at Delaine's elbow. "Be a darling and go first, would you?" he whispered to her. "Help break the ice for the other guests."

Theodosia grinned as Delaine reluctantly allowed herself to be led over to Madame Hildegarde, a sixtyish woman in a flowing purple caftan, who was now ensconced at the small table next to the fireplace.

Some forty minutes later, most everyone had departed. Angie Congdon, who owned the Featherbed House, one of the most popular B and Bs on The Battery, shared the honors for correctly guessing the murderer along with Tom Wigley, one of Drayton's friends from the Heritage Society.

"Drayton," Haley urged, "*you* come have your tea leaves read."

"Oh, all right," he agreed reluctantly.

"Don't be such a curmudgeon," Haley scolded as she slid her chair over to make room for Drayton. "Madame Hildegarde just told me I was going to meet someone *verrry* interesting. Maybe she'll have something equally exciting for you."

"Maybe she'll predict when this storm will end and I can get out and work in my garden," fretted Drayton.

Madame Hildegarde gazed at Drayton with hawklike gray eyes. "Drayton doesn't care for prognostication," she said with a heavy accent. "Doesn't want to look ahead, only behind." She laughed heartily, taking a friendly jab at his penchant for all things historical.

"You know how it works," Madame Hildegarde told him as she poured a fresh cup of tea. "Your teacup represents the vastness of the sky, the tea leaves are the stars and the myriad possibilities. Drink your tea." She motioned with her hand. "And turn the cup upside down. Then I read."

Drayton complied as the remaining guests gathered round him to watch.

"An audience," he joked. "Just what I don't need."

But Lizbeth Cantrell and her aunt Millicent, Theodosia, Delaine Dish, and Miss Dimple and her brother crowded around him, anyway. The rain was pelting against the windows now, and there was no question of leaving until it let up some.

"You want to ask a question or just have me read?" Madame Hildegarde asked Drayton.

"Just read," he said. "Give it to me straight."

"Oh," cooed Miss Dimple, "this is so interesting."

Madame Hildegarde flipped over Drayton's cup and carefully studied the leaves that clung to the bottom inside the white porcelain cup.

"Oh, oh, a love triangle," joked Haley.

Madame Hildegarde held up a hand. "No. The leaves predict change. A big change is coming."

Drayton frowned. "Change. Goodness me, I certainly hope not. I detest change."

Madame Hildegarde was undeterred. "Change," she said again. "Tea leaves don't lie. Especially not tonight."

Drayton cleared his throat somewhat uneasily. "Someone else try," he urged. He was obviously unhappy being the center of attention and having a spotlight placed on his future.

"I'll try," volunteered Lizbeth Cantrell.

"Excellent," said Drayton as he slipped out of his chair and relinquished it to Lizbeth Cantrell. "Another brave soul hoping to have her future divined."

Madame Hildegarde poured a small cup of tea and passed it over to Lizbeth. She drank it quickly, then, without waiting to be told, flipped the teacup upside down and pushed it toward Madame Hildegarde.

"I'd like to ask a question," she said.

Madame Hildegarde locked eyes with Lizbeth as the fire crackled and hissed behind her. "Go ahead," she urged.

Theodosia held her breath. In that split second, she knew what was coming. She knew what Lizbeth Cantrell was going to ask. And she wished with all her heart that she wouldn't. Because, deep inside, Theodosia was afraid of what Madame Hildegarde's answer would be.

"Who killed Oliver Dixon?" Lizbeth Cantrell asked in a whisper.

A hush fell over the room. Madame Hildegarde reached for the cup, her opal ring dancing with fire, and began to turn the cup over slowly.

As she did, the tea shop was plunged into sudden darkness.

A heavy thump at the front door was followed by a loud crash. Then Haley screamed, "Someone's at the window!"

"What's happening?" shrieked Miss Dimple. "What was that noise? Where are the lights?"

A second crash sounded, this time right at Theodosia's feet.

"No one move," commanded Theodosia as she began to pick her way gingerly across the room. Guided by the flickering firelight and her familiarity with the tea shop, she headed unerringly toward the counter. "There's a lantern behind the cash register," she told everyone. "Give me a moment and I'll get it."

Within seconds, the lantern flared, illuminating the tea shop like a weak torchère and catching everyone with surprised looks on their faces.

Haley immediately rushed to the door and threw it open. There was no one there.

"They're gone," she said, confusion written on her face.

"Who's gone?" asked Theodosia as she came up behind her and peered out. Up and down Church Street not a single light shone. The entire street was eerily dark.

"The shadow, the person, whatever was here," Haley said. "It just vanished."

"Like a ghost," said Miss Dimple in a tremulous voice.

"There's no such thing as ghosts," spoke Drayton.

"It *looked* like a ghost," said Miss Dimple rather insistently. "I saw something at the window just before we heard that thump. It was kind of wavery and transparent. Did you see it, too, Haley?"

Haley continued to gaze out into the street, a frown creasing her face. "*Someone* was here," she declared.

Theodosia spun about and turned her gaze on Madame Hildegarde. "The teacup, what was the answer in the teacup?" she asked.

Madame Hildegarde pointed toward the floor and, in the dim light, Theodosia could see shattered fragments strewn across the wood planks.

"Gone." Madame Hildegarde shook her head with regret. "All gone."

CHAPTER 21

❧❧❧

*S*UNDAY MORNING DAWNED with swirls of pink and gold painting the sky. The rain had finally abated, and the few clouds remaining seemed like wisps of cotton that had been tightly wrung out.

The slight haze that hung over Charleston Harbor would probably burn off by noon, but by ten A.M., tourists who'd been hunkered down in inns, hotels, and bed-and-breakfasts throughout the historic district, fretting mightily that their weekend in Charleston might be a total washout, began emerging in droves. They meandered the sidewalks, taking in the historic houses and antique shops. They shopped the open air market and bought strong, steaming cups of chicory coffee from vendors. And they strolled cobblestone lanes to gaze upon the Powder Magazine, one of the oldest public buildings in the Carolinas, and Cabbage Row, the quaint area that inspired *Porgy and Bess*, George and Ira Gershwin's beloved folk opera.

Whipping along Highway 700, the Mayfield Highway, in her Jeep, Theodosia was headed for the low-country. She told herself she was making a Sunday visit to her aunt

Libby's, but she also knew she'd probably do a drive-by of Ford Cantrell's place, too. Sneak a peak, see what all this game ranch fuss was about.

Earl Grey sat complacently beside her in the passenger seat, his long ears flapping in the wind, velvet muzzle poked out the open window as he drank in all manner of intoxicating scents.

With all this sunshine and fine weather, the events of last night seemed almost distant to Theodosia. Of course, even after the power had come back on some ten minutes later, Haley had insisted that someone had been lurking outside. And Miss Dimple had clung hopefully to her notion that a ghost, possibly induced by all the psychic energy they'd generated, had paid them all a visit last night.

Theodosia was fairly sure that if anything had been at the window last night, it had been a window peeper. A real person. Which begged the question, *Who in his right mind would be sneaking about on a cold, rainy night, peeping in windows?*

On the other hand, maybe the person hadn't been in his right mind. Last night's peeper could have been angry, worried, or just frantically curious about someone who'd been attending the mystery tea.

Theodosia frowned and, just above her eyebrows, tiny lines creased her fair skin. Then she made a hard right, jouncing onto County Road 6, and her facial muscles relaxed. She was suddenly engulfed in a tangle of forest, a multihued tapestry of green.

Years ago, more than 150 thousand low-country acres had served as prime rice-growing country, producing the creamy short-grain rice that had been Carolina gold. Fields had alternately been flooded and drained as seasons changed and the cycle of planting, growing, and harvesting took place. Remnants of old rice dikes and canals were still visible in some places, green humps and gentle indentations overgrown now by creeping vines of Carolina jessamine and enormous hedges of azaleas.

Many of these rice fields had also reverted to swampland, providing ideal habitat for ducks, pheasants, and herons. And over the years, hurricanes and behemoth storm surges, the most recent wrought by Hurricane Hugo in 1989, had forged new courses in many of the low-country creeks and streams.

As a child visiting her aunt Libby, Theodosia had explored many of the low-country's tiny waterways in a bateau, or flat-bottomed boat. Poling her way along, she had often dabbled a fishing line into the water and, when luck was with her, returned home with a nice redfish or jack crevalle.

"Aunt Libby!" Theodosia waved wildly at the small, silver-haired woman who stood on the crest of the hill gazing toward a sparkling pond.

"You've brought the good weather with you," said Libby Revelle as she greeted her niece. "And none too soon. Hello there, Earl Gray." She reached down and patted the dog, who spun excitedly in circles. "Come to tree my poor possums?"

Libby Revelle, who loved all manner of beast and bird, spent much of her time feeding wild birds and setting out cracklins and pecan meal for the raccoons, foxes, possums, and rabbits that lived in the swamps and pine forests around her old plantation, Cane Ridge. Of course, when Earl Grey paid a visit, the critters she had so patiently coaxed and cajoled suddenly went into hiding and all her goodwill gestures went up in smoke.

Theodosia put her arm around Libby as they started toward the main house. Theodosia's father, Macalester Browning, had grown up here at Cane Ridge, and her parents had lived here when they were first married.

Built in 1835 near Horlbeck Creek, Cane Ridge had

been a flourishing rice plantation in its day. Now it was an elegant woodland retreat. With its steeply pitched roof and fanciful peaks and gables, the main house had always reminded Theodosia of a Hansel and Gretel cottage, although the style was technically known as Gothic Revival.

"Tell me the news," coaxed Libby as they settled into creaking, oversized wicker chairs and looked out toward the woods from the broad piazza that stretched around three sides of the house. "How are Drayton and Haley?" Libby asked. "And did you ever decide to hire that sweet little bookkeeper?"

"Drayton and Haley are fine," said Theodosia. "Like oil and water sometimes, but they're delightful and caring and keep things humming. Our new bookkeeper, Miss Dimple, is an absolute whiz. What a load off my mind since she's been handling payables and receivables. Why did I ever think I could handle the books myself?"

"Because, my dear, you believe you are capable of handling just about anything. In most cases, you can, but when it comes to the business of accounting, I think that's best left to an expert."

Theodosia smiled to herself. When her mother passed away, Aunt Libby, newly widowed, had stepped in and helped with so many things in the realm of child rearing. One of those was homework. Theodosia had excelled in subjects such as English and composition and history but had foundered at math. Algebra was gut-wrenching, geometry a foreign puzzle. Libby had seen her consternation and struggle with numbers and encouraged her gently. But Theodosia had never really gained complete mastery in that area.

"You heard about Oliver Dixon," said Theodosia.

"I've heard about Oliver Dixon from the horse's mouth," said Libby.

"What do you mean?"

"Lizbeth Cantrell stopped by this past week," said

Libby. "Told me that her brother was being questioned, asked lots of questions about you."

"I figured as much," said Theodosia.

"Did she ask you to help?" asked Libby.

Theodosia sighed. "Yes."

"Are you going to?"

"I told her I'd try. I'm not sure there's much I can do, though," said Theodosia.

Libby leaned forward in her chair and grasped Theodosia's hands. "Don't sell yourself short," she said. "You have a relationship with the investigating officer."

"You mean Tidwell?"

"Yes. Of course."

"I'm not sure I'd call it a relationship," said Theodosia, who considered their standoffish treatment of each other as bordering on adversarial.

"Then call it a nodding acquaintance," said Libby. "But you *are* in a position to affect and impact his thinking."

"I suppose so," said Theodosia, not quite convinced.

Libby smiled. "Good." She released Theodosia's hands and sat back in her chair. "Then do what you do best. Nose about, ask questions, trust in your instincts. You're *good* at solving mysteries, Theodosia. We all know that."

"And if Ford Cantrell really is guilty?" asked Theodosia.

"Then he's guilty," said Libby. "But at least you tried. At least you put forth your best efforts. I know Lizbeth would appreciate that."

Theodosia stared toward the pond. With the sun a great golden orb in the sky now, it caught each gentle ripple and cast diamonds across the water. Around the edge of the pond, bright green fronds of saw grass waved gently in breezes that carried just a hint of salt.

Theodosia shifted her gaze to the left of the pond, to the small family cemetery. Dogwoods were beginning to bloom, and crape myrtle poked over the crumbling stone wall that surrounded the small plot. Her mother and father both rested here, under the ancient live oak that spread its sheltering branches above them. Her mother had died when she was eight, her father when she was twenty. The sorrow she had once felt had long been replaced by gentle sadness, tempered with warm memories that would always be there, always live on.

"Lizbeth Cantrell was around when Mother was so sick, wasn't she?" said Theodosia.

"Indeed she was," said Libby.

"I'd forgotten a lot of that, but now it's coming back to me."

They sat and watched as Earl Grey emerged from the woods, plunked himself down in a sunny spot, and set about chewing at a clutch of cockleburs that clung stubbornly to his left shoulder. There was no need for the two of them to talk. Over the years, they'd said it all. They were all the other had; there were no other relatives. They knew in their hearts how important they were to each other and cherished that knowledge. Their kind of love didn't require words.

Finally, Libby pushed herself up from her chair. At seventy-two, she still had a lithe figure and proud carriage, still walked with a bounce in her step.

"I think it's time we thought about lunch. Margaret Rose baked cranberry bread yesterday, and I threw together some chicken salad earlier. Why not fix trays and eat out here where we can enjoy the view? It'll be ever so much nicer."

Theodosia hit the wooden bridge on Rutledge Road much too hard, almost jouncing her and Earl Grey out of their seats.

"Sorry, fella," she murmured as the dog looked up with questioning eyes. Earl Grey had played and chased and worried critters for the better part of three hours and then fallen asleep on the backseat, which Theodosia had laid flat for this second part of their trip.

"I know the turn for the Cantrell place is *somewhere* along here," she said out loud. "I just haven't been down this particular road in fifteen years, so it's all a little foggy."

Twenty minutes ago, she'd passed the restored Hampton Plantation where Archibald Hampton, the former poet laureate of South Carolina, had lived. She was pretty sure the old Hampton place was on the way to the Cantrells' place, so she had to be on the right track.

"There is it. . . . Oh mother of pearl!" Theodosia cranked the wheel hard to the left and still overshot the turn. Slamming on the brakes, the Jeep shuddered to a halt. At the same exact moment, she felt the right side of her vehicle sink down into squishy soil.

"Nuts," she said. She sat for a moment, staring out the front window, then jumped out and walked around the back of the Jeep to see how bad the damage was.

Not terrible. She'd overshot the turn, and her right front wheel was off the gravel road and sunk midway in oozing mud. Remembering horror stories of quicksand in the area, Theodosia quickly decided her wisest move would be to simply shift into four-wheel drive and muscle her way out.

That would work, of course it would.

She stood by the side of the road, batting at gnats, feeling the heat begin to build around her.

She studied the road and the turn she'd just attempted. This *had* to be the turn to the Cantrell place, she decided.

Woof.

Earl Grey peered out the window, wagging his tail expectantly.

"No, you stay there, fella. I'll have us out in—"

Circling around the back of the Jeep, Theodosia stopped dead in her tracks. Off in the nearby underbrush, she'd heard a rustle. A slight whisper. It was probably nothing. Then again . . .

She began moving quietly, softly, but with purpose, creeping toward the driver's side.

There it was again. Not a rustle, more a soft gush of air. Couldn't be an alligator, they were few and far between out here. Plus those critters barked and moaned and made a terrible racket. No, this was more like . . . a snort?

By the time her brain registered the sound, a new movement was under way.

Hoofs clicking on gravel. Quick, precise, and moving toward her. Fast.

Theodosia scrambled for the car door, pulled at the handle, fumbled, pulled at it again. As the Jeep's door swung open and she struggled to climb in, the boar appeared on the road, not more than twenty feet away. It ran easily, almost mechanically, dainty feet carrying the wild pig with awesome swiftness. Theodosia saw that the creature's sharp, beady eyes were focused directly on her.

Theodosia slammed the door shut and grabbed for the ignition key. As the engine turned over, a loud report sounded.

Wham.

Confusion for a split second, not comprehending what had just happened. Jeep backfiring? Wild pig crashing headlong into her front fender?

Theodosia peered out the window and saw the pig lying motionless on the gravel not six feet from her. Then a pair of dusty boots came into view.

Ford Cantrell. Casually hefting a rifle in one hand.

Theodosia remained in her seat and, with shaking hands, pushed the button to lower the driver's-side window.

"Sorry about that," Ford Cantrell called to her. He waved at her casually, as though he were out for a stroll in the park.

Sinking back against the soft leather of the Jeep's upholstery, Theodosia breathed out slowly. Aunt Libby had once told her the Cantrells weren't happy with a thing unless they could ride it, shoot it, or stuff it. She might have been right.

"This bugger got away from us," called Ford. "I had a mind it might be headed this way. Hope it didn't cause you any problem."

Theodosia climbed down from the Jeep. "Quiet," she told Earl Grey, who was barking at the dead pig and at Ford Cantrell. "Settle down."

"Those things bite?" she asked, pointing toward the dead boar.

"They can take a chunk out of a fellow," Ford Cantrell replied mildly. "Although if you'd let that dog of yours out, he probably would of shagged it away. Most pigs are pretty scared of dogs."

As if to underscore Ford's remark, Earl Grey let loose with a throaty growl.

"Most pigs," repeated Theodosia. Fresh in her mind was the look of *intent* on the boar's curiously intelligent face.

"What are you doing this far from town?" Ford Cantrell asked her.

"I was visiting my aunt Libby." Theodosia waved an arm in the direction she'd just come. "At Cane Ridge."

Ford Cantrell seemed to accept her explanation. "Guess you heard I turned Pamlico Hill into a game ranch, huh?"

Theodosia nodded. She was surprised that Ford seemed to know exactly who she was. Introductions at this point would seem superfluous.

He nudged the dead pig with his boot. "This here's one of my main draws. A classic American razorback. Breeder I got 'em from said they's descended from the swine that Ponce de León brought from Spain. Supposed to be real smart."

"I'll bet," said Theodosia.

"Hear you're pretty smart, too. You've been asking questions about me."

Theodosia didn't back off. "A lot of folks have," she said.

Ford Cantrell squinted in the direction of the sun and swiped his hand roughly at the stubble on his chin. "And I guess they always will. Appears I've always been a lot more welcome out here in the low-country than in town."

When Theodosia didn't say anything, Ford Cantrell continued. "Yeah, I'm gonna be moving my boat over to McClellanville. Those guys at the yacht club are just too snooty for my taste."

Theodosia nodded. A sleepy little fishing village on Jeremy Creek would be quite hospitable to a low-country denizen like Ford Cantrell. And he certainly had to be persona non grata at the yacht club these days. Maybe the board of directors had even forced Ford to resign. She'd have to call Jory Davis's friend Eldon Cook, and ask him if he'd heard anything to that effect.

Ford Cantrell swept his broad-brimmed straw hat off his head and ran his broad fingers through a tangle of red hair. "Funny thing about that to-do," he said, finally looking Theodosia directly in the eye. "Everybody thinks Oliver Dixon and me were on the outs. But I was working for him."

Theodosia stared at Ford Cantrell, stunned by his words. "You were working for him!" she exclaimed. "What are you talking about?" she fumbled. "You mean Oliver Dixon was a partner in the hunting preserve?" That didn't sound quite right, but it was the best she could come up with at the moment.

"No, no," Ford said. "I was doing some work for his new company, Grapevine." He laughed harshly. "Well, not *his* company, the whole thing's very tightly controlled by the investors. Anyway, I had worked on some of the fault-tolerant disk arrays for Vantage Computers. You know, the company over in Columbia that has a lot of contracts with the military? Anyway, Oliver asked me to serve as an outside consultant. As it turned out, Oliver and I didn't see eye to eye on many things. That's why we were arguing that day in White Point Gardens. I'm sure everybody thought it was the old family feud but, in truth, I'd just told him he was a damn fool if he didn't think streaming video would be critical."

"You were working *together?*" Theodosia knew she must look totally unhinged, caught so off guard as she was by this new revelation. And here she'd gone and sicced Burt Tidwell onto Ford Cantrell. Tidwell had followed up, so he had to know about the two men's business relationship.

Had Tidwell been able to find some hard evidence that implicated Ford in Oliver Dixon's death? Or was Tidwell laughing merrily behind her back because she was a rank amateur who had jumped to a wild conclusion?

Theodosia watched as Ford Cantrell carefully leaned his rifle up against a tree stump, then grabbed the boar by its hind feet and dragged it to the side of the road.

"Be back to pick up this big boy later," he told her.

"You worked together," Theodosia murmured again.

"Yes," responded Ford, "but it's a moot point now. The investors have decided to shut Grapevine down."

"I hadn't heard anything about that." *Goodness,* she thought, stunned, *things are happening fast.*

"I just got word late Friday. Come tomorrow, the employees are on the street, and any existing inventory of raw materials is scheduled to be sold off." His eyes, pale blue like his sister's, like a sea captain who'd stared at too many horizons, met hers sadly. "I suppose any technology developed so far will also be sold or licensed."

"But why?" asked Theodosia. "I thought Grapevine was beginning to get noticed as a player in the market."

Ford shrugged. "Who the hell knows why these things happen? Could be a jittery board of directors with zero confidence, now that Oliver Dixon's gone. Or maybe the investors found a better place to make a fast return on their buck." Ford Cantrell traced the toe of his boot in the sand. "Hell, maybe somebody has inside information on what's *really* happening with PDAs and is executing a cut-bait maneuver."

Theodosia nodded. She understood there could be any number of reasons. Business start-ups and spin-offs were constantly being shut down or sold off at a moment's notice. Sometimes there was a solid reason; often it was done on a whim. She'd once developed a marketing plan for computer voice recognition software that showed great promise, only to find the entire project shut down because the product manager resigned to take a job with another company.

"Did your sister know you were working with Oliver Dixon?" asked Theodosia.

Ford Cantrell shook his head slowly. "Nope. Less Lizbeth knows, the better."

"What are you going to do now?" she asked him.

Ford Cantrell grinned crookedly, then shifted his gaze toward the dead boar. "Have a barbecue."

On her way with little more than a muddy fender to show for her mishap, Theodosia drove back toward the city, lost in thought. She wasn't sure if Ford Cantrell's business relationship with Oliver Dixon clearly meant the man was innocent, or if it gave Ford all the more reason to want Oliver Dixon out of the way. Maybe Ford Cantrell had somehow ingratiated himself with Oliver Dixon, gotten the consulting project, then conspired to move himself into the senior slot. If Oliver Dixon were out of the picture, the door would have been wide open. In the high-stakes world of business and technology, a power play like that wasn't unheard of.

But now Ford Cantrell was out of a job, too. Correction, out of a consulting job. For all she knew, his part could have been done. He could have already been paid.

Or fired by Oliver Dixon?

She thought back to what Delaine had said a week ago. She had told everyone at the tea shop that the two men were arguing about fishing, which had sounded exceedingly strange at the time, unless you knew Delaine. But Ford Cantrell had just told her the argument was over video *streaming*. Had Delaine somehow gotten fishing and streaming mixed up?

Theodosia knew that the answer was yes. Probably yes.

Theodosia eased off on the accelerator as the Jeep approached Huntville, a small, sleepy village on the Edisto River. Creeping across a one-lane wooden bridge, she found the way partially blocked by a sheriff's car.

Coming to a complete stop, Theodosia waited as a barrel-chested man dressed in a lawman's khakis crossed the road and ambled over to her.

"Looks like you had yourself a spot of trouble." The man with the sheriff's badge pointed to her mud-caked front fender.

"Overshot a turn back there."

"Yeah, that's easy to do." The sheriff grinned widely, revealing front teeth rimmed in gold. "Good thing this jobby's got four-wheel drive." He put his big paw on her door. "Lots of muck and quicksand around."

And then, because her curiosity usually got the better of her, Theodosia asked him, "Is there some kind of problem here, Sheriff?"

The sheriff shifted his bulk to face the river. "Nah, not really." He pointed to where the river narrowed to a sort of canal that flowed under the bridge. A skinny, young deputy in thigh-high waders was poking around down there.

"Somebody come through here last night in a hell of a hurry," he said. "Must of been a big power launch 'cause he clipped the wood where the sides is shored up, then completely knocked out one of the bridge pilings."

Theodosia looked in the direction the sheriff was pointing and saw two timbers peeled back from the bank, rough edges exposed.

"Probably some good old boys got liquored up, then couldn't steer their way clear," continued the sheriff. "Only reason we're checkin' it out is 'cause we got a heads-up from the Coast Guard. They got tipped some two-bit smugglers might be workin' around this area and decided old Sheriff Billings didn't have enough to do. Send *him* on a wild-goose chase the first nice Sunday when he could be havin' a nice time at the car races over in Summerville."

Theodosia nodded, amused by the sheriff's peevishness. She knew there was a maze of rivers and inlets and swamps to navigate out here. Lots of back country that only the locals were familiar with. "They'd have to know this territory pretty well," she said.

"Sure would," agreed the sheriff.

"Sheriff Billings, if it *is* smugglers, what would they be bringing in?" asked Theodosia.

"If it *is* smugglers, most likely goods from somewhere in the Caribbean. Booze, cigars, cigarettes. Folks just love to avoid that federal excise tax." The sheriff peered down over the embankment. "You find anything down there, Buford?" he hollered to his deputy.

"Nothin'," the deputy yelled back. "Seen a darn cottonmouth, though."

"Well, leave it be," advised the sheriff.

CHAPTER 22

"*ALL YOU SERVE* is tea?" asked the young woman with a frown.

"Come on," said her companion, a young man in blue jeans and a Save the Redwoods T-shirt, "there's gotta be a coffee shop down the street."

"If you don't care for tea, you might find something you like on our Tea Totalers Menu," offered Haley.

The young woman accepted the slip of parchment paper tentatively. "Chamomile, Ginseng, Orange Spice," she read as she scanned down the list. "But these are teas, aren't they?"

"Actually," explained Haley, "they're infusions. Thera-peutic fruits and herbs that don't contain leaves from the tea plant."

"Are they good for you?" asked the girl.

"Rose hips and hibiscus are extremely high in vitamin C, while ginseng and peppermint are energy boosters," said Haley. "Tell you what, I just brewed a pot of rose hips. You can have a taste and judge for yourself."

Haley went behind the counter and poured two small

cups of rose hips. It was early Monday morning, and no
other customers had come in yet. She could hear Theodosia and Drayton talking quietly in Theo's back office.
Her scones and honey madeleines were baking in the oven,
and she could afford to spend a little time with this young
couple.

Their eyes lit up at the first taste.

"This is good," declared the boy. "But I think I'd like to
try the plum. It sounds refreshing. Interesting, too."

"I'll stick with the rose hips," said the girl. "And you
serve pastries here, as well?" Her nose had picked up the
aromatic smells emanating from the back room.

"Have a seat, and I'll bring a pastry tray out," said
Haley. "That way you can see everything."

Drayton stared at Theodosia from across her desk.
"They were working *together*?"

"It would appear so," said Theodosia.

"I can hardly believe it," said Drayton. "Everyone and
his brother has been so sure those two were still engaged
in some dreadful eye-for-an-eye feud."

"Including me," said Theodosia. "I feel terrible about
jumping to such a hasty conclusion."

"Don't beat yourself up over it," advised Drayton. "Tidwell certainly believed you and, in fact, seemed to confirm
your thoughts. And, as you pointed out earlier, Ford
Cantrell could have been secretly scheming to oust Oliver
Dixon. He could have been seeking a permanent solution,
if you get my drift."

"I suppose," fretted Theodosia.

"Frankly, I think you should speak with Tidwell again,"
urged Drayton. "About Ford Cantrell *and* Billy Manolo.
Just the fact that Billy Manolo showed up at Oliver
Dixon's funeral—and Tidwell was a witness to that—is
somewhat suspicious. And I'm very uneasy about the fact
that he threatened you."

"Who threatened who?" asked Haley as she stuck her head in the door.

"It's nothing, really," said Theodosia. She didn't want Haley to get upset over Billy Manolo's cruel remark about her floating facedown in Charleston Harbor.

"When our Theodosia went to Billy Manolo's house last Saturday, he picked up a piece of pipe and threatened her," said Drayton.

"Did you call the cops?" asked Haley. "Any guy looks cross-eyed at me these days, I call the cops."

"What about that Hell's Angel with the overpowered motorbike who hung around here all last summer?" Drayton asked. "He frightened off half our customers."

"Teddy wasn't threatening," said Haley. "He was simply in the throes of an identity crisis. Anyway, he's back in school now."

"Studying what," asked Drayton, "anarchy?"

"If you must know, he's studying to be a paramedic," said Haley. "But tell me more about this Billy Manolo character. Maybe he was the one who was peeking in our window Saturday night."

"You're still convinced someone was up to no good," said Drayton.

"I don't know what they were up to, but *somebody* was out there," replied Haley as the timer on her stove gave a loud ding. "Oops, got to pull this batch out," she said as she sailed around the corner.

By ten o'clock, every table in the tea shop was occupied. Drayton had predicted they'd have a busy morning, even though it had started out slowly, and had readied at least two dozen teapots. Now they were being filled with keeman, puerh, and Darjeeling, and being dispatched to the various tables occupied by tourists as well as tea shop regulars.

Theodosia was behind the counter, manning the old brass cash register and, in between cashiering and handing out change, was scribbling notes she could add later to the "Tea Tips" section of her Web site. When it didn't appear that the Indigo Tea Shop could hold one more customer, she looked up to see the door swing open and Doe Belvedere Dixon walk in followed closely by Giovanni Loard.

"Hellooo . . ." Drayton flew over to greet them, had an obvious moment of panic when he realized there wasn't an available table, then demonstrated signs of palpable relief when he saw that two women were just getting up to leave. "I'll have your table ready in a moment," he assured Doe and Giovanni.

Theodosia waited until Doe and Giovanni had been seated and served before she went over to their table to greet them. Things had settled down somewhat—all the customers were sipping and noshing—and Drayton seemed to be in a perpetual hover mode near Doe and Giovanni's table.

For someone who'd recently lost her husband, Doe appeared to have done an admirable job of pulling herself out of her grief. Theodosia watched as she chatted animatedly with Drayton, then with people at two other tables.

"They say Coco Chanel always took her tea with lemon," said Doe as her elegantly manicured fingertips gently pushed back a swirl of blond hair. "And that she always ordered in toast and jam from the Ritz." Doe glanced up as Theodosia approached. "Hello," she said, sipping delicately from her teacup. "I love your tea shop; it's so quaint."

"Thank you, how nice to see you again," said Theodosia, "although it's unfortunate our first meeting was under such sad circumstances. How are you doing?" Theodosia wondered if Doe would remember that she was the one who'd pushed her about Oliver's knowledge of guns the day of the funeral. No, probably not, she decided.

"I'm feeling so much better," replied Doe. "Everyone

has been so kind." She turned luminous eyes toward Giovanni and smiled.

Giovanni fumbled for Doe's hand and patted it gently. "She's a strong girl, a real survivor," he said.

Doe shifted her hundred-watt smile to Drayton, and Theodosia wondered just how long this girl figured she could get by on her mesmerizing beauty. Perhaps until she married a second time? Then again, Doe also possessed enormous self-confidence. She might just sail through life, as some people did, secure in the knowledge that the world would always deliver its bounty to them.

"Can you sit with us a moment?" Giovanni asked Theodosia and Drayton. "I was just telling Doe what a lovely time I had here last week. How helpful Drayton was with the Edgefield teapot and what a gracious hostess Theodosia had been." He smiled warmly at the two of them. "I feel as though you all are good friends already."

"We were surprised to hear that your husband's business was shutting down," said Theodosia to Doe. First thing this morning, she had scanned the business section of the *Charleston Post and Courier*. There had been a short article, and details had been fairly sketchy, but it did confirm what Ford Cantrell had told her yesterday. Grapevine was being shut down. Not with a bang but a whimper.

Doe blinked slowly, and a tiny furrow appeared just above the bridge of her nose. "The board of directors has been very kind, particularly Mr. Crowley."

"Booth Crowley?," asked Theodosia.

"Yes," said Doe. "He came to inform me in person that it was a business decision prompted solely by Oliver's death." She sighed. "It's comforting to know that Oliver was held in such high esteem and that the company is unable to function without him."

"Oliver Dixon was a brilliant man," said Giovanni. "One our community isn't likely to forget for a long time."

"It's a shame the company is being shut down entirely,"

continued Theodosia. "To keep Grapevine going, to build it into a success, would have been a tremendous testament to your husband."

"Unfortunately, it's just not to be," said Giovanni. His eyes seemed to have taken on a hard shine, sending a not-so-subtle warning signal to Theodosia.

Giovanni's overprotectiveness rankled Theodosia and gave her the impetus she needed to continue.

"Well-planned companies usually have a number of capable executives who can take over at the helm," said Theodosia. "For example—" Under the table, she felt a subtle kick from Drayton. Obviously, he thought she was going too far, pushing a little too hard, as well. "For example," she continued, "it turns out Ford Cantrell was doing some consulting work with your husband. As a former VP at Vantage Computers, perhaps he could have provided the needed interim leadership."

Doe frowned and cast her eyes downward, while Giovanni stared at Theodosia with a cold fury. "I'm afraid we'll be leaving now," he announced. He stood abruptly, and Doe, tight-lipped and grim, stood up as well.

Then Giovanni Loard headed for the door without uttering another word and Doe, bidding them a clipped good-bye, followed on his heels.

"Well, you certainly got a rise out of them," said Drayton as they huddled at the counter. "And some might say exceeded the boundary of good manners."

"I take it you disapprove?" asked Theodosia.

Drayton put one hand to the side of his face and patted it absently. "Not entirely," he said. "Like you, I get a very queasy feeling about a number of people."

"And your suspicions are focused on . . ."

"The girl, yes," said Drayton. "Such a pretty thing. But I can't help feel that beneath that radiant exterior is a very tough cookie."

"A girl who arranged to have her own husband murdered?" asked Theodosia.

"It's true, Doe didn't pull the trigger," said Drayton. "Poor Oliver did that all by himself."

"Rather convenient, wasn't it?" said Theodosia. "And now sweet young Doe has inherited Oliver Dixon's home and all his worldly assets." She turned to arrange a stack of saucers and cups. "Did you get the feeling that Doe knew Ford Cantrell had been working with Oliver Dixon?"

"Hard to tell," muttered Drayton, "hard to tell."

Over lunch at her desk, Theodosia reread the *Post and Courier* article. The byline at the end of the article said J. D. Darling. She knew J. D. Darling wasn't one of the regular business writers and, from the tone of the piece, the whole thing sounded like a quick rewrite of a press release. Probably one that had been issued hastily by Cherry Tree Investments over the weekend, then reworked by one of the copy cubs who pulled the Saturday to Sunday shift.

Theodosia drummed her fingers on her desk. The last line of the article intrigued her. It said that Cherry Tree Investments would continue to focus its efforts on several new high-tech start-ups.

Close down one high-tech company to start another? It happened, but it still sounded strange. Especially in light of all the gut-wrenching front-end work that had probably gone into Grapevine; months or perhaps even years of product development, writing a business plan, creating marketing and media strategies, finding a distribution chain, and developing a sales force strategy.

And, truth be known, high-tech companies weren't exactly the darlings of the venture capital world these days. It wasn't that long ago that the whole dot com thing experienced a disastrous shakeout on Wall Street, and skeptical analysts, probably the most vocal being those who got burned themselves, had stuck dot coms with the kiss-of-death label "*dot bombs.*"

Theodosia set her tuna fish sandwich down and dialed information. Within seconds, she'd obtained the number for Cherry Tree Investments and was dialing it.

"Hello," Theodosia greeted the woman who answered Cherry Tree's phone, "this is Judith Castleworth at the *Post and Courier*. I'm calling to clarify a few facts for one of our business writers, Mr. J. D. Darling?"

"Of course," said the receptionist.

"In Cherry Tree's recent press release regarding the closing of the company Grapevine, you mention that Cherry Tree is undertaking financing for several new high-tech companies. Can you give me the names of those companies?"

"You're talking about our newest underwritings," said the receptionist, not sounding completely sure of herself.

"Yes," said Theodosia.

"Let me see if I even have that information," said the woman. "Shirlene, the regular girl is at lunch, I'm Marilyn. Can you hold for a moment?"

"Of course," said Theodosia.

There was a rustle of papers, and Theodosia could hear the woman coughing gently. Then she was back on the phone.

"Miss Castleworth? I have those names for you."

"Go ahead," said Theodosia.

"The companies are Deva Tech, that's D-E-V-A Tech, two words. And Alphimed, A-L-P-H-I-M-E-D, one word."

"Deva Tech and Alphimed," repeated Theodosia.

"Yes," said Marilyn. "Deva Tech manufactures scanners for the warehouse industry, and Alphimed is a franchised medical testing company. Interim financing for both has already gone through, and Cherry Tree will be issuing a complete story to the media . . . oh, probably next month."

"Would it be possible to speak with your president, Mr. Booth Crowley?" asked Theodosia.

"I'm sorry, Mr. Crowley's at lunch. Could I have him return your—?"

"Thank you anyway, Marilyn," said Theodosia.

Theodosia replaced the phone in the cradle and leaned back in her leather chair. So Booth Crowley was financing two more high-tech companies. And from the way things sounded, they were very close to launching.

Booth Crowley. He was the man who'd handled Oliver Dixon the pistol. He was the man who'd been so hostile toward Billy Manolo at Oliver Dixon's funeral. And Booth Crowley was the big-time venture capitalist who launched Grapevine by virtue of his financing, then pulled the plug after Oliver Dixon was killed.

"You look like you've got a headache," said Haley.

"Getting one, anyway," said Theodosia, her head spinning with possibilities. She was hungry but had only eaten a quarter of her sandwich.

"I have the perfect antidote," said Haley. "Just give me a sec."

Theodosia stared out the window, thinking that *everybody* had suddenly begun to look suspicious.

Haley returned with a teacup filled with pale yellow liquid. "Drink this," she urged.

"What is it?"

"Meadowsweet tea."

"Perfect," declared Theodosia. Meadowsweet was a plant that had been used for centuries to fight fever and tame headaches. Its derivative, salicylate, was the compound that had been chemically formulated to produce aspirin.

"Drayton told me about your genteel conversation with Giovanni and Doe," Haley said, very tongue-in-cheek. "You don't think *she* had anything to do with Oliver Dixon's death do you?"

"I'm not sure what to think anymore," replied Theodosia. "First Ford Cantrell looked suspicious, then Billy Manolo. Although Billy just seems a little crazy."

"But crazy people do crazy things," said Haley.

"Yes," said Theodosia slowly, "they do. And now I'm also having second thoughts about Doe. It would appear she had a lot to gain from Oliver Dixon's death."

"You think the prom queen whacked her own hubby? Gosh, it sounds like tabloid fodder, doesn't it? Or a plot for a B movie."

"It doesn't stop there," sighed Theodosia. "I'm also curious as to what Booth Crowley is up to. It still seems strange to me that he just closed down Grapevine." Theodosia sipped her tea as Haley stared placidly at her. "Haley, tell me more about PDAs."

"What do you want to know?"

Theodosia paused. "There are different kinds. . . ." She wasn't sure where she was going with this.

Haley frowned at Theodosia, as if trying to decipher her thoughts. "You mean different operating systems?"

"I think so, yes," nodded Theodosia.

"Oh that," said Haley. "There's two kinds duking it out right now. Palm versus the Pocket PC."

"And your gizmo uses Palm," said Theodosia.

"Right," said Haley, "because I've got a Palm Pilot."

"What was Grapevine designing applications for?" said Theodosia.

"Not really applications, more like expansion modules."

"For the Palm," said Theodosia.

"Yes," said Haley.

"And now Booth Crowley is going to underwrite Deva Tech, a company that manufactures warehouse scanners. What kind of computer systems do big warehouses generally use?"

"Big stuff, networks," she said.

"No Palm operating system?" asked Theodosia.

Haley smiled. "Hardly."

"So maybe Grapevine was small potatoes," said Theodosia.

"Or Booth Crowley didn't want to tick off the powers that be, the Microsofts of the world. It was just easier to dump Grapevine."

"Or dump Oliver Dixon," said Theodosia.

"Chilling thought," said Haley.

"Which means I need to find out a whole lot more about Booth Crowley," said Theodosia.

"How about tapping into radio free Charleston down the street?" suggested Haley.

"You mean Delaine?"

"Who else? She always seems to have the latest word on everything. Just don't let on that you're *too* interested," warned Haley.

CHAPTER 23

※※※

"THEODOSIA, I JUST got in the most *marvelous* green silk jacket," exclaimed Delaine. "It is to *die* for." Delaine bustled over, delivered a quick air kiss in Theodosia's general vicinity, then scampered off, leaving an aromatic cloud of Joy in her wake.

"Janine!" Delaine yelled to her overworked assistant. "Where did we hang those silk jackets? Or are you still steaming them?"

Janine came rushing out from the back room, bearing silk jackets on padded hangers. Janine always looked a trifle red-faced and out of breath, and Theodosia often wondered if the poor woman had borderline high blood pressure or if her state of nervous excitement was due to six years of working for Delaine. She suspected the latter.

"Here, try this." Delaine pulled at Theodosia's black cashmere cardigan, trying to wrest it off, while she held out the green silk jacket for her to try on. "No, this is a medium, Janine, get Theodosia a small. These jackets run a tad generous, and our girl seems to have lost a couple pounds. Did you, dear?" she asked pointedly.

Theodosia ignored Delaine's question and, instead, slid into the smaller-size jacket. She adjusted it, buttoned a couple buttons, pirouetted in front of the three-way mirror.

"Oh, with your hair, *très élégant,*" gushed Delaine.

Theodosia gazed at herself in the mirror. The jacket was a stunner, she had to admit. Sleek, lightweight, and a very bewitching green. She could see herself wearing it to any number of upcoming outings and parties. Accompanied, perhaps, by Jory Davis?

"I have it in jade green, pomegranate, and, of course, black," said Delaine. "Very limited quantities, so you won't see yourself coming and going." She plucked at one of the sleeves. "And so light, gossamer light, like butterfly wings. Perfect for a cool spring evening."

Theodosia snuck a peek at the price tag and decided she'd have to sell a good sixty or seventy cups of tea to finance her purchase.

"Let me think about it, Delaine," she said, slipping the jacket off and delivering it into the waiting arms of Janine.

Delaine wagged a finger at her. "Don't wait too long, Theo. These jackets will go like hotcakes."

"I know, I know." Theodosia picked up a beaded bag.

"Those are all hand-stitched in Indonesia," Delaine told her. "They come in that leaf pattern or there's a star motif."

"Lovely," said Theodosia as she examined the bag, then set it back down on the little display table. "Doe and Giovanni stopped by the tea shop this morning," she said.

Delaine brightened immediately. "Did they really? How is Doe getting along?"

"Seems to be bearing up quite well," said Theodosia. She didn't want to confide to Delaine that Doe and Giovanni had both exited the tea shop in a somewhat hasty huff. Delaine would probably learn about that soon enough. "And you heard about Grapevine, Oliver Dixon's company? Booth Crowley closed it down."

"Mmm, yes," said Delaine as she fussed over a tray of

scarves, arranging them in artful disarray. "I saw something about that in the paper this morning."

"You haven't heard why, have you?"

"I just assumed the company couldn't get along without him."

"But you haven't heard anyone mention a specific reason," said Theodosia as she fingered the beaded bag again.

"Mmm . . . no," said Delaine as she straightened a stack of cotton sweaters. "Gosh," she said, peeling an apple green sweater off the top, don't you adore this color? Can't you see it paired with white slacks? Yummy."

"Pretty with your coloring," said Theodosia.

Delaine held it up. "You're right." She preened in the mirror. "Anyway, Theo, to get back to what you were saying, Booth Crowley certainly must know what he's doing. He's had his hand in enough different businesses."

"Yes, I guess he has," said Theodosia.

"Do you know his wife, Beatrix?" asked Delaine.

"No, not really."

"Delightful woman, patron of the Children's Theater Company. She buys quite a lot of her clothing here. Of course, she also flies to New York and Paris. I believe she even attends some of the *collections*."

"Wow," said Theodosia, trying to look suitably impressed for Delaine's sake. She wandered over to an antique armoire set against a cantaloupe-colored wall. The doors of the armoire were open, and it was stuffed with a riotous array of silk camisoles, jeweled pins, antique keys strung on ribbons, and Chinese ceramic cachepots. A turquoise silk sari hung down from one side.

"Delaine, your decor is absolutely delightful," began Theodosia. "I've been thinking about giving my shop a bit of a face-lift. Maybe even go for a touch of exotica." Theodosia watched as interest flickered on Delaine's face. "One of the design firms that's been recommended to me is Popple Hill. Are you familiar with them?" She'd tucked Billy

Manolo's Popple Hill connection in the back of her brain and now figured it might be worth seeing what Delaine knew.

"My dear, Popple Hill is *extraordinary*," gushed Delaine. "It's headed by two absolutely brilliant women, Hillary Retton and Marianne Petigru. I know them because they also shop here whenever they can. Both are cultivated beyond belief and *so* multitalented. Do you know Gabby Stewart, who lives over on Lamboll?"

"I think so."

"She's the pretty blond with the really good face-lift whose husband gave her the black Jaguar XKE for her last birthday, which nobody's bothering to count anymore."

"Now that you've described her so precisely, I do recall her," said Theodosia, smiling.

"Well, the Popple Hill ladies took *her* house from early Dumpster to utterly dazzling. Gabby and her husband, Derwood or Dellwood or something like that, inherited that great old house and all the furniture. The wooden pieces were okay, so-so seventeenth-century French that could be refinished and touched up a bit, but most of the dining room chairs were absolutely bedraggled. And *nothing* had been done to the interior, not a speck of paint nor snippet of wallpaper, in ages. Now it's stunning, an absolute showpiece. I wouldn't be surprised if *Town and Country* or *Southern Accents* wanted to do a big spread on it."

"What about the exterior?"

Delaine wrinkled her nose. She wasn't too keen on having her stories interrupted. "Yes, Hillary and Marianne masterminded a restoration on that, too."

"They used wrought iron?"

"Oh, *tons* of it," said Delaine, "because of the huge garden courtyard out back. You know that house, don't you? You've been inside and seen that marvelous oversized fireplace?"

Theodosia ignored Delaine's question. "Do you know any of Popple Hill's craftspeople?" she asked.

Delaine frowned. "Their *craftspeople*? No, I wouldn't know about that. I imagine they're just ordinary workers. Hillary and Marianne are the real geniuses." Delaine paused. "I love that you're thinking about updating your look."

"Mm-hm," said Theodosia, knowing she'd *never* let anyone tinker with the cozy interior she loved so much.

"Come to think of it, Popple Hill did some recent restoration work on Doe and Oliver's home, too," said Delaine as the ring of the telephone perfectly punctuated the end of her sentence.

"Chloe Keenland is on the phone," Janine called to Delaine. "She wants to know if you're still on for this afternoon."

Delaine pushed back her sleeve, glanced at her watch, a Chopard rimmed with sparkling jewels. "Gosh, I'd forgotten all about Chloe." Delaine chewed her lower lip as she gazed at Theodosia. "Garden Fest starts this Friday, and I'm on the opening night refreshment committee," she explained. Swiveling her head toward Janine, Delaine smiled winningly. "Janine, could you be an absolute *angel* and work until five today?"

Janine looked glum. "I suppose," she said.

"Wonderful," declared Delaine. "Perfect."

Back at the tea shop, Theodosia felt more confused than ever. Her somewhat strange and rambling conversation with Delaine hadn't yielded much. And none of the theories she'd been tossing around seemed to make sense, either.

"Haley, did you—" began Theodosia, but her sentence was cut short.

"Don't look now, but it's the prom queen again," Haley muttered under her breath.

Theodosia looked up to see Doe Belvedere Dixon striding into the Indigo Tea Shop for the second time that day.

"Miss Browning," said Doe in a breathless, little-girl voice, "can we talk?"

Theodosia nodded and quickly steered the girl to one of the far tables. "Of course," she said, her curiosity suddenly hitting a fever pitch.

Doe waited until they were both seated and was positive no one was in earshot before she began. "I came back to apologize," she said. "Giovanni is still very touchy about Oliver's death, and he often overreacts rather badly. But you have to understand, he was so very fond of his cousin."

"Second cousin," said Theodosia, watching Doe closely, wondering what the real agenda was.

"Yes, of course," said Doe as she picked a tiny fleck of lint from the sleeve of her perfect buttercup yellow sweater. "But the two of them were extremely close. Giovanni's mother died when he was very young, and Oliver was always like an older brother to him."

"I'm sure he was," said Theodosia, wondering again why Doe had come back. Her apology didn't seem all that heartfelt.

Then Doe leaned forward across the small wooden table and her taffy-colored hair swung closely about her face. "Frankly, I think Giovanni was upset because I told him about Ford Cantrell and me," she said.

Now it was Theodosia's turn to lean forward, the better to catch every word.

"Ford and I met a few years ago at the University of Charleston," explained Doe. "He was a grad student in computer engineering, and I was a Tri Delt pledge." She stopped and smiled wistfully at Theodosia. "Were you ever in a sorority?"

Theodosia stared at Doe. "No," she said.

"Best time of my life," she declared. "Anyway, Ford and I dated a few times, and then I broke it off."

"You *dated* Ford Cantrell?" Theodosia said in a loud whisper.

Doe frowned, as though she were unused to any type of critical remark. "Honestly, Theodosia, it was no big deal." She shrugged. "I *said* I broke it off. If you ask me, Ford Cantrell has never accepted being rejected."

"She *dated* him?" Drayton tucked his chin down and stared over his glasses. His right eyebrow twitched crazily; he did not look amused. "You're making this up," he finally declared in a flat voice. "In a brazen attempt to completely muddle my poor mind."

Theodosia shook her head. "Doe told me so herself."

"Is that what you two were whispering about?" said Haley. "A date she had with Ford Cantrell in college? Hmm, she certainly holds herself in high regard, doesn't she?"

"I think she was just trying to explain why Giovanni got so upset when I started talking about Ford Cantrell this morning," said Theodosia. "In her own way, Doe was trying to be nice."

"She's got a funny way of being nice," grumbled Haley.

"Indeed she has," agreed Drayton.

Theodosia was inclined to agree with them, if the whole situation hadn't been so bizarre. Bizarre bordering on Ripley's Believe It or Not!

And when you tried to look at Oliver Dixon's murder from the standpoint of pure motive, it was also terribly confusing.

Ford Cantrell supposedly harbored a grudge against Oliver Dixon, yet he'd worked for the man as a consultant. Ford had motive only if you took into account the long-standing family feud and their somewhat strange business arrangement, which could have been far from amicable.

Booth Crowley and Billy Manolo had both handled the antique pistol minutes before Oliver Dixon was killed by it.

Both men impressed Theodosia as being short-tempered and snappish.

But as far as motive went, the only connection Billy Manolo seemed to have to Oliver Dixon was through the yacht club and as an ironworker, possibly creating some decorative wrought-iron pieces for Doe and Oliver's home via the Popple Hill people.

Would you kill someone because he might have criticized the scrollwork on your garden gate? She didn't think so.

Booth Crowley was a suspect by virtue of his peripheral connections. He'd handed the pistol to Oliver just moments before he was killed and had put up most of the money for Grapevine. On the other hand, if Oliver Dixon had somehow gotten wind that Booth Crowley was going to shut the company down, he might have been forced to retaliate. That was a theory that certainly warranted more investigating.

As far as Doe Belvedere Dixon was concerned . . . well, Theodosia wasn't sure where Doe fit into the equation, other than the fact that she stood to inherit a lot of money.

Of course, to make things all the more confusing, Ford Cantrell, Booth Crowley, Oliver Dixon, and Billy Manolo were all members of the same yacht club. Well, Billy worked there, but he was still at the club a lot of the time.

So what did all that information add up to? As far as Theodosia was concerned, it totaled a big fat zero.

Puttering about the tearoom for the rest of the day, Theodosia fretted about her inability to draw any kind of conclusion. She was unwilling to let it go by the time evening rolled around and she found herself upstairs with Earl Grey in her little apartment.

As though Earl Grey had psychically picked up on her restlessness and disquietude, the dog paced about the apartment, toenails clicking against kitchen tile and hardwood floors.

They'd already taken their evening walk through the historic district. Starting on Church Street, they'd jogged up Water Street, then wended their way down Meeting Street to The Battery. After Earl Grey had romped in the park, they'd even walked home past the Stewart home on Lamboll Street, where Billy Manolo, according to Delaine, had supposedly created *tons* of wrought iron to enclose their backyard garden.

And still Theodosia was restless.

What to do? she wondered. *Take another walk? Sip some chamomile tea? Fix a tisane of Saint-John's-wort to calm me down?*

No, she finally decided, there was something far better that she could do. She could put it all down on paper. Or rather, computer. She would compose and organize her thoughts, making notations if she was seriously bothered by any glaring facts or strange coincidences. Then she could hit a single key and E-mail the whole shebang to Detective Burt Tidwell. She could put him on the same page with her, so to speak. Get him alerted to or caught up on all the details. After all, she told herself, two heads were better than one. And from the looks of things, her head seemed to have borne the brunt of worrying about Oliver Dixon's death these last nine days. Not even Oliver's wife, Doe, seemed to think the accident hadn't really been an accident.

That resolved, Theodosia sat down at her computer and began the task of putting it all down.

The writing and rewriting took her a good while. But when she was finished and the information sent, it felt like a great weight had been lifted from her shoulders. And Theodosia, sleepy at last, padded into her cream-colored bedroom and slid into bed between indigo cotton sheets that were cool and feather light and infinitely conducive to pleasant dreams.

CHAPTER 24

"*THEODOSIA? IT'S BERNARD* Morrow."

Clenching the phone tighter, Theodosia straightened up in her chair. "Professor Morrow, hello. I've been hoping to hear from you." She glanced out across the tearoom. Haley was sliding gracefully between the small tables with a tray that held samples of their new South African Redbush tea. Drayton was chatting with two regulars who came in every Tuesday morning, dressed to the nines and wearing hats and gloves. Sunlight streamed in through the heavy, leaded panes, lending a shimmering glow to everything. With the morning's sunlight came a ray of hope as well.

"Yes, well, I meant to get your little project dispatched with sooner," said Professor Morrow, "but I've been serving on this confounded academic search committee. Everyone on it worries endlessly about adding new, untenured faculty to the department and pontificates over their own specialized area. All in all, it gives you the sense that your career is drawing to a close, and it's time to take a final bow."

"You're not thinking about retiring, are you?" Theodosia asked in alarm. Professor Morrow was one of the most caring, humane professors she had ever encountered. It would be a profound loss to the University of Charleston if he were to retire.

"Considering it, but not planning my exit in the near future," said Professor Morrow. "Anyway, I didn't call to tell you my problems. You asked me to analyze the material on the linen tablecloth, and I did exactly that. Not the blood, of course, you'd need a chromatograph to do that, and our lab is simply not equipped that way."

"I understand," said Theodosia.

"Anyway, I took a look at the ground-in matter. It's dirt, all right."

"Dirt," repeated Theodosia.

"Not flecks of metal or gunpowder as you had initially suspected. Just garden-variety dirt." He paused. "I could run a couple more tests, see if I can break down the compounds, measure phosphorous and potassium, things like that."

"Would you?"

"No problem. Those are simple chemical analyses I can do with reagents we have right here in the lab. Take me a day or two."

"Thank you, Professor Morrow."

Theodosia hung up the phone and hastily replayed their conversation in her mind. It wasn't what she'd wanted to hear. She'd been fairly convinced that the pistol had been tampered with in some way and that the fine dust on the linen tablecloth would reveal metal shavings or some type of unusual gunpowder.

But *dirt*? What the heck did that mean? Had someone kicked it around in the mud before Drayton snatched it up and stuck it in the trunk of his car?

"You look as though someone just delivered some bad news," said Drayton.

"Professor Morrow just called with his analysis of Haley's schmutz," replied Theodosia.

"And?"

"Dirt," she replied.

Drayton looked skeptical. "Dirt? That's it?"

"That's it. Now you can see why I'm disappointed."

"You're disappointed? *I'm* disappointed," said Drayton. "I've been envisioning endless scenarios involving strange resins or chemicals that could be traced, by means of sophisticated forensics, to a particular suspect who would then be summarily apprehended."

"Drayton, you watch too much crime TV," said Haley, who had been filling teapots and eavesdropping at the same time.

"I rarely watch television," he said with an imperious lift of his gray head.

"I stand corrected. Then you read far too many mysteries," said Haley. She furrowed her brow as if to lend solidarity to Theodosia's dashed hopes. "Sorry the tablecloth didn't lead somewhere," she said.

Theodosia nodded.

"What's next, then?" asked Haley. Boundlessly optimistic, Haley was never one to be discouraged by a little bad news. She was always ready to move on, explore another angle.

"I think I've got to pay another visit to Timothy Neville," said Theodosia.

"You mentioned that a couple days ago, but I haven't seen any forward progress yet," Drayton commented in a dry tone.

Theodosia undid her apron, balled it up, thrust it into Drayton's hands. "On my way."

"Mr. Neville?"

Timothy Neville looked up from the antique map he

was studying, a schematic diagram of old Fort Sumter. "Yes, Claire?"

"Miss Theodosia Browning is here to see you?"

"Is that a statement or a question, Claire?"

Flustered, Claire just stared at him. She loved working at the Heritage Society but had long since decided that Timothy Neville was the strangest little man she'd ever encountered. "Perennially puckish" was how Theresa, one of the longtime curators, had described him, and Claire had the feeling that Theresa had hit the nail squarely on the head.

"It's both," said Claire finally. "She's here. Do you have time to see her?"

Timothy Neville smiled to himself. "Kindly show her in."

"Yes, sir."

"And Claire?" said Timothy.

Claire hovered in the doorway. "Yes?"

"Thank you." Timothy Neville smiled to himself as he carefully rolled up the fragile parchment map and slid it into a cardboard storage tube. He waited until he heard the Browning woman enter his office and cross over to his desk before he looked up. When he did, he was struck by the keen intelligence in her eyes.

"Hello," he said to Theodosia.

Theodosia stared back at Timothy Neville, noting that his eyes were the sad, unblinking eyes of an old turtle. "Hello, Mr. Neville," she replied.

Timothy Neville lifted his gnarled fingers slightly, inviting Theodosia to be seated in one of the French deco leather club chairs that flanked his desk. She did.

Watching her closely, Timothy Neville was somehow pleased that the woman sat poised so straight in her chair and kept her eyes focused directly on him.

"You have questions," he said. "About antique pistols."

"Yes," she said.

Timothy bobbed his head and managed a half smile. "Drayton called just a few moments ago. Begged me to be civil to you."

"Will you be?" she asked.

"Of course. I'm generally civil to everyone. It's false benevolence I abhor."

Timothy Neville sat down at his desk and faced her. Theodosia noticed that they were at eye level with each other and suspected that the small-of-stature Timothy had adjusted his chair to a higher level, the better to be on an equal parity with visitors.

"You have considerable knowledge about the workings of antique pistols," said Theodosia.

"I have a collection of them, a small collection. Two dozen at most. But I've been collecting for more than fifty years, so I have a couple choice pieces that are now exceedingly rare."

"Can you tell me how a person might cause an antique weapon to explode?" she asked him.

"I take it the antique weapon you so coyly refer to is the offending pistol that brought Oliver Dixon's life to a crashing conclusion?"

"That's right," she said, wondering why Timothy Neville seemed to want to footnote everything. She supposed it was his lifelong involvement in all things historical.

"As chance would have it, I have a pistol of the same ilk. Crafted by the old E. R. Shane Company in Pennsylvania. It's not a perfect mate, but it's very, very close."

"Have you ever fired it?" asked Theodosia.

"Not recently," said Timothy. "But to answer your question, the simplest way to cause a pistol to explode is to overpack it." Timothy folded his arms protectively across his thin chest and posed gnomishly, awaiting her next question.

"With gunpowder?" she asked.

Timothy Neville gave her a thin smile. "That's one way. Not the best, though."

"What else could you use?" Theodosia asked. "Dirt?"

"Pack a pistol with dirt, and you're almost guaranteed it will explode," said Timothy.

Pinwheels of color flared in Theodosia's cheeks. *Dirt,* she thought. *Simple dirt.* She leaned back in her chair slightly and envisioned the scenario. You take an old pistol that had been hand-wrought almost two hundred years ago. You pour in a handful of Carolina dirt, pack it in tight, tamp it down. When the trigger is pulled . . . *boom.* The amazing exploding gun trick.

What was it Professor Morrow had called the residue he'd found on the linen tablecloth?

Garden-variety dirt.

Okay, that had to be it. Then, the next big question that loomed in front of her was: Dirt from whose garden?

"Theo, there's someone here to see you," said Haley.

Theodosia had let herself in the back door that led directly from the alley to her office.

"Who is it?" she asked as she tucked her handbag into the desk drawer.

Haley shrugged. "Beats me. Some guy who came in about twenty minutes ago. I gave him a cup of tea and a scone and tucked him at the small table by the fireplace."

Taking a quick peek in the tiny mirror that hung on the back of her door, Theodosia smoothed her hair and decided to pass on the lipstick. The six-block walk back from the Heritage Society had infused her complexion with a natural, rosy glow, infinitely better than anything packaged cosmetics could deliver.

She emerged through the green velvet curtains with a smile on her face and confidence in her step. But her smile froze when she saw who it was waiting to see her: Booth Crowley.

She recovered quickly. "I'm Theodosia Browning," she greeted the man at the fireside table. "How can I help you?"

Booth Crowley stood and faced her. He was a big man to begin with, but wearing a coal black, three-piece suit, he looked even more imposing. His shock of white hair bristled atop his head, a crooked mouth jagged across his square-jawed face.

"I'm Booth Crowley," the man said as he took her hand in his and clamped down roughly. "We need to talk."

Booth Crowley released Theodosia's hand only when she was half seated. By that time, a single word had bubbled to her brain: *bully*. She'd been in Booth Crowley's immediate presence for all of thirty seconds, and already he impressed her as a bully of the first magnitude. But, then again, hadn't she seen him bullying Billy Manolo that day at the church? It certainly looked like he'd been.

"A very unpleasant man, that Burt Tidwell," said Crowley in his strange staccato manner. "Stopped by to see me this morning." His upper lip curled as he spoke, and his pink face seemed to become increasingly florid.

Tidwell, thought Theodosia. *He had received my E-mail and must have found some merit to it. Obviously he had, since he'd already had a chat with Booth Crowley.*

But would Tidwell have confided to Booth Crowley that she was the one who harbored suspicions about him? Doubtful, highly doubtful. If anything, the pendulum swung in the other direction with Tidwell. He was extremely tight-mouthed about investigative details.

But Booth Crowley wasn't nearly finished. "My wife attended a meeting yesterday," he snarled at her. "Ran into a friend of yours. Delaine Dish."

Theodosia groaned inwardly. Leave it to Delaine to chatter about anything and everything. And to Booth Crowley's wife yet! Unfortunately, there was no way she could have known that Delaine sat on the same committee that Booth Crowley's wife did.

Booth Crowley narrowed his eyes at her. "You've been talking about me. Asking impertinent questions," he said accusingly.

"Actually," said Theodosia, deciding to play it absolutely straight, "my questions have been about Oliver Dixon."

"And Grapevine," Booth Crowley shot back, "which most certainly *does* concern me."

"I was sorry to hear you closed it down," said Theodosia, keeping her voice light. "Good thing you have two more companies ready to come out of the chute. What are they? Oh, yes, Deva Tech and Alphimed."

"What do you know about those?" he snapped.

"Probably no more than anyone else," said Theodosia, "unless you'd care to enlighten me." There, she had jousted with him and obviously struck a nerve. Now it was his turn.

Booth Crowley smiled at Theodosia from across the table, but the vibes weren't particularly warm. "You know," he said, suddenly changing the cadence of his voice and adopting a silky, wheedling tone, "my wife, Beatrix, has always wanted to open a tea salon."

"How nice," said Theodosia. *Give him nothing,* she thought, *nothing. Never let them see you sweat.*

"Right now, she owns that lovely little sweet shop Le Bonbon. Down on Queen Street. She has a couple of ladies—dear, trusted souls—who've been with her for years. They make handmade truffles similar to the ones you find at Fauchon in Paris." Booth Crowley took a long sip of tea, wiped his mouth with a napkin, and tossed it down haphazardly on the table. "But a *salon de thé* that serves high tea is her absolute dream." He looked around imperiously. "Of course, it would be far more formal than what you have here. And I have the perfect name for it. Tea with Bea."

"Cute," said Theodosia.

"Yes, she's always wanted a little shop. Somewhere here in the historic district," said Booth Crowley. "I do so love to indulge my wife."

Theodosia knew that Booth Crowley and his wife, Beatrix, could squash her like a bug if they wanted to. Booth Crowley's net worth had to be high, almost astronomical. As CEO of Cherry Tree Investments, he smooth-talked countless investors into providing millions in venture capital for dozens of companies. More importantly, Booth Crowley sat on the Charleston Chamber of Commerce. If he decided to *indulge* his wife, as he had rhapsodized, he could easily persuade the Charleston tour buses to stop at his wife's tea shop instead of hers. It wasn't good, she decided, it wasn't good at all. She'd stirred up a hornet's nest, and now she might have to face the consequences.

Booth Crowley stood up abruptly and, reluctantly, Theodosia stood, too. "Good day," he told her, his grin hard, his gray eyes filled with menace. "If you hear of any vacancies on your block, be sure to let me know. In the meantime, I'll consult with one of the commercial Realtors my firm has on retainer." He spun away from her, heading for the door, then stopped in his tracks and looked back over his shoulder. "I wouldn't go signing any long-term leases, if I were you," he spat out. "Especially with the economy so uncertain and competition breathing down your neck." Then he slammed out the door and was gone.

Theodosia was aware of Drayton hovering behind her.

"What did he want?" Drayton asked quietly. He put a hand on Theodosia's shoulder, gently steering her over to the counter, where they could have some privacy.

"He came here to rattle my cage," Theodosia told him. "To intimidate me." She tried to keep her remark light, but

she realized that, deep inside, she *was* rattled and intimi-
dated.

"Who *was* that big boor?" asked Haley as they all
crowded behind the counter, whispering.

"That was Booth Crowley," Drayton told her.

Haley's eyes went wide. "*Really?* Darn. If I'd known
who he was, I wouldn't have been so pleasant to him when
he first came in." She meant her remark to be humorous,
but she saw the look of consternation on Theodosia's face.
"Just how did Booth Crowley try to intimidate you?"
Haley asked.

"Oh, it was rather indirect at first," said Theodosia. "He
talked about how his wife has always wanted to have a tea
salon somewhere in the historic district. Then he escalated
things, told me not to sign a long-term lease or anything."
She struggled to maintain an outward calm, but she still
came across shaken.

"You've had competition before," said Drayton, trying
to be practical. "It hasn't made a whit of difference."

"Not *real* competition," said Theodosia.

"What about Tea Baggy's over on Wentworth?" Drayton offered.

Theodosia looked thoughtful. "That's different. Tea
Baggy's is retail, and all the charm is in the name. Besides,
they only stock a few canisters of so-so tea. Most of their
sales are in candy and glassware. And gobs of giftware."

"They just added a line of teddy bears," said Haley
helpfully.

"You see?" said Theodosia to Drayton. "It is more retail. Booth Crowley was talking about something entirely
different."

"How much you want to bet he was just bluffing," said
Haley.

"How did your meeting with Timothy go?" asked Drayton, deciding it might be best to change the subject and try
to get Theodosia's mind off Booth Crowley's threats.

Theodosia stared at Drayton as though she wasn't sure what he was talking about. Then she blinked, and understanding came back to her face. "My goodness, I forgot to tell you! I came back here and went rushing into that awful meeting."

"So Timothy was helpful?" said Drayton.

"Actually, he was extremely helpful. And so were you," said Theodosia. "Thank you for calling ahead and smoothing the way."

Drayton waved a hand airily. "Just making sure the ferocious Timothy didn't make mincemeat out of you."

"So what did Timothy Neville say?" asked Haley.

"Basically, he told me it's fairly easy to rig a pistol to explode," said Theodosia. "All you have to do is overpack it."

"Overpack it?" frowned Haley. "With what?"

A sly smile crept onto Theodosia's face. "I think somebody overpacked the yacht club's pistol with dirt," she said.

"Which tracks with what Professor Morrow told you," Drayton exclaimed excitedly. "He said the tablecloth had *dirt* on it."

"Does somebody want to give me the complete story?" asked Haley impatiently.

"Haley," said Theodosia, "Professor Morrow analyzed the tablecloth and said the smudge, or schmutz, as you called it, was garden-variety dirt. Then I talked with Timothy, and he said that if you stuffed a pistol full of dirt, it would probably explode."

"Holy smokes," said Haley. "So maybe the garden-variety dirt—"

"Is really from somebody's garden," finished Drayton.

The three exchanged knowing glances.

"Sounds like we might have to slip into our ninja costumes tonight and visit a few gardens," suggested Haley.

Drayton rubbed his hands together in anticipation. "Like Booth Crowley's, Billy Manolo's—"

"Let's hold off on that for the time being," said Theodosia. "Professor Morrow is going to try to break down the compounds. He thinks he can get a lot more specific than telling us it's just dirt."

"You mean he'll determine pH balance or nitrogen content?" asked Drayton. "That would be fabulous! In fact, it would help launch us in a very specific direction. For example, if we found out the soil was acid-based, we'd look for someone who had, say, a rose garden."

"Pretty slick," agreed Haley. "That would really help narrow it down. When do you think your professor will have those test results for us?"

"Hopefully, tomorrow," said Theodosia.

"Isn't it serendipitous," said Drayton, "that the Garden Fest kicks off in two days?"

"Kind of gives us an excuse to poke around in the dirt," said Haley with an impish grin.

CHAPTER 25

❦

THE NEXT MORNING, they all fluttered about nervously, waiting for Professor Morrow's phone call. But when the good professor hadn't called by ten A.M., Drayton suggested they put their heads together and work on some ideas for an artists' tea.

"I've heard of garden teas and teddy bear teas and, of course, we just had our mystery tea," said Haley, "but what the heck is an artists' tea?"

Drayton's eyes skimmed across the tea shop. Only three tables were occupied, and the customers sitting at them had all been served. Business was a tad slow but, then again, it was midweek.

"I was thinking of holding an artists' tea in conjunction with Spoleto," explained Drayton. "Theme the tearoom with Art Deco table decor, offer a creative menu, invite a few performing artists in. Maybe a jazz trio or string quartet. Or we could have a poetry reading."

"Sounds neat," said Haley.

"Theo?" asked Drayton. She had been arranging sets of

miniature teapots on the wooden shelves and seemed lost in thought. "What do you think?"

"Judging by the success of your mystery tea, I think you could expect standing room only," she said, producing a grin that stretched ear to ear on Drayton's venerable face.

"What if one of the teas we served was badamtam," suggested Haley. "Really make it special."

Drayton feigned mock surprise. "My goodness, our little girl has actually been paying attention. Badamtam is, indeed, a grand Darjeeling."

"We could even invite some fine artists in," suggested Theodosia. "Display their work or actually have them sketching or painting during the tea. You know, in the manner of a plein aire artist, where a small painting is begun and completed in the field, so to speak, all in one sitting."

"How about using sheets of classical music as place mats?" suggested Haley.

"That's the spirit," crowed Drayton as his black Montblanc pen fairly flew across the pages of his notebook. "Now, if I can just jot all these great ideas down—"

"Yoo-hoo."

They all spun on their heels. Delaine was standing there, smiling in her maddeningly, self-important manner.

"Can I get a quick cup to go?" she asked. "Assam, if it's not too much trouble."

"We've got ten different kinds of Assam," said Drayton as he deftly ran his fingertips across the lineup of tea tins that were shelved on the nearby wall. "But this golden tips is by far the best," he said, pulling down one of the shiny brass tins.

"Theo, I'm still holding that jacket for you," said Delaine.

"I know you are. And I'm still thinking about it." Theodosia paused. "Delaine, did you by any chance say something to Booth Crowley's wife the other day?"

Delaine smiled coyly. "Whatever are you talking about?"

"Booth Crowley stopped in here yesterday afternoon. To say he was unhappy would be putting it mildly. He was under the impression that I've been asking probing questions about him." She paused. "When in fact, we were just making conversation, were we not?"

Delaine hesitated for a moment, and Theodosia could see her mind working to formulate a plausible, Delaine-deflecting answer.

Theodosia sighed inwardly. Really, it *had* been her own fault. She knew that Delaine's true nature was to dish out as much information as she could, and still she'd kept pressing her for answers.

"Good heavens, Theodosia," Delaine said finally, "I ran into Booth Crowley's wife a couple days ago, that's all. Beatrix and I are on the same committee. I suppose I *might* have mentioned that her husband's name came up in conversation, but certainly nothing beyond that."

Theodosia gritted her teeth. She *really* should have known better. Delaine thrived on gossip and adored passing it on.

"Drayton," said Delaine, eager to change the subject, "are you terribly excited about Garden Fest? Is there any chance we'll get a peek at your Japanese bonsai trees this year?"

Drayton filled an indigo-colored paper cup with the freshly brewed Assam and snapped on a white take-out lid. "Actually, Timothy Neville has invited me to display a few of my bonsai on his patio," Drayton told her. "You know his garden is very dramatic and Asian-inspired. Of course, there'd be no judging involved, the bonsai would be purely for fun."

"So you'll have your bonsai at Timothy's Garden Fest party!" Delaine exclaimed. "How delightful. You know what? You folks should serve some of your yummy Japanese tea as well. Make it a *themed* affair."

"Yummy isn't the precise term I'd use to describe Japanese green tea, but, yes, Delaine, the idea had occurred to me," answered Drayton.

"We have to *work* at Timothy's party?" asked Haley.

Delaine turned probing eyes on Haley. "You're on the guest list, dear?"

"Well, not exactly," stammered Haley.

"Then serving tea would be an ideal way for you to be in attendance at a major social function, would it not?" said Delaine. "Give you a chance to hobnob with *café* society?"

"It's still work," grumbled Haley as she turned to answer the ringing phone. "Hello?" she said. "Yes, she's here." Haley put her hand over the receiver. "It's for you, Theodosia."

"I'll take it in my office, Haley," said Theodosia, chuckling at Delaine's somewhat pompous reference to café society. It was hard to stay angry with Delaine. She was a sweet woman and a rich source of entertainment. Still, there was no way she was going to have this conversation, or *any* conversation, in front of Delaine Dish. She'd learned her lesson for good.

"Hello?" said Theodosia as she kicked back in her comfy leather chair.

"Theodosia, it's Lizbeth Cantrell."

"Hello, Lizbeth," said Theodosia.

"My brother just told me." Lizbeth Cantrell's words spilled out in a rush.

"Told you what?" said Theodosia.

"That he's been doing consulting work for Oliver Dixon." She hesitated. "I feel like . . . I'm sure I put a great imposition upon you. Not knowing all the facts and then still pushing you . . . Well, anyway, it's over, isn't it? I feel like a great load has been lifted off my shoulders."

"Lizbeth, what do you mean?" asked Theodosia.

"There's no way anyone could be suspicious of Ford now," said Lizbeth, her voice filled with relief.

Theodosia stared at a bright little spot of sunlight that fell at her feet. "Lizbeth, I hate to say this, but your brother is not entirely off the hook."

There was silence for a moment. "I don't understand," said Lizbeth. "He and Oliver Dixon were working *together*. Surely, anyone could see they had a business relationship. Why would anyone believe that Ford wished harm to the man?"

"Yes, but it's not clear what *kind* of relationship they had," said Theodosia. She hated to say it, but she had to. "For all we know, it could have turned adversarial. Your brother made a recommendation that Oliver Dixon didn't agree with. . . . The result was friction between the two of them. . . ."

"Oh," said Lizbeth in a small voice.

"A man like Booth Crowley might even tell police that it reached the point of severely damaging the company," said Theodosia. "Then, what with Oliver's, uh, accident . . . Well, they might just read any business problem as motive."

"Booth Crowley would say something like that?" asked Lizbeth.

Oh yes, thought Theodosia. *The man would lie through his teeth if he thought it would gain him a centimeter's advantage.* Instead, Theodosia said, "There was a lot at stake. An investor might have an entirely different perspective."

"And the issue of the pistol still hangs over my brother's head," said Lizbeth. "All because Ford's an avid collector, because he knows guns. . . ."

Yes, thought Theodosia, *and gun collectors often know*

tricks. If Timothy Neville knew how to mastermind an exploding pistol, chances are, Ford Cantrell did, too.

"I had no right to involve you," said Lizbeth Cantrell. "I feel awful." She sounded as though she were ready to break down sobbing.

"Lizbeth," said Theodosia in as gentle a manner as she could, "you didn't involve me. Truth be known, I involved myself. And, please, also know this. . . . I intend to see this thing through to the bitter end. I will uncover some answers."

"You're going to keep investigating?" asked Lizbeth.

"Yes," said Theodosia.

"In cooperation with the police?" asked Lizbeth.

"That depends on how cooperative the police are," said Theodosia.

"Who's Drayton talking to?" asked Theodosia as she slid behind the counter and poured herself a cup of lung ching.

"Don't know," said Haley. "The other line rang the minute you went in back to take your call. Whoever he's on the line with has been doing all the talking, though."

Drayton hung up the phone, looking sober.

"What's with you?" asked Haley.

"I just had a very strange conversation with Gerard Huber, the manager of the Saint James Hotel," said Drayton.

Haley gave a low whistle. "That's a pretty hoity-toity place. What the heck did they want with you?"

"They just offered me a job," said Drayton unhappily.

"What?" exclaimed Haley.

"You heard me," snapped Drayton. "Gerard Huber asked if I had any interest in coming to work there."

"Doing what?" asked Haley.

Drayton turned a clouded face toward Theodosia. "Executive director of their food and wine service." He reached a gnarled hand out, rested it gently atop Theodosia's. "You know what this is all about, don't you?" he asked.

"Change!" declared Haley boisterously. "This is what Madame Hildegarde predicted the night of the mystery tea!"

Theodosia shook her head slowly. "I'm afraid not, Haley. But what it does mean is that Booth Crowley has started to come after us."

"Booth Crowley?" said Haley, scrunching her face into a quizzical frown. "What does *he* have to do with this?"

"He's one of the owners of the Saint James Hotel," said Drayton. "One of their silent partners, so to speak."

"Oh," said Haley, absorbing this latest information. "Did they offer you a lot of money?"

"Haley," said Theodosia, "that's Drayton's—"

"It's okay," said Drayton as his gray eyes sought out Theodosia's blue eyes. "They said they'd double what I was making now."

Haley gave a low whistle. "Double the salary . . . imagine that."

Drayton's face settled into a look of indignation. "As if I could be bought. What absolute rubbish!"

CHAPTER 26

❦

$\mathcal{D}$ETECTIVE BURT TIDWELL finally showed up midafternoon. Theodosia knew he would. He almost had to, given the fact that her earlier missive to him, her E-mail spelling out her roster of murder suspects, had undoubtedly prompted him into having a talk with Booth Crowley.

Tidwell grasped a floral teacup in his huge paw, took a delicate sip of amber-colored dimbulla tea. "Ah, Miss Browning," he said as he settled back in his wooden chair, "such a civilized respite." Tidwell took another sip and gazed placidly about the tearoom. "With such lovely environs as this, why do you continue to involve yourself in such unpleasantness?"

"You're referring to Oliver Dixon's death?" she said.

"That and your persistent penchant for investigating," said Tidwell. "Why risk exposing yourself to unnecessary danger?"

"Do you think I'm in danger?" Theodosia asked with genuine curiosity.

"Anyone who goes about asking probing questions will,

sooner or later, find their popularity severely compromised," said Tidwell.

What a maddening answer, thought Theodosia as she stared across the table at him. *Tidwell is, once again, jousting with words. He's trying to determine who I think should be at the very top of the list that I sent him.*

"So you believe my questions have exposed a few sensitive areas?" said Theodosia.

Tidwell waited a long time to answer. "Yes," he finally replied. "Although your Mr. Booth Crowley seems to be a tad hypersensitive." Tidwell's eyelids slid down over his slightly protruding eyes in the manner of one who is relaxed and ready to fall asleep. "Interesting man, Mr. Crowley. Did you know he can trace his ancestry back to John Wilkes Booth?"

Theodosia ignored Tidwell's remark. It seemed like everyone in the South could trace their ancestry back to someone who was famous, infamous, or had played some sort of walk-on role in the course of the nation's history. Her own mother had been a great-great-grandniece of Aaron Burr.

"How hard have you looked at Doe?" Theodosia asked him.

"Ah," said Tidwell as his eyes snapped open like a window shade. "Doe Belvedere Dixon. Grieving widow, toast of the town, belle of the ball."

"Don't forget Magnolia Queen," added Theodosia.

Tidwell pursed his lips delicately. "The girl *did* seem to collect beauty pageant crowns much the same way a Girl Scout does merit badges."

"The question is," said Theodosia, "was Oliver Dixon one of her merit badges?"

"Miss Browning, you have a nasty habit of thinking the worst of people."

"As do you, Detective Tidwell," said Theodosia, smiling at him.

"Touché," said Tidwell. "Here's what I *will* share with you, Miss Browning. According to a recent study conducted by our wise friends at the Justice Department, forty percent of so-called family murders are committed by a spouse."

"Do you think this was a family murder?"

"Hard to say," said Tidwell.

"Was there life insurance?" asked Theodosia.

"There was considerable life insurance as well as accidental death insurance."

"Accidental death," said Theodosia. "Interesting." She thought for a moment. "Did anything turn up during Oliver Dixon's autopsy?"

Tidwell lifted one furry eyebrow, and a knowing smile spread across his chubby, bland face. "Your line of reasoning follows that if Oliver Dixon suffered from an incurable disease, the possibility exists that he might have staged his own accidental death?"

"It wouldn't be the first time someone tried to do it," said Theodosia.

"Nor the last," agreed Tidwell. "But no, I studied the medical examiner's report with great care, I assure you. Aside from a small degree of hardening of the arteries and the onset of osteoarthritis in his hands, Oliver Dixon was in relatively good health for a man of sixty-six."

Theodosia reached for the teapot and poured them each another half cup of tea. "Would you tell me about your visit with Booth Crowley?" she asked.

"I think not," he said.

"But you find him a suspicious figure in all of this?" she said.

"I once told you that I regard everyone as a suspect."

"And I once told you that cannot be efficient."

"If efficiency is what you seek, I suggest you cease and desist from your amateur sleuthing," Tidwell told her.

"Since the modus operandi of an investigator is dependent on tedious fact-finding and repetitive questions."

Theodosia decided to try another approach. "Your talking to Booth Crowley indicates you may have shifted your focus away from Ford Cantrell."

"I didn't say that," said Tidwell.

"No, but your actions indicate that," said Theodosia.

"Why do I have the nagging feeling that you're trying to clear Ford Cantrell?" asked Tidwell.

Theodosia sighed. What harm would it do to tell Tidwell, even if he was closemouthed with her? "If you must know, I told his sister I'd do everything in my power to help her."

"Why?" asked Tidwell.

"It's personal," said Theodosia, standing up. "It turns out we go back a long way together. Now, if you'll excuse me, Detective . . ." And she hurried over to where Drayton was folding napkins.

Tidwell continued to sit at the table, sipping tea, enjoying the aromatic smells and the bubble and hiss surround-sound that enveloped him like a warm cocoon. He lived alone, police work filled his days and most of his nights, so it wasn't often that he was able to be part of an environment that felt so pleasant and relaxed.

So the Browning woman had made some sort of promise to Lizbeth Cantrell, Tidwell mused to himself. That was unfortunate, because he still had doubts as to Ford Cantrell's complete innocence. And it especially didn't look good that Billy Manolo was involved.

Or, at least he *thought* Billy Manolo was involved.

He'd instructed the patrol cars in Billy Manolo's neighborhood to keep tabs on the hotheaded young man. Most of the time, when Billy went out at night, it was to drink a couple beers at a desultory little bar called the Boll Weevil. But on two separate occasions, and rather late at night, they'd observed Billy's old Chevy pickup heading out the

165 toward the low country. And the low country was
where Ford Cantrell lived.

*Had Billy Manolo somehow aligned himself with Ford
Cantrell?* Tidwell wondered.

Possibly.

Of course, he was still questioning personnel from the
now-defunct Grapevine, but he'd heard his share of stories
about disagreements between Oliver Dixon and Ford
Cantrell. So Ford *could* have had motive. And Billy *could*
have done the dirty work.

Tidwell had studied the shots that the *Post and
Courier*'s photographer had taken that day in White Point
Gardens. That lovely Sunday afternoon when he'd been
home in his postage stamp–sized backyard, trying to coax
some life from the tulip bulbs he'd planted last fall.

They'd all been watching the sailboat race, the whole
cast and crew. Oliver Dixon, Doe Belvedere Dixon, Ford
Cantrell, Billy Manolo, and Booth Crowley. And Theodosia Browning.

Tidwell took a final sip of tea, pushed his chair back,
and stood, economical movements for a man so large. Re-
moving a five-dollar bill from his wallet, he laid it gently
on the table. Theodosia had never charged him for tea, yet
he felt paying for it was the honorable thing to do. He
knew the young girl Haley probably didn't like him, but
she was always polite and took great pains to serve him
properly. In a world gone mad with indifference, that
counted for something.

"Miss Dimple, you're doing the bookkeeping for a couple other shops on Church Street, aren't you?" asked
Theodosia. Theodosia knew she was, but it seemed like a
good way to kick off the conversation she wanted to have.

It was late afternoon, and the last customers had just
left. Miss Dimple had her ledgers spread out on one of the

tables and was slowly going through the last few of the day's receipts.

Miss Dimple beamed. "Indeed I am. Monday mornings I tally the weekend receipts for the Chowder Hound, and Tuesday afternoons I'm at Pinckney's Gift Shop. Once in a while I even work behind the cash register. It's so pleasant to be around all that Irish linen and crystal."

"Have you heard any rumors about Doe Belvedere Dixon? How she's doing, what she's doing?" asked Theodosia.

Miss Dimple placed the tip of her Ticonderoga number-two yellow pencil between her lips and thought for a moment. "I heard she was selling off some of her art and collectibles. But, then, you already know about that."

"Right," volunteered Haley, who had been unpacking Chinese blue and white teapots from a newly arrived shipment. "Giovanni Loard brought in that Edgefield pot last week."

"I *did* hear something about her changing her name," said Miss Dimple.

"Changing her name?" asked Drayton. He'd obviously been listening, too, as he double-checked the order forms for some covered tea mugs that had caught his eye in a supplier's catalog.

"Yes," said Miss Dimple, her memory coming back to her now. "Word is out that Doe is going back to being just Doe Belvedere."

"You know why I think she's doing it?" asked Haley. "Because Doe Dixon sounds like an exotic dancer."

"Nonsense," said Drayton, a smile playing at his lips. "You determine your exotic dancer name by combining your pet's name with your mother's maiden name."

"Oh, my God!" screamed Haley. "Then mine would be Lulu Rendell!"

"See?" said Drayton.

"You two!" said Miss Dimple, shaking with laughter.

CHAPTER 27

❧

ᏔYNTON MARSALIS PLAYED on the CD player, and she was deep into Pearl Buck's *Pavilion of Women* when Professor Morrow called.

"Miss Browning," he said in his somewhat distracted manner, "I hope I've not phoned too late."

Theodosia glanced at the baroque brass clock that sat on the pine mantel, saw that it was just half past eight.

"Not at all, Professor Morrow," she said, sliding a bookmark between the pages and closing her book. Her heart seemed to thump an extra beat in anticipation of his news. "I'm delighted you called. In fact, I've been looking forward to hearing from you," she told him.

"Good, good," he said. "Took me longer than I thought. But then, everything takes longer these days, doesn't it? I'm teaching a two-week interim course this June, and Kiplinger, our department head, just now suggested I develop an on-line syllabus. So of course I had to scramble—"

"What's the course?" asked Theodosia, trying to be polite.

"Herbaceous perennials," said Professor Morrow.

"Simple to teach, not a lot to prepare, and students always seem to like it."

"Great," said Theodosia. "I really want to thank you for taking time to do this soil analysis.

"Right," said Professor Morrow, "the analysis."

Theodosia had a mental picture of Professor Morrow adjusting his glasses and thumbing through his notes, ready to deliver a short lecture to her.

"I ran a standard micronutrient test, measured levels of sulfur, iron, manganese, copper, zinc, and boron. As far as pH level goes, I'd have to say your dirt came from an area where the soil was quite acidic."

"What kind of plants grow in acidic soil?" asked Theodosia.

"Are we talking flowers or shrubs?" asked Professor Morrow.

Theodosia made an educated guess. "Flowers." In her mind's eye, she could imagine someone stepping out into his garden, shoving the point of a trowel into soft, black dirt, then scooping that dirt into a plastic bag to carry to the yacht club.

"Flowers," said Professor Morrow, weighing the possibilities. "Then you're talking something like verbena, marigold, calliopsis, or nicotiana. Of course, those varieties are all annuals. In perennials, you'd be looking at baptisia, coreopsis, platycodon, or silene."

"Wow," said Theodosia, feeling slightly overwhelmed.

"Of course, roses are also notorious for preferring acidic soil, but you can't have it *too* acidic. The demanding little darlings prefer a pH balance somewhere between 5.5 and 6.5. Any more than that, and they get chlorotic."

"What does that mean?"

"Their leaves mottle," said Professor Morrow.

CHAPTER 28

❈❈❈

"*IT'S A GOOD* thing he faxed you his notes," said Drayton, "otherwise this would be *really* complicated."

For the last hour, Drayton had been poring over Professor Morrow's jottings, checking them against three different gardening books that he'd borrowed from Robillard Booksellers next door. Books, faxes, and pages torn from Drayton's ledger were strewn on one of the tea shop's tables. In between waiting on customers and serving fresh-from-the-oven pastries, Haley hovered at the table where Drayton and Theodosia had set up headquarters.

"I'm going to end up buying these books," Drayton announced. "They're very good, and I don't have them in my collection. Just look at this tabular list of garden perennials and this lovely chapter on bridge grafting. You don't run across information like this every day."

Earlier, Theodosia had shared Professor Morrow's findings with Drayton and Haley, and they had both jumped at the chance to be involved in the investigation. Although it felt like they were heading down the right trail, their task also felt slightly daunting. Professor Morrow had given them so many details and possibilities that one almost needed a degree in horticulture to figure everything out.

"Haley, we're going to need litmus paper," said Drayton. "Can you run down to the drugstore later and pick up a packet?"

"Sure," she agreed. "You're still convinced we can get a handle on who might have overpacked that pistol by testing soil from various gardens?"

"And the yacht club," said Theodosia. "Let's not forget the yacht club."

"Right," said Drayton, then added for Haley's sake, "this is a gamble that *could* pay off. We've got the results from Professor Morrow's tests, so that becomes our baseline. Now what we do is check the various soil samples using the soil testing kits we got from Hattie Bootwright's floral shop down the street."

"So how exactly are we going to pull this off?" asked Haley. She was almost dancing in place, excited at the prospect of being involved in a full-blown investigation and, at the same time, keeping a watchful eye on her tea shop customers.

"Drayton and I already talked about that," said Theodosia. "We'll all be at Timothy Neville's tonight, so that will serve as a kind of home base."

"Right," agreed Drayton. "We'll work from there. Doe lives half a block away, so we can easily scout her garden and obtain a sample."

"You're sure she'll be at Timothy's tonight?" asked Haley.

"Absolutely," said Drayton. "In fact, she'll be attending with Giovanni Loard. He called me yesterday about a silver teapot someone brought into his shop, and he mentioned that he'd be there. If you remember, his garden is on tomorrow night's tour. So he's very excited about the entire Garden Fest event."

"He's not still mad about the other day?" asked Theodosia.

"Never mentioned it," said Drayton.

"Okay then," said Theodosia, getting back to business. "Booth Crowley lives two blocks away on Tradd Street, so his garden should be an easy hit as well. We know he'll be there tonight, since his wife Beatrix serves on one of the Garden Fest committees with Delaine."

"Perfect," said Drayton, rubbing his hands together.

"What about Billy Manolo and Ford Cantrell?" asked Haley. "I thought they were on your hot list, too."

"They are," said Theodosia, "but Billy Manolo doesn't really have a yard. Well, he does, but almost every square inch is littered with pieces of iron or covered with finished metalwork. We can drop by the yacht club, though, that's easy enough."

"And I guess it would be difficult to check Ford Cantrell's place, since he lives on a huge plantation," said Haley. "You wouldn't even know where to start." She turned to scan the tearoom, saw out the window that one of the yellow tour jitneys had just let off a load of tourists, and they were making a beeline for the tea shop.

"I guess we'll just work with what we've got," said Haley as she headed for the door to greet their new customers.

"Actually," said Theodosia, once Haley was out of earshot, "it's *not* all we've got."

Drayton turned his head sharply to stare at Theodosia. Something in her tone told him she might be hatching another idea. "What do you mean?" he asked warily.

Theodosia bent close to Drayton's ear and began to whisper. And as she did, a look of astonishment flickered across his face. When she was done, he gazed at her with admiration.

"It's a jolly good brazen plan, all right," said Drayton. "The question is, will it work?"

Theodosia lifted her shoulders imperceptibly. "It might flush out a fox or two."

"It's also dangerous," he said, adding a sober note to the conversation.

"Agreed," said Theodosia, "But that's also why I like it." She frowned. "Trouble is, the whole plan would hinge on Timothy Neville's cooperation. Do you think we can persuade him to go along with us? And especially at such short notice?"

"You leave Timothy to me," advised Drayton. "I can be very convincing when I have to. And since elections at the Heritage Society are coming up soon, and Timothy is lobbying strongly for reelection as president, he might just listen carefully to what I have to say. So you go call Lizbeth Cantrell and arrange for her to come up with some creative ruse to have her brother present at the party tonight. And leave Timothy Neville to me."

Theodosia tapped her fingers on the telephone. This wasn't going to be easy, she told herself. Because she *could* be setting Ford Cantrell up for a terrible fall. Then again, if Ford really was instrumental in engineering Oliver Dixon's death, justice would be served.

The word *justice* echoed in Theodosia's brain. Lizbeth's wreath of coltsfoot had been intended to connote justice. Funny how that single word seemed to hang over this entire investigation like a sword suspended from a single thread.

Taking a deep breath, Theodosia opened the phone directory, ran her finger down a fairly long list of Cantrells, spotted Lizbeth Cantrell's phone number, and punched it in.

Lizbeth Cantrell was in today; she picked up on the first ring.

"Lizbeth," said Theodosia, the words tumbling out,

"can you bring Ford to a party at Timothy Neville's home tonight?"

"What's going on?" asked Lizbeth, her antennae already at full alert.

"Hopefully, a plan that will reveal Oliver Dixon's killer," said Theodosia.

Lizbeth hesitated. "A plan you want my brother's participation in."

"Yes," said Theodosia, "but I'm afraid I can't share the exact details."

"And if this plan backfires?"

Theodosia had heard fear and worry in Lizbeth's voice and knew exactly what she was thinking. *Backfiring* was Lizbeth's euphemism for Ford being proven guilty. She knew Lizbeth was utterly heartsick over the possibility.

I've got to strongly dissuade her of that thought, Theodosia decided. *Keep her thinking positive.*

"Hopefully," said Theodosia, "this plan will help *clear* Ford's name, once and for all. But it will only work if he's in attendance tonight. At the Garden Fest kickoff party." Theodosia listened to dead air for a moment. "You know where Timothy lives?" she asked hopefully.

"Yes," said Lizbeth.

"So we can count on your attendance?"

"We'll be there," said Lizbeth finally. "Ford won't like it, but I'll think of something."

Breathing a sigh of relief, Theodosia hung up the phone. That hadn't been as difficult as she'd thought it might be. But, then again, Lizbeth Cantrell was one tough lady, made of fairly stern stuff.

It would all play out tonight, Theodosia decided, once her plan was set into motion. Of course, her plan also hinged on a number of critical pieces: all the right people showing up and Timothy Neville's supreme cooperation. Was that too much to ask? She surely hoped not.

Gazing at the wall of photos across from her desk,

Theodosia's eyes were drawn to an old black and white picture of her dad rigging one of his old sailboats, a Stone Horse. And her thoughts turned to Billy Manolo, the surly part-time handyman at the yacht club.

It would be perfect if she could somehow get Billy Manolo to show up tonight as well. Then they'd have all the players. . . .

Yes, it would be perfect, she decided. It was certainly worth a try. But how exactly would she . . . ?

Theodosia punched in the phone number for the yacht club. A crazy idea had popped into her head that, on closer inspection, might not be so crazy after all.

"Yacht club," answered a youthful male voice.

"Is Billy Manolo there?" she asked.

"Oh, he's . . . I think he's out working on one of the boats. I saw him on one of the piers an hour or so ago, but I couldn't say where he is now. I just stopped by the clubhouse to grab a drink of water, and the phone rang. I can't really help—"

"Could you take a message?" asked Theodosia.

"A message. Yeah, I suppose so. Hang on a minute. Gotta get a pencil and paper."

There was a fumble and a clunk as the phone was set down, then the young man came on the line again.

"Okay, go ahead," he said.

"This is for Billy Manolo," said Theodosia. "The note should say, please be at Timothy Neville's home tonight at eight. Address is 413 Archdale."

Theodosia could hear the man softly repeating the message to himself as he wrote it down. "Anything else?" asked the young man.

"Add that it's urgent Billy show up and make a note that it's at the request of Booth Crowley."

"How do you spell that? I got the Booth part, I'm just not sure on Crowley."

"C-R-O-W-L-E-Y," said Theodosia.

"Okay," said the young man. "And who is this?"

Theodosia ransacked her brain for the name of the woman she'd spoken with the day she phoned Booth Crowley's office. Marilyn, the woman's name had been Marilyn.

"This is Marilyn from Booth Crowley's office."

"Gotcha," said the young man. "I'll leave the note in his mailbox."

"Yes, that's perfect," said Theodosia, remembering a line of four of five wooden mail slots that were used by employees, handymen, yacht club commodores, and other folks who spent time there.

CHAPTER 29

❧❧❧

TIMOTHY NEVILLE ADORED giving parties. Holiday parties, charity galas, music recitals. And his enormous Georgian mansion, a glittering showpiece perched on Archdale Street, was, for many guests, a peek into the kind of gilded luxury that hadn't been witnessed in Charleston since earlier times.

Although not an official Garden Fest event, Timothy had been staging his Garden Fest kickoff party for more years than anyone could count. It was a way to bring all the Garden Fest participants together in one place, and it served as a kind of unofficial marker that heralded the arrival of spring. Days were becoming warmer, deep purple evenings held the promise of fluttering luna moths and night-blooming nicotiana. And, once again, everyone in Charleston was more than ready to treat their gardens as an extended room of their house. For Charlestonians adored their gardens, whether they be tiny, secluded brick patios surrounded by slender columns of oleander or one of the enormous enclosed backyards in the historic district, lavishly embellished with vine-covered brick walls, fountains adorned with statuary, and well-tended beds of verdant plant life.

Poised on his broad piazza, dressed in impeccable white, Timothy Neville greeted each of his guests with a welcoming word. Flickering gaslights threw a warm scrim and lent an alabaster glow that served to enhance the complexions of his female guests.

Just inside, Henry Marchand, Timothy's valet of almost forty years, stood in the dazzling foyer. Attired in red topcoat and white breeches, Henry solemnly directed newly arrived ladies to the powder room and gentlemen toward the bar with the grace and surety of a majordomo secure in his position.

"Even though it's not entirely black tie, it's certainly creative attire," exclaimed Drayton as he and Theodosia surveyed the chattering crowd. Most of Timothy's guests were also residents of the historic district and, thus, nodding acquaintances to the two of them. Many were descended from Charleston's old families and had lived in the surrounding neighborhood for years. Others had been drawn to the historic district by their love of history, tradition, and old-world charm and had scrimped and saved to buy their historic houses with an eye toward full restoration. For in the historic district, restoration was always big business. And a major boon to the plasterers, wallpaperers, chimney sweeps, gardeners, designers, and various other tradespeople and craftsmen who were so often called upon to keep these grande dame homes in working order.

Earlier, Drayton and Theodosia had helped Haley get her tea service set up outside in Timothy's lush garden. Ten of Drayton's bonsai had been arranged on simple wooden Parsons tables, creating an elegant, Zen-like atmosphere. Haley was now busily pouring Japanese tea into small, blue-glazed tea bowls and passing them out to those guests who'd come outside to admire Timothy's elegant garden and Drayton's finely crafted bonsai.

"I do love this house," declared Theodosia, as she gazed in awe at the Hepplewhite furnishings, glittering crystal chandeliers, and carved walnut mantelpiece signed by Italian master Luigi Frullini. She'd only given a cursory glance to the oil paintings that lined the walls but had already recognized a Horace Bundy and a Franklin Whiting Rogers. She also knew that the china Timothy displayed in illuminated cases in one of the two front parlors was genuine Spode.

"Timothy's got taste, all right," said Drayton, "and the man has demonstrated a remarkable amount of class. I couldn't believe how willing he was to take part in our little plan."

"I'm relieved that he's agreed to help," said Theodosia. "But I must admit I'm a little nervous about the whole thing."

"Me, too," said Drayton. "But if we stick to our plan . . . Oh, talk about perfect," said Drayton under his breath.

"You bought the jacket!" Delaine Dish's strident voice rose above the buzz of conversation in the solarium where Theodosia and Drayton had wandered in to visit the bar and get flutes of vintage champagne. Clutching an oversized goblet of white wine and wearing a frothy wrapped dress of pink silk, Delaine pushed her way through the crowd to join them.

"When?" she asked Theodosia, her eyes all aglow. "Today?" Her dark hair was done up in a fetching swirl and held in place by a pink barrette. Her shellacked pink toes peeped out of matching pink sandals.

"About two hours ago," said Theodosia. "Suddenly, the jacket seemed like the absolute perfect thing to wear to this party. So I phoned your shop and talked with Janine and, lo and behold, I was in luck. You still had the green."

"And so pretty with your ring," giggled Delaine, noting the cluster of peridots that sparkled on Theodosia's hand. "Is that a family heirloom?"

"My grandmother's," replied Theodosia.

"Inherited jewelry," murmured Delaine, "always the best kind." She turned glittering eyes on Drayton. "No strings attached. Unlike a gift from a gentleman."

"Delaine, any gentleman worth his salt would be quite content to lavish gifts upon you, nary a string attached."

"Oh, Drayton," she cooed.

Drayton bowed slightly. "Now, if you ladies will excuse me, I'm going to head out to the garden. Timothy has asked me to do a short, impromptu talk on the style merits of the windswept bonsai."

"Such a gentleman," said Delaine. She smiled at Theodosia with a slightly glassy-eyed look, and Theodosia knew Delaine was wearing her tinted contact lenses tonight. She was terribly nearsighted and, at the same time, loved to enhance and sometimes change the color of her eyes.

"Delaine," Theodosia began, feeling a tiny stab of guilt at what she was about to set into motion. "You know I've been asking more than a few questions about Oliver Dixon's death. . . ."

Delaine blinked and moved closer to her. "Has something new turned up?" she asked.

"In a way, yes," said Theodosia. "I probably shouldn't—"

"Oh, you can tell me, dear," said Delaine. She put a hand on Theodosia's arm, pulled her protectively away from the throes of the crowd. "I'm as concerned about all this as you are."

"The thing of it is," said Theodosia, "I've stumbled upon the most amazing clue."

"Whatever do you mean?" asked Delaine.

"Remember the linen tablecloth?"

Delaine's face remained a blank.

"The one that Oliver Dixon sort of fell onto during the . . . uh . . . accident?"

Remembrance suddenly dawned for Delaine. "Oh, of *course*. The *tablecloth*."

"Well, I had it analyzed."

"You mean like in a crime lab?" asked Delaine. She glanced around to make sure no one was listening in on their conversation.

"No, a private analysis. But by an expert."

"How fascinating," said Delaine, her face lighting up with excitement, "tell me more."

"One of the theories about that old pistol exploding was that someone *meant* for it to explode. Someone packed it chock-full of gunpowder and dirt."

"How awful," said Delaine, but her face held a smile of anticipation.

"The analysis I had done broke that dirt down into specific compounds. In theory, if we can match the dirt from the weapon with the dirt in someone's garden, we'd have Oliver Dixon's killer."

Delaine's mouth opened and closed several times. "That's amazing," she finally managed. "Astonishing, really."

"Isn't it?" said Theodosia.

"When are you going to do this matching of dirt?" asked Delaine.

"We're working on it right now," said Theodosia.

"So you could know *tonight*?"

"In theory . . . yes," said Theodosia.

"Do the police know? That Detective Tidwell fellow?"

"All in good time," said Theodosia.

Delaine let loose a little shiver. "I'm getting goose bumps. This is just like one of those true-crime TV shows. On-the-spot investigating . . . very exciting."

Theodosia stared across the room into the crowd. She could see Booth Crowley standing at the bar. He had just gotten a martini or a gimlet or something in a stemmed glass with a twist of lemon and was staring glumly at his wife, a small, sturdy woman with hair teased into a blond bubble.

At the opposite end of the room, Ford Cantrell had just walked in with his sister and was glancing nervously toward the bar, probably hoping he could get three fingers of bourbon instead of a glass of champagne and wondering why on earth Lizbeth had seen fit to drag him to this stuffy party where he was probably highly unwelcome.

Across the wide center hallway, Theodosia could see Doe Belvedere Dixon reclining on a brocade fainting couch in Timothy's vast library. Doe was dressed in a sleek cranberry-red pantsuit and was gossiping and talking animatedly with three other young women. Giggling like a schoolgirl, not a decorous widow.

Scanning the rest of the crowd, Theodosia hoped Billy Manolo had gotten the message she'd left him and would also put in an appearance some time this evening.

Theodosia knew that any one of them could have overpacked that pistol. Any one of them could be a cold, calculating killer. And tonight was the night to set a trap and see who stumbled in.

CHAPTER 30

❧❦❧

THE HISS OF the oxyacetylene torch was like a viper, angry and menacing. It was exactly how Billy Manolo felt tonight as he wielded his welding equipment.

He was angry. Angry and more than a little resentful. First of all, he was supposed to have this stupid gate finished by tomorrow morning. He'd been following a classical French design and using mortise joinery, and the project seemed to be taking forever. Marianne Petigru had made it perfectly clear to him that if he missed one more deadline, he could forget about getting any more work from Popple Hill. But Marianne was a snotty, rich bitch, he told himself, who could go stick her head in a bucket of swamp water for all he cared.

At the same time, he genuinely *liked* working on these projects. They were good jobs, substantial jobs, and they usually involved design challenges. It also didn't hurt that he was able to earn several hundred bucks a crack.

And, face it, he told himself, there was no way in hell he could ever *parlaz vous* with those rich folks by himself and convince them to hire a guy like him to create wrought-iron gates, fence panels, and stair rails for their fancy houses. Hell, if he were a rich guy, he wouldn't hire a guy like himself!

The other problem that gnawed at him was the fact that he was supposed to have gone out on another job tonight. And if he wasn't along to practically hold the hands of those dumb yahoos, they'd sure as hell get lost. Because not one of those good old boys was smart enough to find his backside in the hall of mirrors at high noon. That was for sure.

But everything had changed when he received that stupid message from Booth Crowley. Old jump-when-I-say-so Crowley wanted him to meet him tonight at some guy's house. What was *that* all about? Had the plan changed completely? Was he no longer honchoing their little clandestine operation?

Billy reached down with a leather-gloved hand and shut off the valve for the gas. He let the blue white flame die before his eyes before he tipped his helmet back.

Eight o'clock, the note had said. Eight o'clock. He guessed he'd better not cross a guy like Booth Crowley. Crowley was one important dude around Charleston, and Billy knew firsthand that he could also be a pretty nasty dude. Right now, he regretted ever getting involved with Booth Crowley.

Billy Manolo carefully laid his equipment on the battered cutting table. He shut off the lights in the garage, pulled down the door, and locked it.

As he picked his way across the yard, he told himself he had barely enough time for a quick shower.

CHAPTER 31

❦

"*DID YOU GET* the samples?" Drayton asked quietly.

Triumphantly, Haley laid three plastic Baggies full of dirt on the table next to Drayton's bonsai trees. "I did just as you said," Haley told him. "Used the litmus paper first in a half-dozen places. Then, when I found what seemed like a fairly close match for the soil's pH level, I collected a sample."

"Good girl," breathed Drayton as he pulled two little plastic petri dishes out of the duffel bag that held his bonsai tools and copper wire. "You're sure nobody noticed the light from your flashlight?"

"Positive. The yacht club was a cinch, 'cause nobody was there. And when I went into the two backyards, I only turned the flashlight on for a moment when I had to read the litmus paper. And then I cupped my hands around it."

"Sounds like an excellent cat burglar technique," said Drayton.

But Haley was still riding high from her little adventure. "Doe's yard was easy," she chattered on. "Nobody home at all. But I had to scale a pretty good-sized fence in order to get into Booth Crowley's backyard. I had a couple hairy moments that definitely brought out my inner athlete." She paused. "You're going to test the soil samples right now?"

"That's the general idea," said Drayton as his fingers fluttered busily, measuring out spoonfuls of soil from each bag and dumping them into their own petri dishes.

"So we'll know right away?" asked Haley.

Drayton slid the three petri dishes out of sight, behind a large, brown, glazed bonsai pot that held a miniature grove of tamarack trees. "Haley," he said, "*everyone* will know right away if you persist in asking these questions."

"I thought that was the general idea," she said.

Drayton smiled tolerantly. "All in good time, dear girl, all in good time."

Lights blazed, conversation grew louder, the string quartet that Timothy Neville had brought in, fellow symphony members, played a lively rendition of Vivaldi's *Four Seasons*. Theodosia moved from room to room, dropping a hint here, a sly reference there. She was following in Delaine's wake, so all she really had to do was toss out an innuendo for good measure. It was surprisingly simple. And since this was a party where conversation groups constantly shifted and re-formed, it was easy to mix and mingle and get the rumor mill bubbling.

In one of two front flanking parlors, Theodosia ran into their genial host.

"Enjoying yourself, Miss Browning?" Timothy pulled himself away from a group of people that was heatedly discussing the pros and cons of faux finishes and peered at her hawkishly.

"Lovely evening, Mr. Neville," she said.

"I noticed you've been flitting about," Timothy said, pulling his lips back to reveal small, square teeth, "and chatting merrily with my guests. The old marketing instinct dies hard, eh? Fun to be a spin doctor again." His voice carried a faint trace of sarcasm, but his eyes danced with merriment. Then Timothy leaned toward her and asked quietly, "Drayton working his alchemy with the soil testing?"

"Should be," she said, taking a sip of champagne, feeling slightly conspiratorial.

"Why not scoot out and check for results then. If it's a go, we'll launch part two of your little plan."

Theodosia was suddenly captivated by Timothy's quixotic spirit. "Why, Mr. Neville, I do believe you're rather enjoying this," she told him.

"It's a game, Miss Browning, a fascinating game. Truth be known, Drayton didn't have to twist my arm much to get me to play along. But"—Timothy Neville suddenly sobered—"at the same time, Oliver Dixon was a decent man and a friend. He was a generous benefactor to the Heritage Society and lent support to several other worthwhile charities here in Charleston. It was a terrible fate that befell him, and if someone *was* responsible for masterminding such a frightful, premeditated act, that person should be made to pay. If the police haven't figured something out by now, I see no reason why the fates shouldn't intercede. Or at least receive a helpful prod from us." Timothy paused, removed a spotless white handkerchief from his inside jacket pocket, and blotted his brow gently. "Now, when you have an answer, Miss Browning, be sure to tell Henry immediately. He's the one charged with rounding up the troops for my little spectacle here tonight." Timothy reached for a glass of champagne from the tray of a passing waiter, held it up to Theodosia in a toast. "Henry is also who most of my guests fear more than me." He chuckled.

"Drayton, Timothy wants to know if you have any results yet," Theodosia asked somewhat breathlessly. She'd hurried from one end of Timothy's house to the other, then fairly flown down the back staircase into Timothy's elegant garden.

How delightful it is out here, she thought suddenly as she felt the gentle sway of palm trees and bamboo around her, caught the moonlight as it shimmered on the long reflecting pool. *How cool and quiet after the closeness and social chaos inside.*

But Drayton was peering at her with a glum expression. "I've got results, but not the kind you want to hear about," he said, a warning tone in his voice.

Theodosia was instantly on the alert. "What's wrong?"

"What's wrong is that none of our soil samples match with what Professor Morrow took off your tablecloth," he said. He drummed his fingers on the tabletop, obviously irritated.

Theodosia stared at Drayton and saw his vexation and frustration. Haley, who stood poised with a Japanese teapot in her hand, suddenly looked ready to cry.

"I did it just the way you told me to, Drayton," Haley said.

He held up a hand. "I'm not questioning your methodology. The preliminary matches looked good. It's just that . . ."

"What is it?" asked Theodosia.

"When we run a full analysis," said Drayton, "we come up empty."

"So Doe, Booth Crowley, and Billy Manolo are all innocent?" said Haley.

"Innocent of using soil from their own backyards," said Theodosia. "Or the yacht club, in Billy's case." She was bitterly disappointed as well. At the same time, she'd known this whole soil business had been a long shot.

"So that's it?" asked Haley. "We've come this far just to hit a dead end?"

"Not quite," said Theodosia. "The soil samples were really only the lure. Now it's time to have Timothy dangle the bait."

CHAPTER 32

❦

*B*ILLY MANOLO HEARD the laughter and conversation from half a block away. It drifted like silver strands out the open windows and doors of Timothy Neville's enormous home and seemed to rise into the blue black sky.

Billy stopped for a moment and stared upward, half expecting to see something tangible in the night sky above him. Then he shook his head and resumed walking toward the big house on Archdale Street. *Foolishness,* he told himself. *Just plain foolishness.*

Henry met him at the door before he had a chance to knock or ring the bell.

"Mr. Manolo?" Henry asked in his dry, raspy voice.

Billy stared at him. The old guy in the red and white monkey suit had to be ninety years old. He also looked like somebody out of an old movie. A silent movie at that.

"Yeah, I'm Billy Manolo," he answered, his curiosity ratcheting up a couple notches. "Is there some kind of problem?"

"Not in the least," smiled Henry. "Fact is, we've been expecting you."

"Is that so?" Billy eyed Henry warily as he stepped into the foyer and glanced hurriedly around. "Looks like you all have a party going on."

"Indeed," said Henry.

"This is quite a place. You could park a 747 in this hallway."

"Thank you," said Henry. "I shall convey your rather astute observation to Mr. Neville, I'm sure he'll be pleased."

"Booth Crowley around?" Billy asked. "I got some weird message to meet him here."

"Yes, that was nicely arranged, wasn't it," said Henry.

"Huh?" asked Billy sharply.

"If you'll follow me to the music salon, sir," beckoned Henry. "It's time we get started."

The thatch of white hair atop Booth Crowley's head bristled like a porcupine displaying its quills. Then his small, watery gray eyes focused on Billy Manolo, dressed in faded jeans and a black T-shirt, swaggering down the center of the Oriental runner that ran the length of the hallway. Strangely enough, he followed in the wake of Timothy's man, Henry.

"Damn that boy," Booth Crowley muttered under his breath, immediately tuning out the two women who'd been making a polite pitch to him concerning funding for their beloved Opera Society's production of *Turandot*.

Their eyebrows shot immediately skyward. Swearing was not unknown to them, but neither was it customary for a man to display such rudeness in a social situation like this. The eyes of the volunteer coordinator flashed an immediate signal of those of the board member: *Uncouth. Not much of a gentleman.*

But committing a social faux pas was the furthest thing from Booth Crowley's mind right now. His was a personality hot-wired for anger, one that accelerated from rational behavior to utter rage with no stops in between, no chance for a safety valve.

Booth Crowley bulled his way across the room. Leading with his barrel of a chest, he shoved himself between Henry and Billy in an attempt to physically block Billy's way.

"Get the hell away from here," Booth Crowley snarled. His lips curled sharply, his Adam's apple bobbed wildly above his floral bow tie. Several people standing nearby paused to watch what seemed to be an ugly spectacle about to unfold.

Billy gazed at Booth Crowley in disbelief and decided the old fart had to be bipolar or whatever the current pop psycho term was. First Booth had left him a note that was practically a presidential mandate to meet him here tonight. Now the crazy fool was trying to toss him out! *What an idiot,* thought Billy as he shook his head tiredly. But then, everything felt nuts these days, like the world was crashing down around him.

The high tinkle of a bell cut through the raw tension and the sudden buzz of excitement.

"Everyone is kindly requested to convene in the music salon, please." Henry's normally papery voice had suddenly increased by twenty decibels, ringing out strong and clear and authoritative. He sounded like a courtier announcing the arrival of the queen to parliament.

"You old fool," spat Billy to Booth Crowley as the two men were suddenly jostled, then engulfed as bodies flowed past them.

Party guests pushed toward the music room, flushed with excitement, their spirits buoyed by the free flow of the excellent Roederer Cristal Champagne. Billy Manolo and Booth Crowley could do nothing but let themselves be carried along with the crowd. The most they could manage were furious scowls at each other.

Out on the patio, Drayton, Theodosia, and Haley also heard the high, melodious tinkle of Henry's bell.

Theodosia turned bright eyes to Drayton. "This is it," she whispered excitedly. "Keep your fingers crossed."

"Is *somebody* going to tell me what's *really* going on?" complained Haley. "I feel like I'm the last person on earth to—"

Drayton grabbed her by the hand and pulled her forward. "Come on then. Timothy's going to do his little speech. In about two minutes, you'll see exactly what we're up to!"

The three of them scampered up the back staircase into Timothy's house and pushed down the main hallway with the rest of the crowd. Once inside the vast music salon, they jockeyed for position.

Standing center stage, in front of an enormous marble fireplace, Timothy Neville waited as the crowd continued to pour into the room and gather around him. High above him, set incongruously against gold brocade wallpaper, hung a scowling portrait of one of his Huguenot ancestors.

It was a full minute before all the murmurs, coughs, and whispers quieted down. Finally, Timothy looked over toward Henry, who nodded slightly at him. Timothy gazed serenely out into the crowd, found Drayton and Theodosia, but did not acknowledge them. Then he pulled himself into his usual ramrod posture and began.

"Thank you all for coming tonight," he greeted the crowd in a ringing, impassioned voice. "It's always an honor to host a party for a delightful crowd such as this."

There was exuberant applause and several shouts of "Hear! Hear!"

Again, Timothy waited for the noise to die down. "Our Garden Fest event continues to grow each year," he told them. "This year alone we've added six additional garden venues to our program. That gives us a grand total of thirty-eight private gardens in our beloved historic district that will be open, over the next three days, for the public's sublime viewing pleasure."

More applause.

"On a more personal note," continued Timothy, "I sincerely regret that the garden of my friend and neighbor, Oliver Dixon, will no longer be included on the Garden Fest roster. As you all know, we lost Oliver recently, and the memory of his accident still haunts us."

With those few words, Timothy had suddenly gained the complete and rapt attention of the crowd.

"Oliver Dixon was a generous contributor to the Heritage Society," said Timothy. "And more than a few years ago, when I was a younger and far nimbler fellow, I sailed against Oliver Dixon in several of the yacht club's regattas: the Isle of Palms race, the Catfish Cup, the Patriots Point Regatta. Oliver was a true gentleman and a fine competitor. I know in my heart that he would not wish the yacht club's reputation or any of its long-standing traditions to be tarnished by what was truly a senseless accident."

Timothy paused, much the same way a minister would when asking for a moment of silence. The crowd seemed to hold its collective breath, sensing something big was about to happen.

"To celebrate Oliver Dixon's vast contributions and help continue the yacht club's time-honored customs, I am making a special donation in his memory."

The inimitable Henry now strode forth, bearing in his arms a large wooden box. Turning to face the crowd, Henry paused for a moment, then slowly lifted the lid.

Catching the gleam from the overhead chandelier, a silver pistol glinted from its cradle of plush red velvet.

There was a hush at first, an initial shock, as a visceral reaction swept through the crowd. They were surprised, slightly stunned. Then a smattering of applause broke out among several of the men standing near the front. The applause began to build steadily until, finally, almost everyone had politely joined in.

"You were right," Drayton whispered to Theodosia, "it *was* a shocker."

But Theodosia had turned to face the crowd, and her eyes were busily scanning faces.

She caught the look of initial shock, then supreme unhappiness that spread across Doe's young face.

Ford Cantrell, pressed up against the back wall, retained a mild smile that seemed to barely waver. But Theodosia had caught a spark of something else behind Ford's carefully arranged public face: curiosity. Ford Cantrell had taken in the entire scenario and was trying to figure out exactly what was going on, what con was being run.

Booth Crowley's sullen countenance bobbed among the crowd like an angry balloon. He had applauded perfunctorily but seemed nervous and distracted. His wife, Beatrix, at his side, maintained the look of mild bemusement she'd worn all night.

And Billy Manolo, looking like an angry rebel in his black T-shirt among a sea of dinner jackets and tuxedos, kept an insolent smirk on his face.

"What kind of pistol is it?" asked a young man at the front of the crowd. His eyes shone brightly, and he seemed pleased with himself for asking such a bold question.

Timothy's grin was both terrifying and curiously satisfying. "A Scottish regimental pistol. Manufactured by Isaac Bissell of Birmingham, England. See the engraved RHR? Stands for Royal Highland Regiment."

Delaine stood nearby, fanning herself nervously. "Is it loaded?" she asked with a mixture of alarm and fascination.

"Of course," said Timothy, hefting the weapon in one hand and pointing it toward the ceiling. "The cartridge is a traditional hand-rolled cartridge, loose powder and a round ball wrapped in thin, brown paper. It was crafted in the

British tradition by Lucas Clay, one of the foremost munitions experts in the South today." Timothy held the pistol aloft for a moment, then put it reverently back in its box.

There were whistles of appreciation and murmurs as several people pressed forward to gaze at it, lying there, shiny and dangerous, on a bed of red velvet.

They are drawn to it like the hypnotic attraction of a cobra to a mongoose, thought Theodosia. The pistol was troubling yet difficult to resist, on display for all to admire on the library table next to the fireplace.

But the crowd was also beginning to dissipate now, moving out into the center hallway where it was cooler. Most folks were shuffling down the hall toward the solarium for drink refills at the bar.

Booth Crowley had shoved his way through the crowd again and stood talking with Billy Manolo. Or, rather, Booth Crowley was doing all the talking. Billy stared fixedly at the floor while the tips of Booth Crowley's ears turned a bright shade of pink.

Almost as pink as Delaine's dress, thought Theodosia, wishing she were a little mouse who could scamper across the floor and listen in on the tongue-lashing Booth Crowley seemed to be inflicting upon Billy Manolo.

"What do you think?" Drayton asked eagerly as he hovered at her elbow.

"Jury's still out," replied Theodosia.

"I'm going to dash over and grab a word with Timothy," he said. "Be right back."

As the room emptied rapidly, Theodosia moved along with the crowd, straining to keep everyone in view. Just ahead, Doe held an empty champagne glass aloft and, with a deliberate toss of her blond mane, handed it over to Giovanni Loard.

Giovanni Loard.

The thought struck Theodosia like a whack on the side of the head. *Maybe we should have taken soil samples from his garden,* she thought suddenly. After all, Giovanni seemed to get awfully cozy with Doe right after Oliver's death. On the other hand, Giovanni was Oliver's cousin, so he was expected to be sympathetic and solicitous.

She looked back to see where Drayton was, but he and Timothy were nowhere in sight.

"Theodosia!" Delaine's troubled face appeared before her. "Did Timothy not *transcend* the boundaries of good taste tonight?"

Delaine wore a mantle of pious outrage, but Theodosia knew she would deliciously broadcast and rebroadcast tonight's events for days to come.

"Timothy's a true eccentric," admitted Theodosia. "You never know what he's got up his sleeve."

"Eccentric isn't the word for it," sputtered Delaine. "He's downright . . ." She searched for the right word. "Intemperate."

Amused, Theodosia glanced back into the music salon. It appeared to be completely empty now. Drayton and Timothy must have exited via another door, she decided.

"And what's with those soil samples you've been collecting?" asked Delaine. She nudged closer. "Any results you'd care to share?"

Soil samples, Theodosia thought again. *Should get one from Giovanni's garden, just to be safe.*

"Oh my gosh," gasped Delaine suddenly, "there's Gabby Stewart." She craned her neck to catch a glimpse of a pencil-thin woman in a short black cocktail dress. "Will you look at her face; not so much as a single line. Oh, Gabby . . ." And Delaine elbowed her way frantically through the crowd.

Theodosia stood by herself for a moment, watching the last of the guests amble toward the solarium and out onto the enormous front portico. Then she made a snap decision.

Giovanni lived nearby. His garden was highlighted on

the map in the Garden Fest program that had been passed out earlier to all the guests.

She'd go there right now and take a soil sample. What harm would it do? After all, she'd be back in five minutes.

CHAPTER 33

※※※

FLAMING TORCHES ILLUMINATED Timothy's backyard garden, although it was completely deserted at the moment. Beginning life as a classical Charleston courtyard garden, it had, over the years, veered toward an Asian-inspired garden. Now indigenous flowering trees and shrubs rubbed shoulders with thickets of bamboo, stands of lady fern, and Korean moss. The long, rectangular pond was overgrown with Asian water plants. Along the paths, stone lion-dogs and Buddhas stood guard.

Cool breezes swept through the garden as Theodosia stepped hurriedly down a stone walkway. In a far, dim corner, a small waterfall splashed noisily. Arriving at the back wall, Theodosia put a hand on the ancient wooden gate that led to the alley. Pushing outward, the old metal hinges creaked in protest. And in that same instant, Theodosia heard something else, too: light footsteps in front of her.

She hesitated, then turned to peer into the darkness.

A silver moon slid out from behind a bank of clouds and cast faint light on the man standing ten feet in front of her.

Theodosia put a hand to her chest. "Giovanni, you frightened me."

"I meant to," he said.

Theodosia caught her breath. Giovanni's voice was cold and menacing. He was no longer playing the role of the charming and witty antique dealer. Her eyes went immediately to the pistol Giovanni had clutched in his hand. It was the same pistol Timothy had just presented in the music room. Theodosia decided that Giovanni must have waited until everyone had left, then snatched it from the wooden box that looked so eerily like a miniature coffin.

"You think you're so smart," Giovanni snarled at her. "Why couldn't you just mind your own business?"

"And let you get away with murder, Giovanni?" Theodosia faced him with as much bravado as she dared. "Killing your own cousin. What a coward you turned out to be."

"*Second* cousin," corrected Giovanni. He waved the pistol menacingly at her. "But what does it matter how we were related? The fact is, Oliver signed his own death warrant by staunchly refusing to give me any help at all."

"Help with what?" asked Theodosia, determined to draw him out.

"Money," sneered Giovanni. "I needed money. Some very nasty men were demanding immediate payment of a debt. But Oliver, righteous citizen and uptight businessman, wouldn't *give* it to me. Wouldn't even *lend* it to me. Said I was incapable of managing my finances."

"What did you need the money for?" she asked him, knowing full well that greed was a motivator that often outweighed a pressing need for money.

"What does it matter?" Giovanni said petulantly. "The shop, gambling debts . . . Anyway, my problems are almost behind me now."

"And you think you'll get control of Oliver's money by

wooing Doe," said Theodosia. *Keep him talking,* she told herself. *Drayton has to come looking for me.*

"Doe has the mind of a child," said Giovanni scornfully. But she *listens* to me, she *trusts* me. It won't be long before *I'm* calling the shots."

"You think you can make her fall in love with you? Marry you?"

Giovanni shrugged. "Sure, why not?"

"She's not that much of a child," said Theodosia.

"Shut up!" he said with a harsh bark. All pretense of Giovanni's carefully cultured voice had long since been abandoned.

"What have you got in mind?" Theodosia goaded Giovanni. "Another accident? Another exploding pistol?" Fury shone brightly in her eyes; her cheeks blazed high with color.

"Not necessarily," said Giovanni, and suddenly his voice was smooth and hard as ice. "I'm sure this pistol will fire quite nicely all on its own. We have our host, Timothy Neville, to thank for that. Quite the expert when it comes to weapons." Giovanni's eyes darted about the dark garden, but only golden koi peeped at them from the pond. The woman had been stalling for time, Giovanni decided, and he knew he'd better bring this to a rapid conclusion.

"Unlatch that gate." He gestured with the pistol. "You and I are going to take a little stroll down to Charleston Harbor. The water's awfully chilly this time of year but . . ." He chuckled nastily. ". . . You won't be in any condition to notice."

Theodosia faced him square on. "I don't think so," she told him.

Her obstinance infuriated him. "You foolish, snooping woman," he hissed. "Very well, have it your way. You hear them in there?" He gestured toward Timothy's house. "No one's going to come to your rescue. Everyone is having a merry old time, sipping champagne and whispering about your silly soil samples. I'm sure they all think you're quite mad. Especially when they find out you were sneaking about at night, snooping in people's gardens. No wonder you met with such an unfortunate accident."

Theodosia stared at him. Giovanni had become so enraged he was spitting like a cat, and his eyes were pulled into narrow slits like an evil Kabuki mask.

Oh dear, Theodosia suddenly thought to herself as her heart began to pound a timpani solo inside her chest. *Did I push him too hard? I hope he—*

Giovanni's finger tightened about the trigger.

"Giovanni . . ." said Theodosia, extending a hand.

Giovanni Loard squeezed the trigger, flinching slightly as a loud *whomp* echoed in the courtyard. At the same instant, Theodosia's hands flew up in surprise, and she uttered a tiny cry of dismay.

"You fool!" Timothy Neville's voice rang sharply across the garden, bouncing like shards of glass on cobblestones.

Startled, Giovanni whirled to find the grim face of Timothy Neville staring at him from above the barrel of a pistol, a sleek contemporary pistol that looked far more menacing than the one Giovanni held in his hand.

"Miss Browning?" Timothy called. "Still in one piece?" He looked past Giovanni, but his gun never wavered. It remained pointed squarely at Giovanni's heart.

Giovanni snapped his head around toward Theodosia. "What?" he gasped, amazed to find her still standing.

"You're a pitiful excuse for a man," said Timothy, his upper lip curled in disgust.

Giovanni was thoroughly stunned that his shot had been without effect. "It was supposed to be loaded," he stammered. "You said—"

"Assuming you are still in one piece, Miss Browning, would you care to enlighten the recalcitrant Mr. Loard?"

Theodosia lifted her chin in triumph. Her eyes bore into

Giovanni, and her hair flowed out around her like a vengeful wraith.

"We created a special type of ammunition," she told him. "Gunpowder green."

"That's right," added Timothy. "We figured once our killer knew that soil samples were being tested, it was only a matter of time before he, or she, erupted into a full-blown panic and attempted something foolish." Timothy smiled with smug satisfaction. "Witness your own folly just now."

Giovanni Loard's face was black with fury. "You put *what* in the pistol?" he bellowed.

"Gunpowder green," said Theodosia. "Actually a rather pungent and flavorful Chinese tea. But then, what would you know?" Her eyes blazed like a huntress who'd just claimed her prize. "You yourself admitted you were unable to distinguish between Chinese and Japanese blends. We simply assumed your inadequacies ran to gunpowder, as well."

"And we were correct," smiled Timothy.

"You pompous old blowhard," menaced Giovanni. His hands clenched and unclenched, and his eyes sought out the pale skin of Theodosia's neck.

In a split second, Timothy read the cold, calculating menace on Giovanni's face.

"You're not nearly as smart or as quick as you think you are," Timothy warned him. "Consider the fact that this Ruger is loaded with .22 caliber hollowpoints." Timothy's eyes gleamed, almost daring Giovanni to make a move.

When Giovanni continued to stare at Theodosia, Timothy Neville pulled his face into a tight smile and cocked the hammer back. The loud click reverberated off the stone garden walls.

"Timothy . . ." cautioned Theodosia. Fear suddenly gripped her. She was afraid that Timothy Neville, fiery old rebel that we was, might well escalate this standoff into something extremely foolish.

Timothy's dark eyes glittered with cold, hard rage. "Go ahead, Giovanni, why not make a grab for her? With my arthritis and advanced age, my reflexes probably aren't what they used to be, so we could make a game of it, you and I. Never mind that I've cocked the hammer back, which puts you about a nanosecond away from meeting your maker."

Giovanni almost seemed to consider the possibility for a moment. Then there were sudden, fast footfalls across cobblestones as men rushed toward them, and shapes emerged from the darkness. Much to Theodosia's delight, Tidwell's big belly bobbed across the garden courtyard. She'd never been so happy to see that protruding form in all her life.

Along with Tidwell were two uniformed police officers, one with his gun drawn, the other brandishing a set of handcuffs. At the sight of the three lawmen, Giovanni Loard seemed to collapse within himself.

"Detective Tidwell," said Theodosia, surprised and a little breathless, "what are you doing here?"

"I took the liberty of calling him, ma'am," said Henry, Timothy Neville's highly competent old butler, as he stepped out from behind Tidwell. For all his part in tonight's drama, Henry still seemed relatively unfazed.

"Good work, Henry," crowed Timothy, seemingly happy now to relinquish the task of dealing with Giovanni to the police. "Fine work."

Henry turned baleful eyes on Timothy. "Sir, your guests are departing. Perhaps you should come up to the house and bid them a proper good night?"

CHAPTER 34

❦❦❦

"**Y**OU'RE MAKING A terrible mistake!" screamed Booth Crowley as a pair of handcuffs was clamped tightly about his chubby wrists. "One call to Senator Wilbur and your career is finished!"

"Yeah, sure," said the police officer calmly. He turned as Tidwell entered the house. "These two go to central booking?" he asked.

Tidwell nodded. "ATF's been alerted, they're aware they're being brought in."

"Tidwell, you idiot!" screamed Booth Crowley, "I'll have your head on a platter. When I'm finished, you won't be able to get a job as a crossing guard!"

Theodosia couldn't believe the bizarre scene being played out inside Timothy's home. She had just witnessed Giovanni Loard's arrest out in the garden. Now two more uniformed officers had just apprehended and handcuffed Booth Crowley and Billy Manolo and were about to lead them away. And while Billy seemed subdued and cooperative, Booth Crowley was in a vile rage.

"B. C.?" Beatrix Crowley made pitiful little bleating

sounds as she ran helplessly alongside her husband. "What's going on?" she pleaded. "Tell me why this is happening!"

"Shut up with your fool questions and get on the phone to Tom Breedlaw," Booth shouted at her. "Tell that good-for-nothing lawyer he'd better move heaven and earth on this one! Go on, what are you waiting for?" he sputtered.

"What *is* going on?" Theodosia asked Tidwell as a bemused crowd of onlookers, the remains of Timothy's party guests, gawked and whispered as the two men were led away.

Tidwell favored Theodosia with a benevolent smile. "Yet one more piece of business taken care of, Miss Browning. Not to steal credit from Henry, but we were en route, anyway." He paused for a moment to scrawl his name on a piece of paper a uniformed officer had presented to him. "We were coming to pick up those two chaps." Tidwell waved after the departing Booth Crowley and Billy Manolo. "And we ended up with your Mr. Loard, too. A lucky strike extra, I'd have to say."

Theodosia's brows knit together as she stared earnestly at Burt Tidwell. "Explain please," she said as Drayton, Haley, and Timothy crowded around them.

Drayton and Haley had rushed out into the garden just in time to see Giovanni Loard taken into custody. Now they were equally amazed by the arrest of Booth Crowley and Billy Manolo. But, of course, everyone was.

Tidwell gazed into their eager faces. Drayton looked like he was about to collapse, Haley was boundlessly enthusiastic, and Theodosia and Timothy seemed to await his words with a peculiar calm.

"A sheriff and his deputy apprehended a group of smugglers over near Huntville," Tidwell told them. "Not more than an hour ago. The sheriff had been alerted by the Bureau of Alcohol, Tobacco and Firearms working in conjunction with the Coast Guard. Everyone was pretty sure there'd be some activity tonight; they just weren't sure where. Then, when the smugglers ran their boat aground, the sheriff and his deputies nabbed them. Being caught red-handed with the goods, the four smugglers rolled on their ringleader in about five minutes flat."

"Let me guess," said Theodosia, "the ringleaders being Booth Crowley and Billy Manolo." In her mind, Theodosia could see Sheriff Billings questioning the confused smugglers in his laconic, low-key manner. She was glad he'd been the one to bring them down.

"Booth Crowley was the kingpin," said Tidwell. "Billy Manolo was really just hired help. Apparently, Billy was born over in that area, near Shem Creek. He knew the coastal waters and could thread his way through the inlets and channels like a swamp rat. Billy was supposed to serve as guide tonight, but for some strange reason, he ended up here." Tidwell swiveled his bullet head and turned sharp eyes on Theodosia. "Funny turn of events, wouldn't you agree?"

"It is strange, isn't it," she said.

Haley was grinning from ear to ear. "I love it when people get their comeuppance. Leading Booth Crowley out in handcuffs sure had to bring him down a peg or two."

"It couldn't happen to a more deserving chap," commented Drayton. He'd loosened his bow tie and was fanning himself madly, using a palmetto leaf as a makeshift fan.

"But why smuggling?" asked Theodosia. "Booth Crowley had money, a successful company—"

"For a person with a true criminal mind, that's not enough," said Tidwell. "It's never enough. A person like Booth Crowley is constantly looking for a new angle, a new money-making scheme. And this isn't the first time he's run afoul of the law. He and several of his investors are under close scrutiny by the Securities and Exchange Commission because of possible insider trading."

"That's amazing," said Drayton. "And after the big show he made about supporting the arts—"

"I must commend you, Miss Browning," continued Tidwell. "Wresting a confession from Giovanni Loard was an admirable piece of work."

"I couldn't have done it without Timothy's help," said Theodosia. "He helped set the snare with his donated pistol and impassioned speech."

Timothy beamed. "Thank you, Miss Browning," he said, "the pleasure was all mine. I enjoyed being complicit in your little scheme because I sincerely meant what I said earlier in the music room. Oliver Dixon was a fine neighbor and a good friend. If I helped put temptation in front of Giovanni Loard in the form of that pistol, then so be it. I'm a firm believer in poetic justice."

"And Ford Cantrell's name is cleared after all," said Drayton as he grasped Theodosia's hand tightly, almost as though he were fearful some terrible fate might still befall her. "His sister will be eternally grateful to you, I'm sure. Although you gave us all a nasty fright!"

"His sister is more than eternally grateful," said Lizbeth Cantrell, as she approached the group, her brother Ford in tow. "Thank you, Theodosia, you are an interceding angel, truly heaven-sent."

The two women embraced as Ford looked on sheepishly. "Thank you, Miz Browning," he told her. "You're very kind. Very smart, too. If you ever decide to get into computers . . ."

Theodosia shook her head. "Judging by tonight's events, the tea business holds more than enough intrigue for me." She laughed.

"And Doe was proved innovent, too," mused Haley as Theodosia smiled after the departing Lizbeth Cantrell. "Now I feel a little sheepish thinking she might have had a hand in killing Oliver Dixon."

"It doesn't appear Doe was in collusion with Giovanni

Loard," said Tidwell. "She'll be questioned, but I doubt we shall find any ties. I doubt there are any ties."

"Giovanni offered a lot of false sympathy," said Theodosia. "I can see where it was easy for her to lean on him."

"Say," said Haley, "do you suppose that was Giovanni Loard prowling around outside the night of our mystery tea?"

"I'm almost positive it was," said Theodosia. "He had to have been curious about our investigation and worried about how much we knew."

"Goodness, I need a cup of tea," declared Drayton.

"Come," urged Timothy. "Come sit out on the side piazza and relax. We've all had enough high drama for the night."

They all followed Timothy the few steps outside, then collapsed into comfortable wicker chairs and chaise lounges. A few feet from where they sat, a whippoorwill called mournfully from where it had tucked itself among sheltering bows of live oak, and streamers of Spanish moss wafted gently in the night breeze.

"Teakettle's on," Henry announced to the group. "Should only be a moment."

"I couldn't believe Booth Crowley's face when he was led out in handcuffs," said Drayton.

"It was bright red," chortled Haley.

"Like keeman tea," said Drayton.

"I guess Booth Crowley's wife won't be starting that tea shop any time soon," said Haley.

"Right," agreed Drayton, "he's going to have to put his money to better use, like paying attorney's fees."

"And he'll need to focus on mounting a strong legal defense," added Tidwell. "Smuggling is a federal crime. It's not much fun going up against the Justice Department. Those boys do their job because they love it and because they're true believers. They're not in it for the money because, Lord knows, there *isn't* that much money."

Just like you, Theodosia thought to herself. *Just like you, Detective Tidwell.*

Teacups clattered as Henry approached, bearing a silver tray laden with a lovely blue ceramic French tea service. Henry poured steaming cups of tea for everyone, then passed them around.

"Delicious," declared Tidwell, taking a loud slurp. "And what kind is this?"

They turned inquisitive faces to Henry. He had, after all, brewed the tea.

"Why, I prepared the tea Mr. Conneley brought over," Henry said in his papery, proper voice, even as a faint smile tugged at his mouth.

"The gunpowder green!" exclaimed Drayton and Haley together.

Timothy rose to his feet and held his teacup aloft. "I'd like to propose a toast," he announced. "To Theodosia."

"To Theodosia," everyone chimed in.

"Just like her marvelous tea," said Timothy, "you discover what she's really made of when you put her in hot water."

"Hear! Hear!" cried Drayton. "Describes our girl perfectly."

Theodosia just smiled and sipped her tea.

RECIPES FROM
THE INDIGO TEA SHOP

Theodosia's Earl Grey Sorbet
An especially refreshing dessert

1¼ cups water
1 Tbs. sugar
Freshly squeezed juice from 2 lemons plus rind
2 Tbs. Earl Grey tea leaves
1 egg white

Bring water, sugar, lemon juice, and lemon rind to a boil in saucepan and allow to boil for four minutes. Add tea leaves, cover, remove from heat, and let steep until cool. Strain into a bowl, cover, and place in freezer until mixture is slushy and half frozen. Beat egg white until stiff, then fold into mixture. Freeze until sorbet reaches desired consistency. To serve, scoop sorbet into parfait dishes and garnish with fresh fruit or a lemon cookie.

Theodosia's Tea Scones

1 Tsp. baking p.owder
1 Tsp. granulated sugar
1 cup all-purpose flour
¼ tsp salt
1 Tbsp. orange juice
½ cup milk
½ cup raisins

Mix dry ingredients together in bowl, add orange juice and milk. Mix into a dough, then add raisins. Place 8 scoops onto a greased baking sheet, bake in preheated 425 degree oven for 15 to 20 minutes. Serve hot with plenty of butter and jam. Yields 8 scones.

Apricot Tea Sparkler

1⅓ cups strong Irish Breakfast Tea
1⅓ cups apricot nectar
1⅓ cups sparkling water

Combine tea, apricot nectar, and sparkling water. Pour into ice-filled glasses. Make 4 servings.

Theodosia's Chocolate Dipped Strawberries

2 large chocolate bars (Ghiradelli or Dove work well)
12 large, fresh strawberries

Wash and dry strawberries, leaving stems on. Break chocolate bars into bits and place in microwave safe bowl. Heat in microwave on high for 30 seconds or until melted completely. Hold each strawberry by its stem and dip into melted chocolate. Place on waxed paper to cool.

Drayton's Cucumber and Lobster Salad Sandwiches

1 lb. cooked lobster meat
2-3 stalks celery
small onion
Prepared mayonnaise
1 cucumber

Chop the lobster into small pieces. Chop and dice the celery and onion into very small pieces. Combine ingredients in a bowl and add a small amount of mayonnaise. If mixture seems dry, add a little more mayonnaise, then add salt and pepper to taste. Peel cucumber and slice into very thin slices. Spread lobster salad on slices of cocktail bread, top with cucumber, top each sandwich with another slice of bread. Carefully cut each sandwich into two triangles and arrange on platter.

Earl Grey's Liver Brownie Cake

(This is strictly for dogs!)

2 lbs. chicken liver
⅓ cup canola oil
2 eggs
1 fresh clove of garlic
3 cups wheat flour

Mix chicken liver, oil, eggs and garlic in food processor. Pour into mixing bowl and combine with flour. Pour into well-greased 9" x 11" pan. Bake 350 degrees for 40 minutes. When completely cool, cake can be lightly frosted with low fat cream cheese.

Easy tea time treats
you can whip up in your own kitchen.

Serve as many of these as you'd like, but always in small quantities. This is the time to use your fancy glass plates or two-tiered serving tray.

Cream cheese balls rolled in chopped walnuts
Tiny cucumber sandwiches (buy small loaves of
bread and remove crusts)
Thin slices of Swiss or jarlsberg cheese
Wedges of brie or camembert
Deviled eggs garnished with pimento
Cranberry or zucchini bread
Chicken salad on small croissants
Chutney or honey butter on toast points
Crab salad on English muffins
Macaroons
Scones with jam

Setting your tea table.

Unwrap grandma's teapot, round up all your mis-matched cups, saucers and tiny plates. Set out thin slices of lemon, sugar cubes, a tiny pitcher of milk, and a small pot of honey. Gather fresh flowers from your garden or adorn your table with pots of ivy. Light the candles, play a favorite CD, indulge in the relaxing ritual that is tea time.

DON'T MISS THE NEXT
INDIGO TEA SHOP MYSTERY

Shades of Earl Grey

An antique wedding ring mysteriously disappears from the hand of a dying bridegroom. Then a priceless sapphire necklace is plucked from its display at the Heritage Society. Could there be a very dangerous breed of cat burglar prowling the cobblestone pathways of Charleston's historic district? With the Heritage Society under fire and their extravaganza Treasures Show fast approaching, Theodosia is called upon to match wits with a very slippery opponent.

Praise for Death by Darjeeling
The First in the Tea Shop Mystery Series

"Tea lovers, mystery lovers, this is for you."
—Susan Wittig Albert,
author of the best-selling China Bayles series

"The well-drawn plot includes an intriguing amateur sleuth, and the likable cast of characters makes *Death by Darjeeling* a wonderful reading experience." —www.bookreview.com

"*Death by Darjeeling* is a good beginning to a new culinary series that will quickly become a favorite of readers who favor this genre. The cozy and inviting setting will quickly draw readers in and a likable cast of characters will have them eager to return." —*The Mystery Reader*

"Tea lovers in particular will enjoy the arcane world of tea. But these details merely add depth and flavor to the story, never distracting from the likable characters or the nicely crafted plot." —MysteriousStrands.com

Chosen as a featured selection
by the Mystery Book Club

Formerly #1 on the Paperback Bestseller's List of the
Independent Mystery Bookstores

Named one of five "Paperback Best Bets" by
Overbooked.com

Book choice for Yahoo!'s Mystery Book Discussion

**Find out more about the author and the
Tea Shop Mystery Series at www.laurachilds.com**